GUNNER

Also by Alan Parks

The Harry McCoy Thrillers
Bloody January
February's Son
Bobby March Will Live Forever
The April Dead
May God Forgive
To Die in June

ALAN PARKS

GUNNER

BASKERVILLE
An imprint of JOHN MURRAY

First published in Great Britain in 2025 by Baskerville
An imprint of John Murray (Publishers)

1

Copyright © Alan Parks 2025

The right of Alan Parks to be identified as the
Author of the Work has been asserted by him in accordance
with the Copyright, Designs and Patents Act 1988.

All rights reserved. No part of this publication may be reproduced, stored in a retrieval system, or transmitted, in any form or by any means without the prior written permission of the publisher, nor be otherwise circulated in any form of binding or cover other than that in which it is published and without a similar condition being imposed on the subsequent purchaser.

All characters in this publication are fictitious and any resemblance
to real persons, living or dead, is purely coincidental.

A CIP catalogue record for this title is available from the British Library

Hardback ISBN 9781399819664
Trade Paperback ISBN 9781399819671
ebook ISBN 9781399819695

Typeset in Perpetua by Palimpsest Book Production Ltd, Falkirk, Stirlingshire

Printed and bound in Great Britain by Clays Ltd, Elcograf S.p.A.

John Murray policy is to use papers that are natural, renewable and recyclable products and made from wood grown in sustainable forests. The logging and manufacturing processes are expected to conform to the environmental regulations of the country of origin.

Carmelite House
50 Victoria Embankment
London EC4Y 0DZ

www.johnmurraypress.co.uk

John Murray Press, part of Hodder & Stoughton Limited
An Hachette UK company

The authorised representative in the EEA is Hachette Ireland, 8 Castlecourt Centre, Dublin 15, D15 XTP3, Ireland (email: info@hbgi.ie)

In memory of my sister Janice.

A false witness shall be punished, and a liar shall be caught.
Proverbs xix, 9

When you're dead, you're dead. That's it.
Marlene Dietrich

Prologue

It hadn't been this quiet for weeks. He could even hear whatever birds were still left singing in the ruins of the farmhouse. Last time it had been this quiet was the night they had spent in the church, everything at peace, all the pews lined with sleeping bodies. That was the last time he had really slept. 'You were out for the count,' Andy had told him 'Snoring like a bloody rhino.'

Since then, it had been a couple of hours snatched wherever he could. He wasn't even tired any more, just resigned to always being in a kind of half-awake fog. He was sure it was affecting his sight, everything just a tiny bit out of focus, lights leaving trails behind them. In return his other senses seemed to get better, compensating. He could smell wet earth under the permanent stink of cordite, smell the bodies piled under the trees. Could hear better too. Not sure that was a good thing. The screaming whistle of the shells coming in, every scream and moan, every wounded man shouting for his mother ringing louder and louder in his head.

He was trying to get used to Andy not being here. Andy, who was everything he wasn't. Optimistic, happy, slow to take offence. Gunner had held his hand as the blood and the life ran out of him, swore he would go and see his wife in Springburn when he got back, tell her how much Andy had loved her, tell her what happened. Margie, Vulcan Street, number 75. Please, Gunner?

He was finding it hard to think straight. He just did what he was told, put one foot in front of the other and kept going. That was all that mattered now, keeping going. Suddenly there were shouts down the line, sounds of the men getting up. They were on the move again. He was just reaching for his helmet when the first one came in. Noise like a scream, then a whump as it hit, a plume of dirt and smoke rising up about a hundred yards in front of him. Then the air was full of shouts and cries, more shells coming in, a sergeant blowing his whistle over and over. Sky full of flashes and smoke, and he was running, running, the sergeant's whistle all he could hear.

1

Anger is a strange thing. Can come and go in an instant or smoulder slowly until it bursts into flame. Lately Gunner had been suffering from both kinds. A low, permanent anger at what the war had done and sudden rages that swept over him, making him act before he could stop himself. He hadn't been like that before the war, just the opposite. Slow to anger, the one on an even keel amongst his more hot-headed colleagues. Now he felt on edge most of the time, anything could set him off. Now it was the other two blokes in the carriage. Young, new recruits, one of them still with a face full of acne and bumfluff. They'd been at it all night, drinking themselves asleep, then starting again.

The first time Bumfluff stood on his foot on the way back from the train toilet, Gunner bit down, accepted his slurred 'Sorry, pal'. The second time he didn't. The words out his mouth before he had time to think.

'Watch where you're fucking going, ya prick!'

Bumfluff stopped, turned to him. Clearly about to answer back when he saw the expression on Gunner's face. Instead, he held out the bottle of whisky he and his mate were drinking.

Gunner took it, had a good slug and handed it back.

'No happen again,' said Bumfluff.

Gunner nodded and the boy wove his unsteady way back to his pal.

This had been happening to him a lot lately. People backing off, saying sorry, getting out of his way. Something had changed in his expression, the way he held himself. Not the first thing the war had changed in him, wouldn't be the last either.

He was half asleep when the train whistle blew. He yawned, stretched, and looked out the window. They were coming into Glasgow at long last. He stood up, pushed the window of the train door down. A rush of cool air as he stuck his head out, looked around for familiar landmarks. The same soot-covered buildings were still there, some rag-and-bone man with a horse and cart slowly making his way along Hallside Street; could even see the edge of Glasgow Green, people's washing out to dry on the long ropes stretched between the iron poles.

He was back in Glasgow all right, but it didn't take him long to realise how much things here had changed. Barrage balloons were hovering above the city, bobbing up and down on their long wires. What looked like bomb shelters in the middle of every second street, windows of the shops all criss-crossed with tape. They rounded a bend, and he could see a tank parked outside the pumpworks on Weir Street.

A couple of minutes later the train rumbled over the bridge across the Clyde and into the dark cathedral of St Enoch station. Gunner picked up his bag, slung it over his shoulder, stepped over the two snoring boys and went into the corridor. Never been happier to get off a train in his life. He was supposed to have got home yesterday but they'd been held at York station for eleven hours, waiting for six troop trains to load up. The railway guards wouldn't let them off the train, everyone had had to buy cups of tea through the windows, wee boys running back and forward to the cafe for a penny.

An older one somehow managed to get the whisky from somewhere for two Air Force boys, charged them ten shillings for it, not that they cared. They ended up sitting in the station all night, nothing to do but look out the window, watch the rows and rows of white-faced lads in uniforms that were too big for them boarding trains to God knows where. All laughs and shouts and shoving each other, heading off for a big adventure. A couple of them had seen his uniform, given him the thumbs up. He'd given it back. Why not? They'd find out what it was really like soon enough.

A whistle, the hiss of brakes, clouds of steam and suddenly all the doors were swinging open, people desperate to get out onto the platform, away from the stale smell and fusty air of the two-day train ride. Gunner stepped down from the train, stood there for a minute on the platform. Glasgow may have looked different, but it smelt the same. Factory smoke, yeast from the brewery over by Glasgow Green and fried food wafting over from somewhere. He joined the crowd shuffling towards the platform gates and told himself it would only be half an hour until he saw Chrissy again, half an hour to be in the big double bed in her flat.

He'd just walked through the gates when he saw him. He couldn't believe it, didn't want to believe it. But there he was, standing by the newsagents, Detective Inspector Malcolm Drummond.

Unlike Glasgow, his old boss hadn't changed a bit. Looked just like he always looked. Trilby perched on the back of his head, tweed suit that looked like he hadn't taken it off for weeks and the usual Player's cigarette jutting from the corner of his mouth. For a minute Gunner thought of trying to lose himself in the crowd but he was too late, the decision already made for him. Drummond had seen him. No way he could escape now. Next thing Drummond had dropped his cigarette on the ground, stood on it and was walking towards him, hand held out, ready to shake.

There wasn't much else he could do, so Gunner took his hand. Shook it.

'Fuck happened to you?' asked Drummond peering at him. 'You look like a fucking pirate.'

Gunner sighed, finger automatically going to the patch over his left eye.

'Shrapnel.'

Drummond looked unimpressed.

'Daft bugger. Should have kept your head down like I told you.'

He took a hanky from his pocket, blew his nose, inspected it, then stuffed it back into his pocket.

'Come on,' he said. 'Need you to come with me.'

'Hang on,' said Gunner. 'You forgotten something? I don't work for you any more.'

Drummond looked pained.

'Don't be a smart-arse. A body's turned up. Need you to have a look at it.'

'You're joking, aren't you?' said Gunner. 'You want me to look at a dead body?'

The last thing he wanted to do was see another body. God knows he'd seen enough of them in the past two years, more than enough to last him a lifetime. Then it struck him.

'What are you looking at a body for anyway? Last I heard you'd retired.'

'I did,' said Drummond. 'Last year. Even bought a bloody caravan in Girvan. But they called me back in. Force is full of us now, we're all that's left. Just old guys like me that they called back and weans that don't know their arses from their elbows. Been like that since everyone your age fucked off to the war and left us high and dry. You were just about to be made detective when you went. Clever boy. So, much as it pains me to say it, I need you to help me out.'

Gunner shook his head, he had to nip this in the bud, quick.

'Can't help you. I've got things to do.'

'Like what? Get your hole?'

'Among other things,' said Gunner.

'Aye well, that's not going to happen,' said Drummond. 'Bad news. Chrissy's gone. Went to Newcastle with some Air Force captain she met at the dancing.'

Gunner tried not to show his surprise. Suddenly the absence of letters over the past month made sense. More fool him.

'It's too early for the shebeens,' said Drummond. 'You come with me, help me out and I'll drop you off after. There are a few new girls in town. All these fucking troop trains to accommodate.'

Gunner couldn't think of much reason to say no. All his plans had revolved around Chrissy and their great reunion. They'd met each other at the dancing, both thinking it was a one-night thing, but it turned into something more than that. Or so he had thought. Didn't blame her though, girls like Chrissy had to take their chances when they turned up. Still, he was going to miss seeing her.

Drummond turned, started walking towards the station exit.

Gunner swore under his breath, picked up his knapsack and followed. Couldn't believe he was back with Drummond, knew he wouldn't be any different. Same old schemes and fiddles, anything for a quick buck.

The roof of the station was filthy from years of smoke and soot but the sunlight still managed to make its way through the glass, bright shafts piercing the steam and smoke, lighting up the chaos below. The big concourse was packed with army lads sitting on the ground, leaning on their packs, half of them asleep. Twenty or so French sailors were standing along the far wall, smoking, joking, watching the girls. The canvas departure boards were flapping, changing every two minutes: Newcastle, London, Carlisle. There was even a zebra standing on a wooden platform with a sign around its neck: ZEBRA CIGARETTES IN THE BLACK AND WHITE PACK.

A man was holding it on a rope, surrounded by kids with labels on their jumpers, gas-mask boxes around their necks. The zebra looked like it was deciding which one of them to kick first. A board went up saying *Liverpool* and a sergeant started shouting at the army lads. They got up, stretching and yawning, trying to form themselves into some sort of line.

It had been almost eighteen months since Gunner had left Glasgow, 1939, from this same station. Then it was still early days, the war hadn't changed things yet. He'd stood in the station, uncomfortable in his stiff uniform and buzz cut, watching men and women waiting for trains to their work or back home,

Askit and Red Hackle whisky billboards everywhere, newsagents still full of papers and sweeties. Now half the kiosks were shut, billboards replaced by the usual Government stuff. *Keep Mum*; *Dig for Victory*. There was one cafe left in the corner; he could see rolls and cheese lined up, even some scones. His stomach turned over at the thought.

'This way, ya clown!'

He cursed, followed Drummond out the station entrance and blinked in the sudden sunlight. It was warm already, so he unbuttoned the top buttons of his blouse. Fuck it. No one was going to care now. Shook his head when he saw where Drummond had parked the Morris, remembered what an awkward bugger he could be. He'd parked it right in the middle of the taxi rank, didn't give a fuck about anyone that wasn't a polis. God's chosen men as far as he was concerned. Everyone else could fend for themselves.

Gunner ignored the dirty looks of the taxi drivers, opened the passenger door and got in, trying to bend his leg without wincing. The shrapnel tracks on his face weren't the only scars he had, but he didn't want Drummond to know about them.

The Morris was a mess as usual. He pushed old chip wrappers and an empty Tennent's bottle off the seat before sitting down. The back seat was covered in police reports held together with elastic bands and a couple of balled-up shirts. It was Drummond's car all right, even smelt like him. Cigarette smoke, hair oil and beer.

'What was it like, then?' Drummond asked him as they drove off.

'Seen the newsreels, have you?' asked Gunner. 'Just like that.'

Drummond swerved round the rag-and-bone man's cart and accelerated up the road.

'Still the funny bugger, I see. They no feed you over there? You're all skin and bone.'

Gunner sighed. Wasn't sure if Drummond was really so ignorant about what the war was really like or whether he was just taking the piss.

'Army food's not much cop,' he said.

'Ha ha,' said Drummond. 'Cannae be any worse than it is here. You can't get a hold of anything. All fucking powdered egg and here's your two ounces of butter and that's you.'

Gunner nodded. He wasn't really listening; it was hard to stop looking out the car. Change everywhere. An ack-ack gun was sitting outside the Grand Hotel, a nest of sandbags around it. Two uniformed guys behind it smoking and reading the paper, looking all of fifteen. There were sandbags everywhere, piled up against doors, in mounds at the side of the street.

He pushed down the window, let some air in. If he was being honest with himself he wasn't that surprised that Chrissy had left. Anything was better than being stuck in a damp flat in Glasgow married to some docker who spent all his wages on a Friday night.

'Where we off to anyway?' he asked, watching three drunk lads in Air Force blues weave their way down the street.

'The Kelvin Hall.'

'Why? What's on? The circus back, is it?' asked Gunner.

Drummond looked at him as if he were mad, and then it dawned. 'You've been on a train all night, you don't know.'

Gunner looked puzzled. 'Don't know what?'

'We got hit. Fucking German bombers came last night.

Hammered us. Out Clydebank way mostly, a bit of Maryhill. So many dead we're having to use the Kelvin Hall as a temporary morgue. Can't fit the buggers in anywhere else.'

Gunner sat back in his seat. He'd thought he was coming to Glasgow to escape the war, hadn't really thought that it was happening here too. Last thing he needed.

'Anyone we know?' he asked.

Drummond got a hanky out his pocket, wiped his sweaty forehead. 'Hard to tell. Loads of bodies still unidentified, in pieces most of them, not sure they'll ever know what's what. It's a right fucking mess. Most of the boys from the Maryhill shop are accounted for, Tanner's no in but chances are he's just lying pissed somewhere as usual. Clydebank are missing a— Fuck!'

Drummond stepped on the brakes, braced his arms on the steering wheel and they skidded to a halt. Gunner got his hand up just in time, stopped his face hitting the windscreen.

'Fuck's sake, Drummond!'

It wasn't difficult to see why Drummond had hit the brakes. Up ahead of them, Argyll Street was closed off. Ropes across it and a couple of bollards painted red. Fire wardens and guys in boiler suits were looking up at one of the tenements by the old bakery.

'Sorry about that,' said Drummond. 'All this shite wasn't here five bloody minutes ago.' He pushed his window down.

'Fuck's going on here?' he barked.

A fireman the size of a brick shithouse wandered over. Couldn't have looked at Drummond with more contempt if he tried.

'What's going on here, sir, is that a fire has rendered this building unsafe,' he said. 'So we've closed the road. That OK with you, is it?'

'I'm a polis,' said Drummond.

The foreman smiled. 'That right? I'm a Partick Thistle supporter myself. Now fuck off.'

Drummond muttered something about 'bloody jumped-up arseholes' and spun the car around. Gunner looked out the window, not wanting Drummond to see the big grin on his face.

Argyll Street wasn't the only one. They had to go round the houses, half the roads on the way to the Kelvin Hall were blocked off, oil drums and planks of wood, a row of the Home Guard behind them. Drummond wasn't one to give up easily, but to give them their due, the old boys held firm, even in the face of his shouting, swearing and flashing his police card.

They were just coming along Dumbarton Road when they ground to a halt again. The traffic ahead of them had stopped completely, horns were blasting, drivers stepping out of their cars trying to see what the hold-up was. At first Gunner thought it was just another roadblock, then he saw them. It seemed like hundreds of people were coming along Dumbarton Road, weaving their way through the cars and trams, making their way towards the Western Infirmary.

Nurses were running amongst them, blowing whistles when they found the worst off, directing the doctors, getting the porters to put them on stretchers or in wheelchairs. An old man stepped out in front of Drummond's car, stumbled and steadied himself on the bonnet. He was a mess. Snow-white hair thick with blood and dust, left arm hanging at his side, bone poking through the skin and his shirt. He looked at them without seeing and kept going.

Gunner watched the bomb victims walking past while Drummond swore and sat on the horn. It was like being back in France again. Refugees on the roads. The first couple of times he'd seen them, he'd tried asking who they were, where they were going. After a couple of weeks, things had changed. Soon he didn't even notice them any more. There were just too many. Women, kids, old men pushing prams and carts full of piled-up belongings. All of them walking heads down, all of them exhausted, none of them knowing where they would end up.

The nurses and doctors in Great Western Road finally managed to get most of the walking wounded into the wee road up to the hospital and the traffic started moving again. Drummond eased the car forward, only gone a few hundred yards when they were stopped again, right by the hospital entrance. Six army vans were parked up on the pavement, soldiers unloading bodies on stretchers out the back.

'Christ. How many bombs were there?' Gunner asked.

'Fuck knows, they just kept coming all night. Incendiaries did the most damage, half of Clydebank's still burning.'

Drummond leant on the steering wheel, shook a cigarette out the packet and did his usual trick of lighting it off the one in his mouth. He peered through the windscreen at the clear blue sky. Looked glum.

'It rains in Glasgow every fucking day, then the one day you really want it to, it's like a bloody picture postcard. This weather better change soon or we're fucked. The last thing we need is another clear night and those cunts coming back for round two. We cannae cope as it is.'

'I don't get it,' said Gunner, looking at the flow of casualties.

'There must be hundreds of dead bodies in the Kelvin Hall. What have I got to look at one for?'

Drummond turned to him, grinned.

'This one's a bit different. Not that many bombs that manage to cut someone's fingers off one by one.'

2

The Kelvin Hall was an imposing red sandstone building in the west end of the city. The frontage had towers at either end framing a row of columns facing onto the street. It was where the city held exhibitions, big boxing matches, trade fares. A civic palace built to show Glasgow's wealth and importance. It didn't look like that now though, now it looked like a castle under siege.

The front steps and the road in front of the hall were in chaos. Cars, coal lorries, fruit barrows, anything that could be used to transport the dead had been requisitioned and put to use. The crowd was growing by the minute, more blocked traffic, horns blaring. Some people had delivered their dead already and were now sitting on the pavement, quietly crying. A wee boy was screaming, trying to wriggle away from a nurse; half of his clothes were torn off, skin red and weeping. A woman with a baby on her lap was sitting on the step staring into space, dress and baby's blanket covered in blood. Stunned survivors were everywhere, clothes ripped, wide eyes, hair full of brick dust. They were holding bits of paper, signs, photos, anything to try and help them find out where their sons or husbands or grannies were.

Drummond sat on the horn, forcing the car inch by inch through the crowd. The sea of people parted slightly and Gunner saw an ARP in his blue uniform trying to clear a path for two women carrying something in a light blue candlewick bedspread. One of them stumbled, let go of the corner, and a child's arm rolled out onto the pavement. Gunner looked away quickly.

'Fuck this,' said Drummond, and stopped the car.

They got out, left the car in the road and battled their way through the crowds towards the hall. All the chaos and suffering wasn't bothering Drummond one bit. He was happily pushing people aside shouting 'Police!' every few seconds. Gunner followed in his wake, trying to look like it wasn't his fault he was with him.

What looked like an overgrown schoolboy in some uniform Gunner didn't recognise was stationed at the big front doors. He was standing on a wooden crate trying to direct the people carrying bodies through one set of doors and the people looking for relatives through another. As far as Gunner could see he wasn't having much luck. The boy caught sight of Drummond and started waving, shouting over the noise:

'Chief Inspector Drummond, I don't know what to do with these—'

Drummond held up his hand, silencing him.

'Catch yourself on, Fraser, you're doing fine. Just keep at it, we'll be back soon. Ten minutes.'

The boy started to protest again, and Drummond shut him up with a reassuring pat on the back.

'Don't worry, son, you're doing a grand job.'

An old man pulled Fraser aside, asking him what door he

should be queuing at, and they took their chance and pushed their way forward. As soon as they were inside, Gunner pulled the sleeve of his battledress over his mouth, couldn't help himself. The stink of human excrement and burnt flesh was overwhelming, as bad as it had been in France. Drummond grabbed at him and pointed to the back of the hall.

'This way!'

The huge hall was filled with neat rows of bodies. Some of them covered, some just lying there. Drummond and Gunner picked their way through the rows, desperate not to stand on one. There were bodies with limbs missing, bodies that weren't much more than mangled flesh, even a headless man with a football-shaped object wrapped in a bloody sheet next to him.

Seemed all Gunner had been doing since the war started was looking at bodies and blood. The last thing he thought he'd be doing in Glasgow was looking at more of them. A woman in a man's overcoat over her nightie broke free from an ARP and ran up to him, thrusting a creased photo of a wee boy in a cowboy outfit in his face.

'Have you seen him? Have you, son? He's got to be somewhere, he's only nine, he's—'

Gunner shook his head but she clung to his arm, her eyes wide.

'They won't tell me anything, they won't—'

Drummond pulled them apart, shoved the woman aside.

'Up this way, Gunner, that's where the Maryhill bodies are.'

Gunner looked back as the ARP held on to the woman again, let her cry and scream in his arms. The noise started dying down as they walked through the hall and away from the chaos at the entrance. The hall began to seem more like a morgue and less like some charnel house. Gunner couldn't quite take the scale of it in. There must have been at least a hundred bodies in there, never mind the ones still being delivered at the front of the building. He could only imagine what Clydebank must look like now.

The Maryhill dead were laid out in two rows, twenty or so of them, KILMUN STREET chalked on the wooden floor beside them. Gunner knew Kilmun Street well. It was only a couple of hundred yards from the station, a wee street of tenements up by the canal. Drummond walked along the row and Gunner followed behind, scanning the bodies, hoping he wouldn't see anyone he knew. Drummond stopped at a body with a bloodstained floral curtain over it.

'Here he is,' he said. 'Found lying in the rubble in Kilmun Street last night.'

He looked at Gunner. 'I'd watch out – he's no a pretty sight.'

'I'm not the squeamish one,' said Gunner. 'Just get on with it.'

Drummond bent down and pulled the curtain aside. Gunner winced, couldn't help himself. Drummond was right, he wasn't a pretty sight; in fact he was a right bloody mess. The body was a middle-aged man, tall, thin. He'd a torn and bloody white shirt on, a pair of undershorts, and one black sock on his left foot. His body was covered in a dusting of powdered glass that was glistening and twinkling like frost in the sunlight streaming through the big skylights.

Gunner squatted down, tried not to grimace at the pain in his leg, and took a closer look. He picked up the man's right hand. It was cold, already starting to stiffen up. The tips of the fingers were missing, only five bloody stumps left. He looked over; the same scenario with his left one.

'See what I mean?' asked Drummond.

There was a clean cut across each finger, just below the top knuckle. Cutting through bone like that took some doing. You would need to be very strong and very determined. Would have to use garden shears, industrial scissors, something like that. Gunner let the hand drop, steeled himself and looked up at the man's face.

Not that there was much of a face left. The front of the skull had been caved in, was just a mess of blood and bone fragments. The man's eyes were wide open, full of powdered glass and brick dust. His lower jaw was only attached at one side, the rest of it hanging down on his chest leaving the bottom half of his face a gaping hole. A bluebottle circled round the blood and Gunner waved it away.

He heard Drummond light up behind him. 'Whoever did this didn't want him identified.'

Gunner looked up at him. 'It's no wonder they brought you back, Drummond, force must have been lost without you.'

'Aye, very good, Gunner, very good . . .' He hesitated. 'Oh Christ, what are you doing now?'

Gunner thought he'd seen something. He bent right over the body and stuck his hand into the gaping hole that was the corpse's mouth. He pushed his fingers in. It was cold, wet. He felt around, no real teeth left, just a few broken fragments. He stuck his fingers further in. Drummond was groaning behind him, the squelching noises making him squirm. Gunner could definitely feel something, just couldn't get his fingers to it. Took his hand out and wiped the blood and saliva on the curtain.

He took his toothbrush out the top pocket of his battledress jacket, pushed it deep into the corpse's mouth. He wriggled it around, felt it catch on something, jammed it up against the side of the throat, trapping whatever it was, and slid it up to the mouth. He held up the toothbrush, a wire bridge with three false teeth hanging from it.

'Must have battered him so hard it went right down his throat.'

He put the bridge on the man's chest and stood up. His knee cracked; he groaned inwardly and dusted himself off. Realised he was still holding his bloody toothbrush, wiped it on the curtain, went to put it back in his pocket.

'Fuck sake!' said Drummond.

Gunner looked at the toothbrush, dropped it into a nearby bin overflowing with bloody clothes and bandages. Nodded down at the man.

'You want to find out what happened, you need to get a proper autopsy done,' he said.

Drummond looked around the hall, finally saw what he was looking for. A doctor and an ARP warden were huddled together over a body a few rows away. He stuck two fingers in his mouth and whistled, piercing noise echoing around the big hall. The two of them looked up and Drummond waved them over. The doctor was young, late twenties, looked like he hadn't slept in days, dark circles around his eyes and a bloodstained white coat over crumpled pyjamas. The ARP was an old boy, blue uniform neatly tucked into his rubber boots, gas-mask carton over his shoulder.

'What you two up to?' he asked.

'Death certificates,' said the doctor, already bristling.

Drummond nodded down at the body. 'I need a proper

autopsy on this poor bugger soon as. Needs to go down to Montague Street now, tell them I need the results by the end of the day.'

The doctor looked at him, laughed, and waved around the hall.

'Just in case you haven't noticed, I'm busy. Working. And because of the Glasgow Police's inability to organise a piss-up in a fucking brewery, I've got relatives who shouldn't be in here grabbing me every five minutes asking me if I've seen their dad or their sister Ivy or fuck knows who. So, you'll pardon me if I don't jump.'

He was practically spitting, eyes starting to well up. The ARP was holding on to his arm, trying to get him to calm down. He shook him off, moved in on Drummond, started poking him in the chest. All his frustration and anger welling up.

'Eighteen hours I've been here, eighteen hours of wading my way through blood and shit and children burnt alive in their beds. Don't you dare speak to me like I'm one of your cadets to boss around.'

He stood there, breathing heavy, eyes brimming with tears.

Drummond reached into his pocket, took out a packet of Player's and lit one off the cigarette in his mouth.

'You finished?' he asked blandly. 'So what you're telling me is you've been doing your job. What were you expecting? A bloody medal?'

He blew smoke into his face, moved in closer. 'I'm doing my job too and you don't hear me greeting about it.' He nodded down. 'This is a murder victim, so that's a priority, so get it fucking done. Right?'

The doctor was shaking, fists clenched, looked like he was

deciding whether to hit him or not. The ARP moved in between them, promised Drummond the body would be at the morgue in an hour.

Gunner watched them walk away, the ARP's arm around the doctor's shoulder, talking him down.

'You really are a bastard, Drummond.'

A big smile broke across Drummond's face and he clapped Gunner on the back, very pleased with himself. 'Sure, you wouldn't have it any other way. So, you're going to help me out, then, find out who did this to the poor bugger?'

Gunner shook his head. 'I'm not a polis any more—'

'Aye, and you're no in the Army now either so what else are you gonnae do?'

'It's not that easy, Drummond. Things have changed, I've changed—'

'Like what? Your face looks like a dog's dinner, so what. It's done now. You're still my best bet.'

Gunner shook his head. 'I can't, Drummond, I—'

'Christ. You're going to make me say it, aren't you? I need you to do this, Gunner, please. I've naebody else.'

His eye. If only that was all it was. He looked down at the body lying on the curtain. At the mutilated hands and what was left of his face.

He nodded. 'Aye, all right then, but remember what I said. Things are different now.'

Drummond dropped his cigarette into a puddle of blood congealing on the floor. 'Good man,' he said, looked up at him. Grinned.

'Christ, but you want dinner and a swirl around the dance

floor before you get fucked, don't you? A proper lady right enough.'

Gunner shook his head. Should have known better. Drummond hadn't changed a bit, the same prick he always was, had to get the last word every time.

3

Gunner left Drummond and the boy with the uniform at the Kelvin Hall and said he'd see them at the autopsy later. He had other things on his mind than dead bodies with no fingers. His stomach was empty and growling, he had to find somewhere to stay, and he had to eat something. Shebeen could wait until tonight. He made his way back through the crowd outside the hall and started walking up Byers Road in pursuit of both.

Byers Road itself hadn't changed that much, the entrance to the closes were covered in baffles now, queues of women outside every butcher's and greengrocer: other than that it was the same busy street. No students from the University though, maybe that had closed down. No kids either. The city seemed a bit dead without them, too quiet, too well behaved. God help the poor country folk that were being invaded by evacuated kids from Glasgow, they wouldn't know what had hit them.

There was a mobile canteen set up at the junction of Great Western Road by the train station. It was the usual thing you saw everywhere. A van with Government posters slapped all over it and two good-looking girls behind the counter. He approached and they both smiled.

'Cup of tea and a bacon roll,' he said.

The women looked at each other, started laughing.

'Can do you a tea all right,' the one on the left said. 'But bacon? Are you kidding yourself? No bacon for months.'

The other one took the lid off a biscuit tin, held it out for him to look. Two miserable-looking Bath buns sat in a pile of crumbs.

'Could do you a scrape of marge on one?' she said.

Gunner nodded. Looked like this was as good as he was going to get.

He stood at the counter, supping his tea, listening to a couple of French sailors in uniform who'd turned up trying to chat the girls up in broken English. They weren't doing too badly as far as he could make out. The Bath bun was stale but he ate it anyway, chewing it up as much as he could. The Botanic Gardens by the canteen had definitely changed. No more neat flower beds and smooth grass. It had been dug up, big park now planted with rows and rows of potatoes and turnips.

He dug a bit of stale bun out of his teeth with a matchstick and wondered what Drummond was really up to. He had always operated two agendas, Drummond, the one he wanted you to know, the official one, and the one he didn't. Always had some side deal going on. Gunner finished his tea, put the tin mug back on the counter and headed up for the Barracks. No doubt he'd find out what it was soon enough.

The sun was hot on his back as he walked up Queen Margaret Drive, the River Kelvin making its sluggish way below him as he crossed the bridge. His leg was starting to ache, but the doctor had told him to try and walk on it. Easy for him to say, his leg hadn't been half blasted off by a bomb. He could feel the sweat starting to run down his back; whether it was from the sun or the pain he wasn't sure.

He hadn't sorted out anywhere to stay before he arrived, thought he would be tucked up at Chrissy's. Was going to give himself a couple of weeks to work out what he was going to do next. A medical discharge was nothing to be ashamed of, he supposed. He'd been wounded in battle, after all. He was a hero. Not that that was going to do him much good. He was a hero who was out on his ear.

If he wasn't fit enough for the Army then chances were he wasn't fit enough to go back into the police either. The problem was he had no idea what he was going to do next. He'd only ever been a polis since he left school. They would probably give him a desk job if he asked, but he didn't think he could face sitting on his arse all day while other lads did the real work.

He waited to cross the road and a bus passed, sign for Springburn on it. Remembered what he'd said to Andy. Promised to Andy. He'd go and see his wife when he got back to Glasgow. Seemed long ago now, the war did, except when some memory jumped out at him or he woke up from a dream where he was back in France. Still, a promise is a promise. He sighed, turned round and headed for Springburn. Took him twenty minutes or so to get there. Wasn't quite sure what he was going to tell her. Not what had happened, that was for sure.

Number 75 was next to a grocer's with bugger all in its window. Some sad-looking cabbages and a sack of potatoes. Was still a queue outside though, times must be hard indeed. He asked a wee boy coming out the close which flat Mrs Munn lived in. Top floor, he told him. Gunner sighed, started walking up the stairs.

He got to the top landing, stood for a while trying to get his breath back and to let the pain in his leg subside. Knocked on the door. Was just about to knock again when the door opened and a young woman with a baby in her arms was standing there.

'Mrs Munn?' he asked. 'My name's Joe Gunner. I served with your husband. With Andy.'

Five minutes later he was sitting at the kitchen table, mug of tea in front of him, sleeping baby in the cot, framed picture of Andy on the wall, black ribbon around it, Margie Munn looking at him. And he was lying.

'He was a good guy, Andy. Everyone liked him. One of the boys.'

She nodded, tears rolling down her cheeks.

'We were out on patrol. Andy thought he saw something, he shouted and we all got down. Hadn't been for that shout we would all be dead. Germans heard him, let go a shot and . . .'

Gunner stopped. Looked at her. What was the use in saying one minute he was there, next he was in pieces? Didn't help anyone, even if it was the truth. Made himself say it.

'He saved the lot of us.'

Margie reached out and held his hand.

'Thanks for coming here, Joe, it means a lot.'

She got up, went to pour another cup of tea. Gunner felt like a fraud, but the lie was better for her, and that was what mattered. Now she could tell everyone her Andy died a hero, one of the soldiers that was with him at the end had come all the way to tell her.

'What's your plans now?' she asked.

'Going to find myself somewhere to stay,' said Gunner.

'I've got a spare room,' she said. 'Was looking for a lodger, you could take that.'

Gunner thought about it for a minute. Knew it was a bad idea. She was lonely, a wee baby, a widow. Knew what would happen. He'd come home one night after a few drinks, and she'd be waiting up.

'Thanks, Margie, but I need somewhere on my own. Need to take it easy, try and get better.'

Sounded like an excuse the minute he said it. She nodded, tried to smile.

'Just an idea,' she said. 'Don't worry.'

He left her there. Promised he'd come back and see how she was doing, both of them knowing he wouldn't, and walked back down the stairs into the sunshine.

Twenty minutes later he was walking past the Vaults, could see the Barracks looming up in the distance. His next idea. The Barracks had been there since the turn of the century, a huge place, almost a separate village in the city. The official base of the Scots Greys Regiment. More than two acres of ugly brown buildings and exercise yards. Home to a thousand people, in peacetime, God knows how many now. A tall wall ran round the whole compound, more to keep the soldiers in than any intruders out. Officers had quarters across the street for when their wives visited. The 'knocking shop', as it was known to the ordinary men who got no such privileges.

When the war broke out, that's where Gunner went to join up. All he had to do was walk across the road from his station and sign on the line. Just like that. Seemed the easiest option. And now he was back.

He nodded at the armed guards at the gates, showed his

identity card and headed for the wee offices round the back of the main building. He'd find MacGregor, the staff sergeant, see if he remembered him, ask if he could find him somewhere to stay for a few days, just until he found somewhere permanent. Chances were it would be a no to both, but it was the only idea he had.

Gunner skirted around the parade ground, kept close to the walls and out of the road where new conscripts were being shouted at, trying to march in time. He had to admit, even by new conscript standards, they were bloody awful. A tall ginger boy was in tears, sergeant screaming into his face. Supposed it was easier for people like him, that had been in the police, already had half an idea of what the Army was going to be like. Not these guys though, half of them looked shell-shocked already.

There was a kick-about going on round the other side of the ground, everyone down to their vests, sound of shouts and boots clattering on the cobbles, echoing off the surrounding buildings. Like being back at school. He wondered how many of these guys would still be playing football next year, how many of them would be here at all. He stood for a minute watching the game. Used to be pretty good. He'd been good at football, good at most sports. Not any more. Played for the Police First XI. Not any more, not with what had happened. Still, he was here and he was alive, luckier than a lot he had known.

It turned out the expression was true, wonders never ceased. MacGregor did remember him, recognised him straight away.

'Gunner, Joseph, 1542686. Never forget a face,' he said, holding out a hand to shake. 'Or a big bastard with blond hair.'

MacGregor himself wasn't easy to forget either. Big round

face, wee glasses, strawberry birthmark on his neck, black hair cut into the wood. It seemed like MacGregor had come up in the world since the last time they'd met when he was herding new volunteers around the place, showing them where everything was. He even had his own office now, even if it was only marginally bigger than a cupboard, brass nameplate on the door and everything.

After the usual questions about what was going on in France, MacGregor got down to business. He sucked the air through his teeth and flicked through the papers on the desk in front of him. Scribbled something with a blunt pencil.

'How many days again?' he asked.

'A week?' asked Gunner, chancing his arm.

'Christ, not asking much, are you?' MacGregor flicked through his papers again. Spotted something. Grinned.

'You, Gunner Joseph, 1542686, are a lucky man. I can squeeze you in. Just don't spread the word, we're no a bloody hotel,' he said. 'I'll get a rocket up my arse frae the Boss if he finds out.'

McGregor stood up. 'C'mon, let's get you in there before the daft bastard gets back from his lunch.'

They navigated their way back across the parade ground, stopping every two minutes as someone else stopped MacGregor and asked about wrong-sized uniforms or lost gas masks or where the infirmary was. Funny that a wee guy who had been charged with making sure there was enough toilet roll and uniform trousers was now the real power in the barracks. The man who knew everything.

'Where are you taking me, then?' asked Gunner.

'Married quarters for the Major. The stupid old bastard's

been sent to North Africa so they've been requisitioned for transferable use.'

Gunner wasn't following. 'Eh?'

'Odds and sods,' said MacGregor. 'Waifs and strays. People who turn up out the blue and need to be put somewhere. He wiped his brow with his sleeve, looked up at the sky. 'Fucking weather, sun's splitting the sky.'

They both knew what that meant. More raids.

'You'll have some pals, mind you,' said McGregor. 'Two blokes up from London, posh bastards working for the Ministry of Food.'

4

The Major's quarters consisted of a little suburban house backing onto the barracks' walls, a small garden in front complete with a lawn, a white fence, and a row of parched-looking rose bushes. They walked up the path and MacGregor knocked on the door. They waited. No reply.

'Laurel and Hardy must be out,' said MacGregor as he selected a key from the twenty or so on a chain around his waist and opened the door. They went in, shouted hello. No reply. Gunner looked round the living room. Floral wallpaper, three-piece suite with antimacassars, upright piano in the corner. Various African masks stuck up on the walls and an antelope skin rug on the carpet.

'He was in India or somewhere before here,' explained MacGregor. 'Hence all this shite.'

'Africa,' said Gunner. 'Think it was Africa.'

'That right? Fuck knows, but wherever it was, the old bastard went on and on about it,' said MacGregor. 'Wish he'd bloody stayed there. Come on.'

The souvenirs continued upstairs, a shield with crossed spears on the wall by the bedrooms, wooden statues of antelopes and cheetahs sitting on the bookcase on the landing. MacGregor pushed one of the doors on the landing open.

'Sorry,' he said. 'It's a bit poky but you're lucky to get it.'

Gunner peeked in. He wasn't complaining, he'd been expecting a cot at the back of a crowded dorm. The wee box room was going to be the most luxurious place he'd stayed in quite a while, it definitely beat sleeping in a bombed-out barn in the French countryside or a tented dormitory surrounded by the noise of fifty blokes snoring. A bed with a flowery cover filled up most of the room, two pillows on top, lamp on a table beside them. Next door to it was a bathroom with a full-sized bath and a pile of towels on a shelf.

'Hot water?' Gunner asked hopefully.

MacGregor looked at his watch. 'You'll need to be quick, goes off at one.' He started down the stairs. 'I'm off, got another twenty stupid Polish bastards arriving this afternoon and nowhere to put them. I'll leave you to introduce yourself to the food boys.'

Soon as MacGregor had gone, Gunner filled the bath near enough to the top; fuck the regulations and the wee line showing five inches deep painted on the side of the bath, he'd earned it. He stripped off his uniform, the smell of smoke and the dead from the hall still clinging to it, and eased himself into the hot water. Lay back. Tried to remember last time he'd had a proper bath rather than a two-minute shower in cold water surrounded by twenty other blokes.

There was a bar of Pears soap on the side of the bath. He picked it up, smelt it. Better than the carbolic stuff they had in the latrine blocks. He started washing himself, sure he could still smell the hall clinging to him. The mirror on the wall opposite the bath caught his movement. He couldn't help but look at himself in it.

He pulled the bathroom curtain across and took his eyepatch off. Doctor had told him he had to keep it on unless he was in dim light. His eye couldn't cope with normal light, it was like staring at the sun all the time. The hope was, in a couple of months the eye would be back to normal. Scarred flesh around it would always be there though, nothing they could do about that.

The scar on his face wasn't the only one he had, not by a long shot. There were two burns, patches of shiny red skin about the sizes of saucers, on his chest. They looked worse than he'd thought they did now he could see them in a mirror. He shifted in the bath, looking away. Seeing them, he remembered how he'd got them. He could feel his hands start to shake, made fists, waited for it to pass, sank down into the water.

The bomb that did it, that gave him the map of scars, killed the bloke next to him. Arthur somebody, couldn't remember his second name. Gunner had only met him that morning. He'd a broad Birmingham accent, kept blabbering on about wanting to get home to his racing pigeons. He was telling Gunner about how he was going to build a new coop when there was a whump, a sudden heat, and then Arthur Somebody's body was flying up in the air, coming down in two separate pieces. That flying body was the last thing Gunner remembered before he passed out. And it was the first thing he remembered when he came to in the field hospital.

He lay for a minute. Hadn't been lying when he told Drummond he wasn't sure he was up to it. Even if Drummond didn't believe him, Gunner was a changed man. He looked down at his left leg. A scar ran from mid-thigh to mid-calf, shiny pink, width of a penny. Ended in a furrow about six inches long and about an inch deep. The doctors had started off hopeful, talked about him being back to normal in a couple of weeks, then they told him it was going to be a long time in rehabilitation, wasn't healing as it should, and then they didn't really talk to him any more at all. He reached for the soap and winced in pain. The warm water was helping, but not enough. His leg still hurt like fuck. Time to fix it.

He leant over the side of the bath, took the wee cardboard box out of his drawstring washbag and shook it. Only two left. He'd been trying to ration them out since he left the hospital but he hadn't done very well. It was half the reason he was angry most of the time, the pain was constant. He took the syrette out of the box and fitted the wee needle that came with it into the top. Read the label the same as he did every time. *Solution of Morphine Tartrate. May be habit forming.*

Maybe it was. After five weeks in the hospital, it was hard to tell. He pinched the skin on his stomach, pulled it out and stuck the needle in. Then the familiar cold feeling as he squeezed the tube and the solution flowed down through the needle and into his body. It only took a minute or two to start working. He lay back in the bath. The pain in his leg went immediately and then the warmth spread through his body. And then there was nothing. Nothing but a knowledge that for a while at least he wasn't going to be thinking about the bomb or Arthur Somebody or the pain in his leg or the fact there was only one syrette left in the box.

He lay there for an hour or so as the water cooled, just

enjoying the quiet, his mind empty, body not hurting for once. It was one of the strangest things about the Army: you were always surrounded by noise and people, never got any time to yourself. The Army didn't like people being left on their own, it meant they might start thinking for themselves. He stood up, shook the water off and caught sight of himself in the mirror again. He'd lost weight, too much weight. He'd always been a big guy, strong. It came in handy. Being a polis in Glasgow was a physical business. Had to be able to give as good as you got. Wasn't sure he could do that any more.

He dried himself, treating himself to two towels. He was just about finished shaving when he heard the front door opening downstairs, voices. He wiped the soap off his face, wrapped one of the towels around his middle, put his patch back on and walked down the stairs to meet his new neighbours.

Gunner opened the living-room door and whatever conversation had been going on stopped abruptly. Two men turned to face him, both looking surprised. One was in his late forties, ordinary looking, grey suit. The other was younger, about Gunner's age, late twenties. He had a mop of messy blond hair, tweed suit, build like a rugby forward. He looked Gunner up and down.

'You seem to be dripping on the Major's best Axminster. Just as well he's in Iraq,' he said, holding his hand out. 'Giles Nickerson.'

Gunner had met some posh officers in his time, but this guy took the biscuit. He sounded like an announcer for the BBC. He wiped his hand on the towel around his waist and shook hands.

'Joseph Gunner. I've been moved in for a couple of days.'

Nickerson looked thoughtful. 'Gunner? Swedish? You don't sound like it?'

Gunner shook his head. 'Glasgow born and bred. Swedish father, hence the name.'

'Ah! I was close,' said Nickerson, looking pleased with himself. 'Excellent. More the merrier, eh? This is my colleague, Anthony Moore.

Gunner held his hand out. Moore shook it, looking none too happy.

'No one notified us that someone else was going to be staying here.'

'It was a last-minute thing,' said Gunner. 'They billeted me in the box room, nowhere else to put me.'

Moore just stared at him.

Gunner held up his hands. 'If you want to check, be my guest.'

'No need, no need,' said Nickerson quickly. 'Perfectly understandable. Space is an absolute bugger.' He looked Gunner up and down, a beat too long, and stopped on his scars.

'Well, you have been in the wars. No doubt about that.'

Gunner shifted uncomfortably, pulled the towel tighter around his waist. 'I've just got to get dressed, then I'm out your way.'

Moore ignored him, spoke to Nickerson. 'Have we got everything we need? The driver should be here any minute.'

'I'll double-check,' said Nickerson, and scuttled up the stairs leaving the two of them standing there in awkward silence. Moore took a silver cigarette case out of his inside jacket pocket and flipped it open. He was about to take out a cigarette, then paused and stepped forward, holding the case out to Gunner.

'Thanks,' Gunner said, taking one.

Moore lit up, waved the smoke away from his face. Held his lighter out. 'Sorry if I seemed a bit rude, you took us rather by surprise.'

'That's understandable.' Gunner exhaled a cloud of smoke. Decent cigarette for once, not the usual army issue rubbish. 'You're Ministry of Food?'

Moore nodded. 'Bit of a dry job but someone's got to do it.'

'What are you're doing up here?' asked Gunner.

'It's a feasibility study on enlarging the sheep population. Whether there's enough land that can be changed to grazing, et cetera.' He smiled, suddenly seemed a bit less of a dry stick. 'Absolutely fascinating stuff, as you can imagine.'

'Got them! I'd left them on my bed.' Nickerson had re-appeared holding a pile of dun-coloured files.

'Gunner, fancy a drink in the mess later?' he asked. 'Be good to hear what's going on from someone with first-hand experience. Does us back-room boys good to know.'

Gunner nodded. 'Long as you're buying. I'm skint.'

Nickerson clapped his hands. 'Excellent!'

Moore turned and looked out the window: a black Jaguar was drawing up outside.

'That's the car,' he said. 'See you later.'

He opened the front door and they left. Gunner watched them climb into the back of the car, bald driver in a pinstripe suit holding the door open for them. He may have been half full of morphine, but Gunner still had some of his polis instincts left. If those two were from the Ministry of Food, then he was a Russian sailor.

5

'Jesus Christ. The Viking's back!'

Archie Taylor leant over the counter and held his hand out to shake. He'd been the desk sergeant at the Maryhill police station since Gunner could remember. He still looked much the same, same ginger hair combed into a neat shed, hangdog expression, but he looked older. Supposed everyone did.

'Good, Archie, good,' said Gunner, shaking his hand.

He looked round. The station hadn't changed much since he'd been gone. Old and cracked green lino on the floor, the metal bench bolted to the wall, a bucket and mop in case the jakeys didn't make it to the toilets in time. The only new additions were on the walls. Loads of them.

'Got some new posters, I see.'

Archie shook his head. 'Ministry of Defence. You'd think they would have better things to do than send new ones every week. It'll be knit a bloody soldier for Christmas next.'

He looked at Gunner again. 'What happened there?' he asked, touching his own left eye.

'There?' said Gunner. 'Nothing, should have seen the other bloke.'

'Not a scratch on him?' asked Archie, grinning.

'Beat me to it,' said Gunner. 'My clothes still in my locker?'

'They should be. Unless that sticky-fingered bastard Barbour's managed to get in there.'

Archie looked up at the clock over the double doors. 'My shift's about done. Why don't we go for a pint and you can tell me how many Jerries you sent packing.'

'Good idea, just going to see if any of my clothes are still here.'

Gunner lifted up the gate and walked back towards the locker room. The place smelt the same as always, sweat and carbolic soap. He sat down on the bench and looked at his locker. Still had the initials J. D. carved into the wood, whoever J. D. had been, long before his time. A wee room with wooden slats on the wall, five lockers and worn lino on the floor. Even so, he was going to miss it. Miss the joking and the insults, he'd even miss the station chancer Barbour trying to tell everyone what a hero he'd been that day. What was it they said? You don't miss something until it's gone. Wise words. He ran his fingers along the top of his locker, found the key where it always was. Looked like Barbour hadn't had any luck.

He opened the locker up. His police uniform, a suit and a couple of shirts were hanging from the rail. A pair of leather brogues with balled-up socks stuffed into them were sitting on the shelf below. It all looked a bit sad somehow; was that all he added up to? Some worn clothes and a pair of socks balled up in the hope they would last another day? He heard Archie shouting through, telling him to hurry up. He did.

The Punch Bowl across the road from the station was the polis boozer, always had been. They waited to cross the road, still a few ambulances rumbling in from Clydebank. It was getting properly hot now, sun high in the sky. The women waiting outside the butcher's were down to sleeveless dresses, wee kids in shorts and plimsolls holding their mum's hands and looking bored.

The smell of stale beer and Woodbine smoke hit Gunner as soon they walked into the pub. He hadn't smelt a pub in a long time; smelt great. Archie sat down and Gunner went up to the bar. Jackie wasn't in his usual place behind the bar, God knows where he was now, hard to keep track of anyone these days. Instead it was a young barmaid he didn't recognise. She took his order, smiled, moved the chewing gum around her mouth as she poured the pints.

Gunner looked at himself in the big TENNENT's gantry mirror while he waited for them. It was strange to see himself in a suit and tie, he'd been wearing a uniform for so long. Suddenly realised how much he looked like his father. Same blond hair, same height, same big build. He had been the age Gunner was now when he was born. The barmaid plonked the two pints down on the bar, he handed over two bob, told her to keep the change and carried them over to where Archie was sitting.

'Cheers,' he said, clinking glasses and sitting down.

'You hear about the bombing last night?' asked Archie.

Gunner nodded. 'Drummond met me off the train.'

'Christ, what a welcome back,' said Archie. 'Nae luck.'

'You up there, were you?'

Archie nodded. 'Fucking hellish it was. We couldn't even get the van properly into Clydebank, couldn't get near it, roads were all blocked, we had to get out and walk. I'll tell you this,

Gunner, it was like walking through the fires of hell. The whole place was blazing, bright as bloody daylight it was. And you could hear the people stuck in their houses screaming blue murder, screaming so loud you could hear them over the noises of the fires and things collapsing.'

He shook his head, stopped for a minute.

'I've never heard such a horrible sound in my life. Half of them had to drop their kids out the bloody windaes just to save them. Never seen anything like it.'

He took a draught of his pint, looked into space for a minute. 'They're saying the bastards'll be back tonight, another clear sky.'

'You at the Maryhill bombing too?' asked Gunner.

Archie nodded, wiped a foam moustache away.

'Couldn't do much in Clydebank so we came back, heard Maryhill was hit. Shiskine Street, Kilmun Street, all around there. It was nowhere near as bad as Clydebank but a couple of the tenements are down, half of the ones still standing'll need to come down an' all. Not safe any more.' He yawned. Smiled. 'Christ, I don't know if I'm going to be able to finish this pint before I nod off. There's a cot at the station, been staying there most nights, no really worth going home these days. There's so few of us left I've been on back-to-back shifts for months.'

'You take any of the bodies out of Kilmun Street?' asked Gunner, lighting up.

'Aye,' said Archie. 'Helped load them onto the van the ARP boys had. Bloody horrible, like a butcher's shop it was, people no more than pieces, would turn your stomach.'

'You see a man's body there? No fingers, face caved in?'

Archie shook his head immediately, didn't even have to think about it. 'Naw, would have remembered that. I remember them all.'

Not what Gunner had expected to hear.

'You sure?' he asked. 'No body found like that in Kilmun Street? Around there maybe?'

'Oh, I'm sure all right,' said Archie. 'I'll remember everything about last night as long as I live. Every dead body, every woman screaming for her dead weans. I couldnae forget it even if I wanted to.'

He yawned again, tried to stifle it.

'Away you go,' said Gunner. 'Get some sleep. You deserve it.'

'You sure?' asked Archie. 'Sorry, Joe. We just got here. I haven't even heard your news.'

'I'm sure. My news'll keep until next time. Go. God knows you need as much beauty sleep as you can get.'

'Cheeky bugger!' Archie stood up, put his jacket on. 'We'll do another night, eh? Have a proper go of it?'

Gunner nodded, shook his hand and watched him go. If Archie was right, and he'd no reason not to believe him, the body didn't come from Kilmun Street after all. Which begged the question, where had it really come from? And why was it in the Kilmun Street section in the Kelvin Hall?

Gunner drained his pint, stood up. Had a feeling that Drummond wasn't telling him everything he should be. It didn't surprise him, up to his usual tricks. But this time it was different; he was in the driving seat, and if Drummond didn't come clean he was off. Like he'd told him, he didn't work for him any more.

6

Despite its grand title, the Mortuary of the City of Glasgow didn't look like much. A long low building at the corner of Montague Street down by the Clyde. Chances were you wouldn't notice it if you walked past. Maybe that was the point.

By the time Gunner got there it was just after three. He had walked down through the middle of town, still couldn't get over how different it looked. All the shop windows were taped up, criss-crosses of black tape. Seemed like every bit of green space he passed had been dug up to plant vegetables. The streets were quiet for the middle of the day. Just the distant rumble of army trucks heading out of town and a few forlorn blasts of ships' horns from the Clyde.

The morphine was still in his system, he felt pleasantly content, happy to be back home. Needed to get this stuff with Drummond out the way and do what he really wanted to do. Simple stuff. Get drunk, eat some fish and chips. Pay a visit to the shebeen on Gardener Street. See if Ailsa was still there, spend the last of his money, enjoy himself.

He was still wondering about what Archie had said. He seemed pretty definite, no body like the one he'd seen in the Kelvin

Hall had come from Kilmun Street. Gunner had no reason to believe he was mistaken. Which only left one conclusion. Drummond had some answering to do.

Gunner heard someone call his name, turned and squinted into the sunshine, trying to see who it was. The young uniform from outside the Kelvin Hall was running down the street towards him.

'Mr Gunner!' He was trying to shout through the panting. 'Hold on!'

Gunner stopped, waited for him to catch up, wondered what could be so urgent.

The boy stopped running, looked flustered, hair plastered onto his forehead with sweat. 'I just caught you . . .' A few deep breaths. 'Mr Drummond sent me . . .' Another breath. 'He's running late, said you should just go in.'

Gunner shook his head. 'Don't tell me, that bastard up to his old tricks again?'

'What?' said the boy, wiping the sweat off his brow with his sleeve.

'Drummond. Never was keen on a visit to the morgue. Hasn't got the stomach for it. Let me guess, he's running late because he's sitting round the corner in the Old Ship Bank having a fly pint.'

The boy reddened. Nodded.

'What's your name again, son?' asked Gunner.

'Fraser,' said the boy. 'Fraser Lockhart.'

Gunner laughed. 'Fuck me. You're no from Glasgow with a name like that, are you?'

Fraser shook his head. 'Just outside of Perth.'

Gunner looked him up and down. He seemed fit enough,

almost as tall as he was, looked like he'd be happier playing cricket than running about Glasgow after Drummond. He still had no idea what his uniform was supposed to be.

'What are you, son?' he asked. 'Some sort of cadet?'

The boy straightened himself up, tried look official. 'I'm in the Auxiliary Police Force. Joined up straight after school.'

Gunner was none the wiser. 'That a new thing, is it?'

Fraser nodded. 'The police force needed bodies; they've only got old guys now.'

'Don't let Drummond hear you saying that.' Gunner pulled the mortuary door open. 'You coming?'

'Me?' asked Fraser, looking surprised.

'Aye, you, you want to be a polis, don't you? Come on.'

Normally the mortuary put Gunner in mind of a church. It was always quiet and dimly lit, people talking in hushed tones. Not today. Today it was bedlam. The noise was echoing off the bare walls, shouts, the clatter of trolleys, the occasional curse. The corridors were full of people all jammed up against the walls, barely enough space to get a stretcher through.

Gunner told Fraser to stick with him and started trying to make his way to the examination room. Told him to follow behind as shouts from two ambulancemen trying to drop off more bodies at the back door started rising above the general noise. Two mortuary attendants and an ARP were having an argument over a body draped in a green sheet, toe sticking out, two labels tied to it. One more than there should be. They shuffled up the tiny space left in the middle of the corridor and made it to the door at the end. Gunner knocked on the frosted-glass window and they went in.

Robert MacAdam was standing in the middle of the bright white room, wellies and a white lab coat over a tweed suit and a spotty bow tie. He was a dapper wee man in his early sixties, moustache as grey as his neatly trimmed hair. He was frowning and holding what looked like a brain in his left hand.

Gunner turned to Fraser.

'Golden rule. If you're going to be sick or pass out, make for the door. Don't do it in here or MacAdam will crucify you.'

Fraser nodded; he didn't seem that queasy or scared, quite the opposite. He was looking at MacAdam and what he had in his hand with interest.

'So, how's you, Bobby?' asked Gunner.

MacAdam gently eased the brain onto a weighing scale, peeled off his rubber gloves and shook hands.

'Gunner! I thought you were off fighting the Germanic hordes?'

'I was,' said Gunner. 'Back here to recuperate. Said I'd help Drummond out for a few days.'

'More fool you,' said MacAdam, putting his hand on Gunner's chin and moving his face into the light to get a better look at his scars by his eye. He frowned. 'What did they use on that? Darning needle? A fish hook?' He stepped back and looked at Fraser. 'You're not him,' he said. 'So where is the fat oaf?'

'Running late,' said Gunner.

'There's a surprise,' said MacAdam. He nodded over at one of the marble slabs, draped body on top. 'So you're the one responsible for moving this poor unfortunate to the head of the queue?'

Gunner nodded. 'Blame the fat oaf.'

MacAdam pulled the sheet aside and Fraser let out a gasp.

Gunner didn't blame him. Injuries always looked worse in here somehow, laid out for examination. The man's mutilated hands were lying on the pale marble, what was left of his face in sharp detail under the sunlight streaming in from the windows in the roof. A large Y-shaped incision in his chest didn't help much either, big black stitches standing out against his pale chest.

MacAdam hitched himself up on the neighbouring slab and took a swig from a silver hip flask he had produced from his pocket. He grimaced as it went down and handed it to Gunner. He swallowed a mouthful and gave it back. It was good malt whisky, no rubbish for MacAdam. MacAdam held the flask out to Fraser. He shook his head vigorously, seemed more scared of the flask than of the bodies around him. MacAdam shrugged. 'Please yourself.'

He nodded over at the body.

'Somewhere between forty and forty-five, I would estimate. He was in reasonable good health. Some evidence of endo-carditis—'

'Eh?' said Gunner.

'Sorry,' said MacAdam. 'Inflammation of the inner layer of the heart, wouldn't have been a problem for another few years. Just under six feet tall, fourteen stone four, sans weight of fingers that is. Fortunately for him they were removed post mortem. Garden shears or something like that.'

'Nasty,' said Gunner.

'Very. The cause of death itself is no great mystery. Major and multiple trauma to the skull. Blunt instrument. A big blunt instrument in this particular case. A brick, mallet, something along those lines. Whoever did it hit him with some amount of force, destroyed the front of the skull, lower jawbone, teeth.'

'So it was a big bastard, then?' asked Gunner.

MacAdam nodded, slipped off the table. 'Or a particularly strong small one.' He pointed at the wreck of the man's head. 'Injuries consistent with an attempt to prevent identification.'

'Looks like they succeeded,' said Gunner.

MacAdam smiled, took the man's dental bridge out of his pocket.

'Almost,' he said. 'Almost but not quite.'

7

'He was what?' Drummond's normally ruddy face had turned pale.

'You heard me,' said Gunner. 'He was a German.'

Drummond took a matchstick out of the box sitting on top of his cigarettes, broke it in half and started rooting around in his back teeth with it.

'That's all I fucking need,' he said. 'How does MacAdam know?'

'The bridge in his mouth,' said Gunner. 'They make them a different way over there. MacAdam had seen one before. An old German guy that had that tailor's in Virginia Street. The one that killed himself. He did the autopsy. Same kind.'

The Old Ship Inn was filling up around them, workers pouring in from the fish market and the cargo warehouses all along the river. One half had white coats and pink scrubbed hands, the other half were in rolled up shirtsleeves, hands black with tar and dust.

The three of them were sitting at a wee table up the back, out the way of the crowd. Drummond leant forward as if someone were listening in.

'Christ, you don't think he was a spy, do you?'

Gunner shrugged.

'There's something else that's weird too,' he said.

Drummond rolled his eyes. 'Christ, what else?'

'I spoke to Archie at the station. He helped get the bodies out of Kilmun Street and our guy wasn't one of them. No middle-aged man with no fingers and a smashed-in face.'

'For fuck sake,' said Drummond, looking even more glum. 'This is turning into a grade one shite show. What was he doing in the Kelvin Hall then?'

'You were there,' said Gunner. 'You saw it like I did, it was chaos. People were dropping bodies off all the time no questions asked. The perfect cover.'

'Aye, and it would have been if some arse of a doctor hadnae called me in. Wish he hadn't bloody bothered.' Drummond ground the end of his cigarette into the tin ashtray on the table, flicked his zippo open and lit another. 'So what do we do now then?'

Gunner sat back on his stool, took a sip of his pint. 'That's up to you. Tell the big boys I suppose. MI5 or whatever it's called. London.'

Drummond looked pained. 'I cannae do that, they'll be all over me like a rash.'

If Gunner knew Drummond, and he did, he'd be using the chaos of wartime to run scams all over the shop. Fake ration books, confiscated petrol coupons, taking a cut of stuff going missing from the docks. The war was one big opportunity for people like him. The last thing he would want was the big boys from London having a snoop around.

'There is another possibility . . .'

Gunner and Drummond turned toward the young chap's voice. Fraser was already going red.

'There's a what?' asked Drummond.

Fraser put his lemonade down on the table. 'He could be a German POW from one of the camps. There are quite a few around Glasgow. He could have escaped and come into town.'

'That's not a bad idea,' said Drummond. He thought for a minute, then spat his chewed matchstick onto the floor. 'I tell you what, Gunner, you take young Fraser here and go and check the camps, will only take you a day or so. Then if Herman the German's no from there we can call the MI5 boys in. That way it'll look like we've been using our initiative.' He grinned at Gunner. 'Make sense?'

'Fuck off,' said Gunner.

'What?'

'I told you I'd look at a body as a favour, no sign on full time.'

'One fucking day, that's all I'm asking. After all I've done for you.'

Gunner snorted. 'Like what?'

'I let you take the credit for the Wilson case.'

'Because I solved it.'

'Still, I was the superior officer, could have claimed it. Besides, young Fraser here can't drive. How's he going to get to . . . Where was it again?'

'Nearest one is Thornliebank, I think,' said Fraser. 'Over on the Southside.'

'Thornliebank?' asked Gunner. 'You sure?'

Fraser nodded.

'OK. One day and that's it,' said Gunner.

'Knew you would come to your senses,' said Drummond, looking smug.

'Is your motor outside?'

'Aye, but you cannae take it,' said Drummond. 'You can get a car from the station—'

Gunner held his hand out. 'Keys.'

Drummond swore and started digging in his trouser pocket. 'You be careful, that's my good motor.'

Gunner took the keys and handed them to Fraser. 'Away out and sit in the car for a minute.'

He waited until Fraser had made his way through the crowd and was out the door before he turned back to Drummond.

'Something you're not telling me, Georgie boy?' he asked.

Drummond held his hands out, tried to look innocent. 'It's only a bob or two here and there, black market stuff, that's all, it's nothing—'

'Not about that. About the other dead body MacAdam showed me.'

'Ah. That.' Drummond stood up. 'Pint?'

The other body MacAdam had shown Gunner was one Andy Innes. No great pity he was dead, he was a nasty piece of work, it was the way he'd died that was the problem. He'd been brought in a couple of days ago, found in the bushes behind the swing park by Saracen Street. Two shots, one to the head to kill him and one up the arse just to rub in the disrespect. There was only one person in Glasgow that went in for that sort of stuff, and the last Gunner heard he was still locked up in Barlinnie Prison. He should know, he was the one who put him there.

Drummond appeared back with the pints and sat down. Got in first.

'Look, Gunner. I was gonnae tell you Sellars was out. I just haven't had the time yet. Didn't want to get into it in front of the young lad.'

'How the fuck is he out?' hissed Gunner. 'He should be in for another five years.'

Drummond supped his Tennent's.

'His brother organised some big lawyer, didn't he. Employed some hotshot frae Edinburgh. The lawyer put in an appeal, it has been going on for a while, but some High Court judge finally ruled on it. Sellars got out a couple of weeks ago.'

Gunner shook his head.

'So what happened?' he said. 'Sellars finally found a High Court judge he could buy off? What was he doing? Fucking one of his girls?'

Drummond nodded. 'Clever you. Turned out she was fourteen. And they had photos.'

'Christ,' said Gunner. 'So what did Andy Innes have to do with it?'

'Innes? Nothing,' said Drummond. 'But he worked for Con McGill, didn't he, and Sellars is going through his boys one by one. There's more than one bloody war going on in Glasgow, you know.'

'Sellars is going up against Con?' asked Gunner. 'Is he fucking daft?'

'Daft or fucking suicidal, either way he's doing it.'

Gunner shook his head. 'I was sure that bastard was away for years.'

Drummond sat back, looked at Gunner.

'You know, it might do to watch yourself, Gunner. Sellars'll no forget who put him away. And someone will have earned a fiver by now for telling him you're back.'

'What's that supposed to be?' asked Gunner. 'A warning?'

Drummond held his hands up. 'Don't fucking take it out on me. Advice is what it is. Take it or leave it.'

Gunner stood up. 'Thanks for the heads up, Drummond. Thanks a fucking lot . . .'

'Come on, Joe. I'm just trying to . . .'

But Drummond was talking to Gunner's back.

8

Gunner didn't say much on the way to the camp. He had things on his mind. Sellars mostly. Sellars was a pro, took prison as a part of the deal. Him and his brother had been at it since they were teenagers. To them the polis were just doing their job the same as he was, they wouldn't carry a grudge. At least, that was what he was telling himself; didn't fancy spending the next few days looking over his shoulder. Sellars was Malky Sellars, Sunday name Malcolm Sellars. His brother was Matthew. Matthew was supposed to be the brains behind the outfit; Gunner had never met him, wasn't sure anybody had. He'd kept his profile lower than low, let his wee brother do the talking. And the shooting.

Gunner had put Malky Sellars away in August '39 just before the war started. Sellars had got careless and Gunner had got lucky. That was all it took. Gunner pulled him over on a fishing expedition, just the usual low-level harassment. One of the headlights on his car wasn't working, reason enough. Gunner wasn't expecting anything much – least of all to hear a thumping from the boot when he checked the tyres. It turned out a wee toerag called Eck Peters was bundled up in there, doing his best to kick his way free. Gunner opened the boot and there he was, hands tied, gag in his mouth, a broken arm. There was a bonus too. A sawn-off shotgun in a burlap bag beside him. Malky Sellars got sent down for seven years. And now he was out.

'You're going the wrong way,' said Fraser, watching the sign for Thornliebank disappear behind them. 'You should have turned off back there.'

Gunner nodded. He knew he should have turned off but he was heading for Newton Mearns, a small village another mile or so beyond Thornliebank.

'We need to go somewhere first,' he said. 'It'll no take long.'

Gunner was watching the side of the road, waiting for the sign. He almost missed it; it was half hidden in the long summer grass. Chipped black paint on a white wooden board. FLOORS FARM. He turned off the road and onto a muddy track. The Morris lurched and juddered, springs doing battle with the bumps and potholes.

'Who lives up here, then?' asked Fraser.

'My brother,' Gunner replied.

The road to the farm ran led them up a hill through fields of sheep and spring lambs. Gunner rolled down the window and the country smell of manure and cut grass filled the car. There was a break in the hedges and he caught sight of a straggly group of men digging with spades and pickaxes. He pulled the car onto the side of the track, told Fraser to stay put, slammed the car door shut behind him, cutting off his protests, and headed off.

There were a dozen or so men in the potato field, different ages, but all of them dressed the same. They were a ragbag group, all old suit trousers and vests with holes in them. Gunner found a gap in the hedge, squeezed through, and walked across the field towards them. The ground was soft and wet beneath his feet, his shoes were covered in mud after just a few steps. He cursed and rolled up his trousers, trying to keep the mud off them at least. The men stopped working and leant on their spades, stood and watched him approach. One of them took a pair of specs from his trouser pocket and pulled them on. A big smile broke across his face.

'Joe Gunner? Is that you?'

Gunner walked up and shook his hand. 'None other.'

It was only now he was this close that he realised what a state the men were in. One had a broken nose that looked recent, a couple had black eyes, and one of them had his arm in a grubby sling. The man with the glasses was Walter Sweet, his brother's pal. He hadn't fared any better. His hair was shaved to the wood, cuts and stray tufts of hair on his naked scalp. He'd a tooth missing at the front, looked like he's lost a couple of stone.

'I thought you were in away with the Army' said Sweet.

Gunner tapped his eyepatch.

'Some Jerry bomb decided to do its worst.'

'Anyway, what's happened to you?' Gunner asked, looking Sweet up and down. 'You look like a bloody refugee.'

Walter shrugged. 'Same thing that happened to everyone else.' He nodded over towards a group of buildings in the distance. 'The bloke that owns the farm? He gets his mates over on a Friday night, them and his two big bastards of sons. They all get pissed, think it's great fun to come in the barn where we sleep, start shouting the odds. Gets out of hand sometimes, couple of us get a beating.' He smiled. 'I can take the names, it's the fists and boots I'm not so fond of.'

'Can nobody do anything?'

Walter smiled again, squinting up at the sun starting to go down over the hills. 'We're conscientious objectors, Joe, or bloody cowards to most people. Nobody gives a fuck about us. He can do what he wants, starve us, let his sons kick fuck out of us. We're the lowest of the low.'

Gunner spat on the ground. 'I'll talk to him, get it sorted out.' He looked around. 'Where's Vic?'

Sweet looked surprised. 'I wondered what you were doing here. Has nobody told you?'

'Told me? Told me what?' asked Gunner.

'He's gone, Joe. Did a runner a few weeks ago, said it would be him or that bastard farmer if he stayed.'

Gunner cursed under his breath, this was all he needed. 'Where'd the stupid wee prick go?'

'You got any cigarettes?' asked Walter.

Gunner fumbled in his pockets, pulled out an army-issue tin, shook it. 'There's a few left in there, been there a while though.'

Walter didn't take them, looked apologetic. 'I can't take those Joe, I just—'

Gunner rolled his eyes, put his army-issue packet away, searched again, found a crushed Player's in his top pocket. 'This do?'

Walter grinned and lit up, inhaled deep. 'That's magic.' He coughed, took another draw. 'Glasgow. That's where he's gone. It's easy to lose yourself there. Between the soldiers passing through and the blokes who came home on leave and never went back there's a good chance you'll just disappear into the crowd.'

'Why'd you no go too?' asked Gunner.

Walter dug into his vest, pulled out a wooden cross on a bit of string. 'I have my faith. Vic was here because of his politics, wasn't enough to see him through.'

'He still spouting all that "workers of the world unite" stuff?' asked Gunner.

Walter laughed. 'Oh yes, every chance he gets.'

Gunner nodded, turned to go.

'Springburn,' Walter said. 'Try up there, that's where he was spending most of his time before the war. He was organising up there, trying to get something going at the St Rollox Works.'

Gunner said his goodbyes and walked back to the farmhouse. As if he didn't have enough to worry about without his stupid bloody brother on the loose. Victor was five years younger, the bright spark of the family. He had even done a couple of years at the University. Fat lot of good that did him. Still spent all his time standing outside factories trying to convert the world to his way of thinking. Capitalism was the great evil. Communism the only way forward.

A dog started barking as he approached the farmhouse, thin black-and-white thing with an evil look in its eye. Barked enough so that the door opened and a middle-aged man in a mucky boiler suit stepped out.

'What's bloody up with you, Smokie—'

Stopped when he saw Gunner standing there.

'Can I help you?' he asked.

'No' said Gunner, and punched him in the face. The farmer's nose exploded and he went down. Smokie yelped and ran for the barn.

The farmer sat himself up, sleeve across his bloody nose.

'What was that f—'

Didn't get the chance to finish his question before Gunner

kicked him square in the stomach. Hurt his leg but it was worth it. Had to stop himself getting a few more in. Lucky for the farmer he still had enough morphine in his system to stop the red mist descending. He knelt down, grabbed the man by the hair and held his face close to his.

'If I hear you or your pals have gone near they conchies again I'll be up here with a few pals, turn the tables, eh? Maybe we'll take you into the barn and kick fuck out of you, see how you like it. Understand me?'

The farmer tried to nod.

'Can't hear you,' said Gunner.

'Sorry.'

Gunner let him go.

'You fucking will be if I have to come up here again. Remember that.'

He walked back towards the car. His leg hurt and his knuckles hurt but it felt good. Felt like he was a polis again. He opened the car door, threw Fraser a look to back off and started up the car. He turned it round, bumping it up on the hedge, scraping the side on a tree.

Drummond wouldn't be pleased, but at this point he didn't much care. He straightened the wheel up, headed back towards Thornliebank.

'Were those men in the field conchies?' Fraser asked after a while.

Gunner nodded, kept his eyes on the road.

'Is your brother a conchie?'

'Nope. He was, and now he's just another stupid bastard on the run. Where is this bloody camp anyway?'

9

After half an hour's driving on unmarked country roads and a couple of wrong turns they finally stumbled across a hut by the side of the road. Next to it was a row of barrels filled with rocks blocking the entrance to a side road. A big NO ENTRY sign on the fence.

'I think this is it,' said Fraser.

'Looks like it,' said Gunner. 'How come you know all about POW camps anyway?'

'My Uncle Cameron is in the Army, he helped set them up,' said Fraser. 'Researched the sites, drew up plans, that sort of thing. He wasn't supposed to talk about them but once he had a few drinks he wouldn't shut up.'

'You a posh boy, are you, Fraser? Uncles setting up camps, name like Lockhart.'

Fraser started reddening again.

'Not really,' he said. 'Some of my family are, Uncle Cameron for one, Sir Cameron Lockhart to give him his full title, but we were the poor relations. Scottish boarding school, not an English one. Just a house, no land.'

'Not that bloody poor.'

'How about you?' asked Fraser. 'Where did you grow up?'

'The Calton. Heard of it?'

Fraser shook his head.

'Wouldn't have thought so. Bit of a dump but we got by. My dad was in the Swedish Navy, met my mum one night at the dancing and never went back. Come on, let's see if this is where we're supposed to be.'

A military policeman stepped out of the hut as they approached. It looked like they were in the right place right enough. Gunner turned the engine off and the MP motioned him to wind his window down. He leant down to the car, stuck his head in.

'This is a restricted area, sir, members of the public aren't allowed up here,' he said in a broad Yorkshire accent.

Gunner took out his badge. 'That's OK then, I'm not a member of the public.'

After looking less than sure and going back into the hut to call someone on the radio, the MP eventually dragged the barrels aside and waved them through. They drove another five hundred yards or so on a temporary road, were waved through another security check and then they were there.

They parked the car in behind some army trucks, got out. A sign saying PATTERTON CAMP 16 was stencilled on the front gates in white paint. More NO ENTRY signs everywhere.

'You'd think they would say *No Exit*,' said Fraser. 'Would make more sense.'

'Nothing the Army does makes sense,' said Gunner. 'When we get in there, you just sit there, listen and say nothing. Got it?'

Fraser nodded and they walked up to the gate.

Gunner had never been in a prisoner-of-war camp before,

but apart from the fences and barbed wire it looked much the same as any other army camp he'd been in. There were ten or so curved Nissen huts clustered together, corrugated roofs already covered in brown rust, a latrine block surrounded by wooden walkways, a mess hall, the usual set-up. Behind two sets of wooden fencing wrapped in barbed wire, fifteen huts were laid out in rows, prisoners' quarters he supposed. Through the fencing they could see men, must have been a hundred or so at least, some in foreign army uniform, some in civvies. They were gathered in groups outside the huts, smoking, sitting on the steps, some of them kicking a ball around.

'They must be the Germans,' said Fraser.

'Aye,' said Gunner. 'Don't get too close, they might bite.'

After another few rounds of flashing his badge, Gunner and Fraser ended up on a bench in the corridor outside the office of one Colonel Reginald F. Skinner, head of the camp. In contrast to the warm and sunny afternoon outside, the camp's office block was dark and gloomy, smelt of newly cut wood and creosote. Gunner lit up and the young guy behind the desk looked up from his typewriter and frowned. 'Colonel Skinner doesn't allow smoking in here.'

'That right?' said Gunner, continuing to puff away.

The officer tutted, went back to stabbing at the typewriter with two fingers. Gunner looked at him. He was a big guy, looked fit, in his twenties. How did people like him end up with cushy jobs like this? Seeing out the war in a wee wooden hut ten miles from Glasgow with a stove and cups of tea. How come he wasn't in Egypt getting his arse shot off? A buzzer went off, interrupting his thoughts, and the officer nodded to the door.

'He'll see you now.'

The minute they walked into the office Gunner realised why Skinner had his easy job. The Colonel stood up behind his desk and offered his left hand. He had to, he didn't have the right one. His whole arm was missing, sleeve neatly folded over and pinned to his shoulder. It didn't end there. The poor bastard had terrible shiny burn scars all over the side of his face and neck, left eye pulled half closed and weeping.

Gunner awkwardly clasped the Corporal's hand. 'I'm Gunner, Glasgow Police, and this is Lockhart, one of our auxiliaries.'

The Corporal pointed at two seats in front of his desk, and they sat down.

'Incendiary bomb,' he said. 'Always better to get that out the way I think. I was home on a seventy-two-hour leave, came out of a pub in Fleet Street and the bloody thing landed twenty yards away.'

He wiped at his weeping eye.

'You?' he asked.

'Bomb,' said Gunner. 'Dunkirk.'

Suddenly it felt like they were two schoolboys comparing scabby knees in the playground.

'What was is it Shakespeare said?' asked Skinner. '"Such as we are made of, such we be", something like that anyway. No use worrying about what's done. And now the bombs are raining down on poor old Glasgow.'

Gunner nodded.

'How are the casualties? All we hear out here is rumours.'

'High,' said Gunner. 'Clydebank got it bad, very bad.'

Skinner nodded at the blue sky through the dusty window.

'I fear they might be back tonight, the good weather seems

to be holding.' He looked across at them. 'I'm not quite sure why we merit a visit from the Glasgow Police Force, not entirely sure how you managed to get yourself in here, to be frank. So what can I do for you, Mr Gunner?'

Gunner started the story. 'Do you have a prisoner missing from the camp? German national, mid-forties, six foot or so?'

The Corporal shook his head. 'No. Why do you ask?'

'We found a body in town, badly mutilated. Identification is difficult, but we believe it to be that of a German national. Thought was, he might be an escaped POW so we're checking the camps around Glasgow. It seemed the logical place to start.'

Skinner put the hanky down, sat forward in his chair. 'Roll-call was complete this morning. No absentees.'

'You sure?'

'Of course I'm bloody sure, man, what do you take me for?'

Gunner knew exactly what he took him for but knew it was better to keep it to himself.

'Didn't mean to offend,' he said. 'Just that it's an important case for us, that's all. Would you mind if we took a look around?'

'Yes I would. This is a prisoner-of-war camp, not a bloody sightseeing trip for the Glasgow Police. Rest assured it's a tight ship I run here, we don't have prisoners escaping, with or without anyone noticing. And besides, as I said, this is Ministry of Defence property, I'm not entirely sure you have any jurisdiction here, let alone permission to accuse me of not doing my job properly.'

Gunner tried to sound apologetic. 'No offence, sir, we just have to check these things.'

Skinner nodded curtly. 'Perhaps so. Now if you'll excuse me . . .'

He bent back over his papers.

Looked like their interview was over.

10

Gunner and Fraser walked down the office block steps and back across the campground. Gunner stopped, looked back at the hut. 'I'm not sure if we got the bum's rush because he had something to hide or because he's just another arsehole officer.' He looked around. 'C'mon, let's take a walk. We're here now, might as well see what's going on before they chuck us out.'

There wasn't anyone stopping them, so they headed for the double line of barbed wire and the prisoners behind. They were still a couple of yards away when someone broke away from the crowd of prisoners and walked towards the fence.

'Mr Gunner! What are you doing here?'

Gunner groaned inwardly. Of all the fucking people . . .

'Paolo, what are you doing here?' he asked. 'You're as Scottish as I am.'

Paolo held up his hands, made a face. He was a ratty wee man, dressed as usual in a pair of old tweed trousers, a dirty white shirt and a baggy cardigan. The only difference was that this time his trousers had a big white *P* painted on the leg. Gunner had known Paolo for years, he was a small-timer, hung around the big boys, tried to make himself useful. He was a tout as well, played both sides. He'd been put away a few times for taking nudey pictures of girls young enough to be his daughter. One actually turned out to be his daughter, if Gunner remembered correctly.

'Twenty-six years I've been in Glasgow,' said Paolo. 'Not long enough for the fucking Home Office. Stupid fucks. Because I wasn't born here, to them I'm an enemy alien.' He spat on the ground, rubbed at it with his shoe. 'So I'm stuck here like a fucking prisoner, a fucking *prigioniero. Ficas!*'

He spat again, then looked up as if realisation had just dawned.

'I thought you were in the Army now?' he asked.

'I was,' said Gunner. He looked around at the gateposts and barbed wire. 'What's it like in here anyway?'

Paolo shook his head. '*Merda.* Got any fags?'

Gunner took one out for himself and lobbed the rest of the army-issue packet over the fence. Seemed all he had done today was give away his fags. Paolo pounced on them as soon as they fell, stuffed them in his cardigan pocket, looked round, made sure nobody had seen.

'What are the Germans like?' asked Fraser.

Paolo shrugged. 'They keep themselves to themselves. We're a white camp.'

'A white camp?' asked Gunner. 'What's that?'

'Lowest-level security. White camps are mostly for civilians that have been caught up in all this shite. People like me. Black camps are where the real bastards are, the real Nazis. There's one out at Lennoxtown.' He looked at Gunner again, eyes narrowed. 'You still haven't said what you're doing here.'

'You're right, ' said Gunner. 'I haven't. Anyone go missing from here? Break out?'

'Break out?' Paolo laughed. 'Walk out, more like. We work on the farms round here. One guard for twenty men. Wouldn't be hard.'

'What's that over there?' Fraser was pointing at a small hut in the corner of the camp. It stood off by itself, yet another ring of barbed wire round it.

'Nosy wee bastard, aren't you?' said Paolo. 'That's Purgatory. Where they keep the Black Germans before they take them up to Lennoxtown. They don't let them mix; it causes too much trouble. There's a couple of them in there now, brought them in last night.' He looked back at Fraser. 'No offence, son, but gonnae fuck off a minute? I need to speak to Mr Gunner.'

Fraser glanced at Gunner, who nodded. Fraser wandered back towards the car looking pissed off.

'So, Paolo, what's up?' said Gunner wearily.

'Nice to see you back, so maybe you and I can do each other a favour. I can do a lot for you, Mr Gunner, I hear things, see things in this camp. I can pass things back, help you out, then you can help me.'

He tried a smile, cracked yellow teeth making it more of a grimace.

Gunner shook his head. 'Don't think so, Paolo, I don't need to know what goes on up here.'

'No problem,' he said quickly. 'I still hear what goes on in Glasgow. I'm still connected back there.'

Gunner laughed. 'What, from behind three layers of barbed wire in the back arse of nowhere? Thanks, but no thanks, Paolo. See you later.'

He turned to go.

'Please yourself, Mr Gunner. Your loss.' He grinned again.

'There was one thing I did hear. Sellars knows you're back in town and he's not a happy man.'

Gunner turned. Paolo stood there, a satisfied smile on his face.

'That got your attention, eh? News travels fast, Gunner, even to the back arse of nowhere.'

He tapped his nose, walked back to the prisoners.

Gunner watched him go, flicked the last of his cigarette against the wire fence and walked back to the car.

'What was all that about?' asked Fraser.

'Nothing, just Paolo and his usual shite.'

'You think Skinner's lying, don't you?'

Gunner nodded. 'Through his teeth.'

'I do too,' said Fraser. 'Did you notice he kept looking away when he was talking to us, kept looking at the papers on the desk?'

'So?'

Fraser was all enthused. 'So it means he was lying, it's a classic indicator.'

Gunner turned to him.

'What the fuck are you on about?'

The inevitable reddening of Fraser's cheeks started.

'Edgar Wallace,' he said. '*The Door with Seven Locks.*'

Gunner burst out laughing.

'Fuck me, where did Drummond get you from?'

'I graduated first in my year at the college,' Fraser said, trying to make up ground. 'First in my year.'

Gunner started the car. 'That right?' he said. 'Christ knows what the rest of them must have been like, then.'

The road back to Glasgow took them round the back of the camp, close to the far perimeter. They passed close to the hut for the Black prisoners and Gunner pulled the car over, leant over the steering wheel and stared out.

'What do you think goes on in there, then?' he asked.

Fraser shrugged. 'Interviews. I suppose, trying to find out who the real Nazis are, find out what they know.' He thought for a minute. 'Despite what Skinner says, I think the man was a POW. He got out of here, made it into Glasgow, then gave himself away.'

'And then somebody stoved his face in and then cut off his fingers?' Gunner shook his head. 'It doesn't make sense. If he was a POW, why go to all that trouble to conceal his identity? And why sneak him into the Kelvin Hall? Someone had a good reason to kill him, and it wasn't just because he was a German.'

'Why then?' asked Fraser.

Gunner started the car.

'That, Special Auxiliary Lockhart, is what we need to find out.'

He started the car again and pulled out into the road, checked his rear-view mirror. Someone was going into the Purgatory hut, climbing up the wooden stairs. Gunner stepped on the brakes and twisted round in his seat. Too late. He only caught a glimpse before the man disappeared into the hut and the door shut behind him.

'What's up? What you looking at?' asked Fraser, craning round too.

'Nothing,' said Gunner starting the car up again. 'Nothing.'

They drove over the peak of the hill, Glasgow laid out in the valley below, a pall of smoke from the factories and the chimneys of the houses lying over it, barrage balloons gently bobbing on their ropes.

There was something about the man going into the hut that he recognised, something familiar, couldn't put his finger on it.

For want of anything else to say, Gunner made the mistake of asking Fraser how he came to be working for Drummond. He kept at it all the way into town, how his dad was dead and his mum was dependent on him so he wasn't allowed to join up so he'd joined the Police Auxiliary, how he was living in digs in Kelvinbridge, how Drummond never told him what was going on, how—

Gunner slapped the dashboard. 'Bald!' he said. 'He was fucking bald.'

11

'You're supposed to knock,' said Drummond, looking up. The man himself was sitting behind his desk, slurping tea from a tin mug, a half-eaten Empire biscuit and a copy of *Tit-Bits* lying open in front of him. They were in Central, the big police station at St Andrew's Square. Drummond's new domain. He picked up the rest of the biscuit and shoved it into his mouth.

From the look of things it hadn't taken Drummond long to get his feet under the table. He'd colonised the unused boardroom, the biggest room in the station. He'd also managed to make it into a pigsty already. There were cardboard boxes stacked up in the corners, packets of shirts spilling out of them, bulging files piled up everywhere. Drummond's dress uniform and a couple of pairs of trousers were hanging from a nail hammered into the wood panelling. And for some reason two stuffed and mounted stag's heads were propped up against the wall behind him.

'Sorry, didn't realise you were so busy,' said Gunner.

'Fuck off,' Drummond said through a spray of crumbs. 'Any luck up the camp?'

Gunner pushed a pile of dirty socks off a chair and sat down.

'According to the man in charge, one Corporal Skinner, all's shipshape and smelling of roses. No way could there be a missing prisoner on his watch. But . . .'

'But . . . ?'

'But according to Paolo Rossi—'

'Paolo Rossi?' asked Drummond. 'I wondered where that wee shite had got to.'

'Well, the Thornliebank camp is where he's got to, and according to him, the place is as leaky as a banana boat. A prisoner could get out of there any time. You don't even need to escape; you just walk away.'

Drummond grunted. 'Might have known. Bloody Army fuckers, couldnae run a piss-up in a brewery. Leave that!'

Gunner turned. Fraser had picked up one of the files in the pile beside his chair, was flicking through it.

'I just wondered what it was,' he said feebly.

'Aye well, don't. I know where everything is. I don't want it moved. Just sit on your arse and shut up. Right?'

Fraser nodded, put the file down, went red.

'What else?' asked Drummond.

'There's a special hut up there for "Black" prisoners,' said Gunner. 'That's what they call the proper Nazis. They keep them there before they transfer them out to somewhere out Stirling way. I'd say if he came from anywhere, he came from there. That's the only kind of prisoner Skinner is going to want to keep quiet about losing. Don't think he would care if it was just some waiter from Ferrari's that had wandered off.'

'Christ,' said Drummond, lighting up a cigarette. 'This is getting worse and worse. A bloody Nazi.'

'And that's not all,' said Gunner. 'The blokes I'm staying with? I saw their driver up there. Big head, bald as an egg and a pinstripe bloody suit.'

'I thought they were from the Ministry of Food?' said Drummond.

Gunner shrugged. 'You tell me why two guys from the Ministry of Food are staying in a military barracks and why their driver would need to be at a prisoner-of-war camp. Ministry of Food, my arse.'

Drummond sucked air through his teeth, ran his fingers through his greasy black hair. Which was what he always did when he was nervous. Or about to lie. Gunner would have to teach Fraser that clue someday.

'Looks like I'll have to report it officially,' said Drummond. 'I'll put a call in to the Met. Whoever the stupid fucker is, he's still a murder victim on our patch. He's in the files now. You keep going, find out what you can. If those English fuckers come up here, we need to look like we're doing all we can.'

'No,' said Gunner.

'What do you mean, "no"?'

'I'm sick of telling you, Drummond. I don't work for you. You and Fraser'll have to do it.'

'Give us a break, Gunner. What if the Met come up here and there's a fat bastard and some wee boy in charge of finding a bloody Nazi?'

'I'm not a wee boy,' Fraser protested. 'I'm an auxil—'

'Fuck up, Fraser, you know what I mean.'

Gunner shrugged, began to get up.

'All right,' said Drummond. 'What's it going to take to get you to stay?'

Gunner sat back down.

'Funny you should ask.'

'If it's money you're looking for, there's a war on, we're strapped for cash. I can get you a few quid but—'

'It's not just money,' said Gunner. 'I want you to help me find my brother.'

Drummond scowled. 'I thought he was a conchie? Is he no working out on one of they farms with all the other cowards?'

'Not any more he's not,' said Gunner. 'He took off.'

Drummond let out a low whistle. 'Naughty boy, your Victor.'

'I want to find him before the MPs do,' said Gunner. 'He's a stupid arse but he's still my wee brother.'

Drummond snorted.

'I wouldnae worry too much about that. Do you know how many men there are in this city that shouldnae be here? Thousands of them. All sorts of the buggers. We've got deserters, runaways, AWOLs. The whole town's full of them. The MPs aren't going to be looking for your brother, believe me, he's just one more coward on the run.'

Gunner stood up, decided not to take the bait.

'Springburn,' he said. 'Chances are he'll be somewhere up that way, that's where his pals are, the commies and the shop stewards. One of them will know where he is. You want me to help you out, you help me out.' He held out his hand. 'Deal?'

Drummond shook it with as little enthusiasm as he could. 'Fine. I'll find the wee shitebag. You find the big bastard with the garden shears and the brick.'

Fraser dropped Gunner outside the barracks, was going to

go and get Drummond's car washed before he gave it back. Gunner waved him off and walked across the yard yawning, realising just how tired he was. His leg was still flaring up and he'd been on bed rest for so long maybe he just wasn't used to a full day up and about. A kip in his wee room with clean sheets seemed like a good idea.

He pushed the door of the Major's quarters open and the two Ministry of Food men turned to look at him. They'd obviously been having a conversation, one that they weren't going to continue while he was standing there.

'Sorry,' said Gunner. 'I'll get out your way, just came back for a sleep.'

Moore nodded, stepped aside to let him through to the stairs.

Gunner stopped.

'Mind if I ask you something?'

Nickerson smiled. 'Ask away.'

'I know you boys work for the Ministry of Food, but you must run into other Government blokes from time to time, hear things us guys don't. Think there are any German spies in Glasgow?'

Nickerson laughed. Moore just smiled.

'I wasn't expecting that,' said Nickerson. 'Why do you ask?'

'We found a body, think he's a German, wondered what he was doing here.'

Nickerson started to speak but Moore cut across him.

'We're Ministry of Food, Gunner, you know as much about spies as we do. I'd say he's probably a German teacher, something like that, been here for years.' He walked over to the window, a parade was going by, more recruits trying and failing to march in time. 'Haven't you identified him yet?'

'Not yet,' said Gunner. 'But we will, still early days.' He started walking up the stairs. Wondered how daft they thought he was.

'Night, gents.' He said. 'Good luck with the sheep.'

12

Gunner woke up a couple of hours later, reached over to the table for his cigarettes. It was just starting to get dark outside; he could hear the starlings gathering on the roofs of the barracks for the night. He looked at his watch. Half eight. He listened but he couldn't hear anyone downstairs, just the creaking of the house and the distant sound of Joe Loss on the radio drifting over from the mess hall across the way. Ministry boys must have gone out.

He blew a smoke ring up at the ceiling, scratched at the scar on his leg, tried not to think about the fact there was only one syrette left. Maybe he could get some more up here? He could always ask MacGregor if there was a doctor in the barracks, tell him how much pain he was in. Might work. He knew he couldn't go on like this, but he couldn't face life without the syrettes, not just now. He had too much else to worry about.

He watched the shadows of the trucks move across the wall as they drove into the barracks. Tried to think about something besides the morphine. It seemed to him that Moore had been just a little bit too casual about asking whether he knew who the German was. He'd tried too hard to sound unconcerned, yet his eyes told a different story, never left Gunner until he answered him.

If he had something to do with what had happened, what were British agents doing killing a German prisoner of war? Maybe the man was dangerous, an SS officer or something like that. It didn't make sense, though, there were easier ways of doing it than all this found-in-the-rubble stuff. Gunner knew as well as anyone else what 'killed while trying to escape' really meant. It was the standard way it was done.

It had even happened once in France. Ten men went out on a patrol, only seven of them came back, covered in the blood of their pals. Three of them killed in one afternoon. Andy Munn was one of them, the joker of the patrol, only eighteen, the one everyone, even Sergeant Mitchell, liked. He'd bled out in front of them crying for his mum and Jesus and anyone else he thought could save him. Nothing anyone could do but watch, the wound on his abdomen was so huge it was all over in a matter of minutes.

The patrol got back with their minds half gone on grief and the idea of revenge. Matthew Cook grabbed one of the three prisoners tied up by the tents waiting for the truck to pick them up and untied the rope around him. Told him he was free and to start running. The bloke didn't want to do it, knew what was going to happen, but Cook hit him a few times with the butt of his rifle, and eventually he ran. Got about three hundred yards before Cook shot him in the back. The funny thing was, three weeks later Cook was dead too. Hung himself in a barn in the middle of the night.

Gunner sat up, rubbed at his eyes. The last thing he wanted to do was think about France, he needed to get up and get going before the memories got too much. The war damage wasn't just physical. He was different now, harder. Hadn't hesitated to hit that farmer, hadn't even given him a chance to take a verbal warning. Had to admit that some part of him had enjoyed hitting him. Made him feel alive again.

He swung his legs out the bed, stubbed his cigarette out in the buffalo horn ashtray. Least he thought it was an ashtray. Time to stop thinking about syrettes and the war and everything else. Time for a wash and a shave, then a trip up to Springburn to see if anyone had heard from his brother. He knew he'd have to do most of the legwork himself. Despite what Drummond said, he couldn't see him devoting much time to finding Victor. As far as Drummond was concerned, being a conscientious objector was just a way of getting out of doing one's duty.

Gunner got up, put his eyepatch back on and padded through to the hall in bare feet and pyjama trousers, with a towel draped round his shoulders. He yawned, gave himself a shake and pushed the bathroom door open. Took him a minute to realise what was going on. MacGregor was facing him, back against the sink, trousers and skivvies around his ankles. Nickerson was kneeling in front of him, head bobbing up and down. MacGregor saw Gunner and froze. Nickerson stopped, looked up at MacGregor.

'What's up with—'

He followed MacGregor's gaze, to Gunner standing in the doorway.

'Shit,' he said, sitting down on the bathroom floor. 'Shit.'

Gunner sat in one of the armchairs in the living room, lit up a fag from a packet lying on the table and waited. MacGregor appeared down the stairs first, glasses and trousers back on.

He sat down at the dining table.

'Am I fucked?' he asked.

'You're joking, aren't you?' said Gunner. 'You got me a place to stay, a place with a bath and all. Far as am concerned you can do what you like, MacGregor. You're my hero.'

MacGregor grinned.

'I just about shat myself when you opened the door. Thought my number was up.'

'Did look a bit pale, to be honest.'

MacGregor stood up.

'You ever need a place to stay again, anything else I can pilfer from this dump you let me know.'

He walked over, held out his hand for Gunner to shake. He did.

MacGregor looked at his watch.

'Fuck, need to find twenty extra cots from somewhere before six o'clock. See you, Gunner.'

Nickerson came down a couple of minutes later, tie half undone, the tail of his shirt hanging out his tweed suit trousers. He sat on the couch opposite, smiled nervously, held out his cigarettes. Gunner shook his head and Nickerson lit one, hands trembling.

'Sorry about that,' he said. 'Things progressed rather quicker than I imagined. I thought you were asleep.'

'I was,' said Gunner. 'I woke up.'

Nickerson nodded. 'Yes, bad timing on my part. Sorry, it won't happen again.' He fiddled at his cufflink, twirling the metal bar round and round. Looked over at Gunner. 'There's no real need to take it any further, is there? No damage done.'

Gunner looked at him. He didn't much care what Nickerson got up to, didn't share some of the men in the force's zeal for raiding public toilets or investigating nasty wee notes from next-door neighbours. He'd always had enough real polis work to do. Still, Nickerson was right to be worried; Gunner was a policeman, after all. For all Nickerson knew, he could be in a cell in half an hour, career over and looking down the barrel of four years of hard labour. Or he could be facing a lifetime of blackmail. Gunner could promise not to tell the authorities just as long as he got cash in the post every month. Knew men it had happened to, being bled dry month by month by dirty cops.

He shook his head.

'Just don't be so careless again. It might not be me who walks in on you next time.'

Nickerson exhaled; relief spread over his face. 'Much appreciated, very decent of you, very decent indeed.' He stood up. 'I need a drink.'

He went over to the sideboard and poured two whiskies from the crystal decanter, handed one to Gunner and sat back down. He swallowed half the glass down quickly, thought for a minute, then made up his mind to say it.

'Obviously I'm not supposed to tell you this, but a telegram is going to arrive here for you tomorrow morning, from your regiment.'

'How do you know that?'

Nickerson shook his head. 'Doesn't matter, what matters is I do. It will say your medical discharge has been revoked. Orders to return immediately.'

It was the last thing Gunner expected him to say.

'Has it?' he asked. 'How can it—'

'It hasn't' said Nickerson. 'Of course not. It's just a ploy to get you out the way. Someone wants you out the picture, out of Glasgow.'

'Me? Why do they want me out of Glasgow?'

'Simple. You're getting a bit too interested in our German friend from the rubble.'

'I don't get it. That's what I've been asked to do. Drummond asked me.' He stopped, looked at Nickerson. 'Why are you telling me this?' he asked.

Nickerson smiled, pointed up in the vague direction of the bathroom. 'One good turn deserves another.'

Gunner shook his head.

'Bollocks,' he said. 'That's not all, is it?'

Nickerson drained the whisky, walked over to the sideboard, poured himself another.

'Not entirely, no,' he said. 'These are dangerous times, Gunner. You must pick your sides and I don't mean us or the Germans. Unfortunately, there are far more sides than that.' He smiled. 'This is the British Secret Service, after all.'

'How would you know?' asked Gunner. 'You work for the Ministry of Food, don't you?'

Nickerson grinned, held up his glass. 'Touché.'

He walked over to the radiogram and switched it on. Waited for it to warm up a few seconds, then the Tommy Dorsey Orchestra and Frank Sinatra were playing 'I'll Never Smile Again'. He came over and sat down on the couch by Gunner. Spoke just loud enough to be heard.

'I'm telling you this because I want you to keep going on the case, keep digging.'

'Keep digging at what?' asked Gunner, beginning to feel adrift. 'The German, you mean?'

Nickerson nodded.

'Do you know who he is?' asked Gunner.

Nickerson shook his head.

'But I rather think Moore does, and that's what worries me.'

'Moore does?'

Nickerson nodded.

'We're supposed to be working together but the opposite seems to be happening. He's been keeping me in the dark and I'm not sure why.'

'I thought you two were on the same side?' asked Gunner.

'As I said, Gunner, there are sides and sides. Nothing is ever quite so straightforward as it should be.'

'I saw your driver up at the POW camp,' said Gunner. 'What was he doing up there?'

Nickerson raised his eyebrows. 'I don't know,' he said. 'He's not my driver, believe me, hardly acknowledges my existence, he's some thug of Moore's. However, it wouldn't surprise me one bit. I wondered what he was really doing here, plenty of local drivers we could have employed. Not sure why we had to bring one from . . .'

Nickerson stopped, cocked his head.

'Bugger, I think that's the car, I need to go.'

He stood up, pulled his jacket on, and went to the window.

'I'll go out and get in the car before Moore comes in and sees you.'

He looked back at Gunner.

'Don't come back here,' he said. 'Find somewhere else to stay. If they can't find you, they can't give you the recall orders.' He opened the front door. 'I'll stay in touch.'

'Nickerson! What's going on? I can't—'

Nickerson shook Gunner's hand.

'Be careful. Behind the upright façade Moore is a vicious bugger, a real vicious bugger. Avoid him at all costs.' Then he dropped his hand and opened the door, waved at Moore sitting in the back of the Jaguar looking impatient. Ran to the car and got in.

Gunner stood behind the curtain and watched it drive off. Wasn't sure whether to believe what Nickerson had said or not. Least he wasn't pretending to be from the bloody Ministry of Food any more. What he needed to do was find out who Nickerson really was. If he'd lied about the Ministry of Food, he could be lying about the Secret Service as well. Time to do some digging, starting with his bedroom.

13

Nickerson's bedroom wasn't what Gunner expected. He stood in the doorway looking in. The bed was unmade, bedside table piled with books with a half-bottle of whisky on top. There was some sort of Picasso-type picture that looked like it had been ripped out a magazine pinned above the bed. An overflowing ashtray on the floor amongst the shoes and balled-up red socks. A mess.

Whole room smelt of tobacco and some sort of cologne. He walked over to the dressing table and picked up a glass bottle with a stopper in it. Penhaligon's Blenheim Bouquet. He took the stopper off and sniffed. Smelt expensive. Probably was, as were the monogrammed shirts hanging from the handle of the wardrobe.

He pushed a pyjama top to the side, sat on the bed and tried to work out what he was looking for. All the room was doing so far was telling him what he already knew. Nickerson was posh and obviously finding it hard to keep the mess at bay without some butler or nanny or whoever it was that usually tidied up after him.

There was a notebook on the bedside table. He opened it and tried to read what was inside. Wasn't easy. Nickerson's writing was like some mad scrawl, he could only make out a few words:

Closing in   remember to ask Driberg about   Cairo?
Dinner at White's

None of which made any sense or helped him. He put the notebook back and opened the drawer. A couple of monogrammed hankies, roll of aspirin, a male physique magazine, bag of Mint Imperials. He shut the drawer. This was a waste of time. If Nickerson was hiding anything he wasn't stupid enough to leave it anywhere Gunner would find it. Though he'd been pretty stupid about other matters.

Moore's room was the opposite: bed made, clothes put away, a glass of water and a copy of *The Telegraph* folded to the half-completed crossword on his bedside table. There was a file on the desk, which he opened: 'A Feasibility Report on Increasing Sheep Population'. He closed the file and smiled. Moore had forgotten his prop. He walked over to the window and had a look out at the yard. More recruits making a mess of drill. MacGregor emerged from a door in the main building, started walking towards the mess hall. Gunner watched him go, being stopped every two minutes as usual. Suddenly an idea struck him. He hurried down the stairs, out the door and onto the big yard.

'Gunner!' said MacGregor as he approached. 'You following me?'

'Aye, right,' said Gunner. 'Got a question for you. The driver for your pal, where is he bunked?'

'He's in the main barracks, no way was that posh cunt Moore having a driver sharing a house with him. That's why you've got a room. Why?'

'No reason. Just wondering.'

'Bollocks you were. His bed's right at the back, beside the big water pipe and the window, just in case you were going to take a look or anything.'

'Thanks, MacGregor,' said Gunner. 'I owe you.'

'Not as much as I owe you. At least a couple of beers.'

'Done,' said Gunner, and left MacGregor trying to deal with a tearful young soldier who'd lost his kitbag.

He walked towards the main barracks, not quite sure what he was going to do if the driver was there. Ask him what he was doing at the POW camp? Even if he admitted he had been there, there wasn't a chance in hell he was going to tell him why. He pulled the big double doors open and went inside. Would just have to think on his feet.

The main barracks was a vast sea of cots, a metal locker beside each one. They must have been expecting an inspection, place was immaculate. Beds were made so tight you could bounce a penny off them, lino floor shining, kitbag under each bed. Gunner made his way towards the back, realised one of the beds was occupied. A boy, late teens, was leaning up on his pillows, smoking and watching Gunner's progress towards him, eyepatch on his eye.

'All right, mate,' he said in a cockney accent. 'What happened to your eye, then?'

'Shrapnel,' said Gunner. 'Hopefully it'll sort itself out. You?'

'Detached retina,' he said. 'Pain in my bloody arse. Not supposed to move much until it reattaches. I'm climbing up the bloody walls, been lying here for two weeks, nothing to do but have the occasional wank and stare at the ceiling. What you doing in here anyway?'

'Looking for a bed,' said Gunner. 'Big guy, a driver not a soldier.'

'Ah,' said the boy. 'That cunt. He's over by the window.'

Gunner weaved his way towards the window.

'Next one on the left, mate,' said the boy.

Gunner nodded, sat down on the driver's bed.

'Be good if you were asleep when I was here, didn't see a thing,' he said quietly.

'Fine by me,' said the boy, tapping the side of his nose. 'Haven't seen a bloody thing. Eye's not great anyway, right?'

Gunner got a penknife out his pocket, folded out the smallest blade and wiggled it into the lock in the door of the locker. Didn't take long for him to find the right depth, turn it and open the door. Some folded underwear and vests, copy of *Titter* magazine with a redhead on the front. Tin of toothpowder, a couple of pairs of socks, laundry ticket. In other words, nothing. He closed the door locked it again.

'No luck?' asked the boy.

Gunner shook his head. 'Know him, do you?'

'Unfortunately,' said the boy. 'Never heard anyone talk such arse in my life. Keeps trying to drop hints he's on some kind of secret mission. Wanker's just a jumped-up taxi driver.'

Made Gunner think.

'His car. Do you know where he keeps that?' he asked.

'He's got a space at a garage in Lochburn Road, just over the way. The stupid twat keeps boasting about all the women he fucks in the back seat of the car, picks them up in town, parks in there for the dirty deed, then drops them back off.'

Gunner thanked him and wandered back through the beds. Garages had bolt cutters, all sorts of stuff that could take a man's fingers off. Maybe that's why the driver was really here, to do Moore's dirty work. Still had no idea why, though. Why would Moore kill and mutilate a German prisoner of war?

He'd just opened the barracks door when he heard it. The low moan of an air-raid siren starting up. First one, then another. Felt his stomach drop. He looked up at the sky, nothing to be seen. Yet. Within seconds the yard was full of people running in all directions, looking up at the skies, panic on their faces. Two drill sergeants were shouting loud enough to be heard above the din, trying to get everyone into the shelters. One turned, saw Gunner standing there and waved him towards the shelter entrance.

Gunner pretended he hadn't seen him and started running. There was no way he was going to sit in a damp box with a bunch of army lads waiting to be bombed. Only one place he could think to go. He ran across the yard, through the gate, and headed for the Maryhill station.

14

Gunner pushed the big wooden doors of the station open, stood there trying to get his breath back. The front office was empty, no Archie on the desk. He made his way through the corridors to his wee den at the back, the only other place he could think he would be. He heard muffled voices and pushed the door open.

'Well, well,' said Drummond turning towards the door. 'We are honoured, Gunner's finally turned up. Where the fuck have you been all afternoon, lying in your bloody bed?'

'Fuck off, Drummond,' said Gunner. 'I said I'd help you out, I didn't say I—'

'Is that them?' asked Archie, cocking his head.

They all stopped, stood still. Listened.

'Fuck,' said Drummond. 'Sounds like it.'

All Gunner could hear was a faint hum, like the sound a radio made when it was warming up. It was starting to get louder.

'Right,' said Drummond looking glum. 'This is it, get your stuff.'

They started gathering up tin hats, gas-mask cases, torches. Fraser's hand shaking as he tried to tighten his helmet strap under his chin.

'You all right?' Gunner asked, doing it up for him. Fraser nodded. Didn't look it.

'Just keep your head down, don't try and be a hero. OK?'

Fraser nodded again, put his gas mask over his shoulder, and they headed out of the station.

Out in Maryhill Road, everything had changed. Chaos of a few minutes ago had been replaced by an eerie silence. The streets were deserted, everyone in the shelters now. No lights in any of the buildings. No cars running on the road. Everything was quiet, just the occasional squeak and flutter of wings from the crowds of starlings whirling around the roofs.

It felt more like being deep in the countryside than being a mile or so from the centre of town. A fox appeared from the back of the dairy, eyes shining in the dark. Trotted across the road and disappeared into the bushes. Fraser and Drummond headed off down the street making for the Anderson shelter round the back of the Baths. Gunner held back, not sure what he was going to do.

'You no fancy the shelter either?' Archie grinned. 'Don't blame you. C'mon with me, I need to go up to the canal.'

They set off up the hill, Gunner's eyes slowly getting used to the evening gloom. They cut around the back of the Thomson works, stumbled across the waste ground, tripping over bricks and broken bits of masonry. They'd just about made it to the other side when Archie stopped dead. Looked up at the sky.

'Jesus Christ,' he said. 'Jesus bloody Christ.'

Gunner looked up, tried to take it in. The sky above them was filled with planes, rows and rows of Junkers and Heinkels coming in from the east, must have been fifty odd of them at least. Fifty odd dark shapes against the last pink of the dying sun. A deafening crack, a flash of lights and fire from ack-ack guns shot up into the sky. Was like a huge flashbulb lighting up the bombers and the barrage balloons, going off every few seconds.

'Quick!'

Archie grabbed Gunner and they ran up towards the canal. A woman was lying on the pavement crying, screaming that she couldn't go inside the shelters, two ARP men trying to pull her up. They skirted around them and kept going up the hill.

The ack-acks started up again and they heard the first high scream of a bomb dropping and the distant boom as it exploded. They kept running, trying not to stumble in the dark. Gunner could just about make out the canal up ahead, barges moored back to back as far as he could see. Archie made his way along the bank, heading for a new-looking set of solid iron gates half submerged in the water.

'What are we doing here?' Gunner shouted, trying to be heard above the noise of the planes and the ack-acks. He pointed at the gates. 'What are they?'

Archie pulled him in close, shouted in his ear. 'There's forty thousand tons of water in this wee bit of the canal. If a bomb hits and it gets breached the water will run down the hill like a bloody tidal wave. It'll cause more damage than the bombs.'

He pointed along the canal. In the light flashes, Gunner could see a set of the big gates every couple of hundred yards.

'They put in new breakwaters,' said Archie. 'They go all the way along to Port Dundas. If a section gets hit, we have to pull the levers, close the gates, stop the rest of the water escaping.'

They sat down on the grass next to the nearest gates and watched the sky. The noise from the planes was now a horrible low roar that you could feel in your bones. Gunner had never seen so many. In France, they came in groups of three or four, came in quick, got out quick. These planes were different, slow and deliberate, and they just kept coming. From up on the hill, they could see all of Glasgow below, could see how near the planes were now, must be over the East End. Suddenly flames started shooting up in the city beneath them.

'Incendiaries!' shouted Archie.

They watched as the planes flew over and Glasgow caught fire beneath them. Sudden huge jets of orangey flame towering up from the buildings that had been hit, followed by clouds of thick oily smoke a few seconds later. The ack-acks were still going but they didn't seem to be having much effect. The planes just kept coming, dropping more and more incendiaries. A giant column of flame rose up from the centre of town, the boom taking a second or so to reach them. Had to be one of the warehouses by the Clyde, must have been full of barrels of oil, something like that.

The first wave of planes was directly overhead now. Gunner craned his neck, could even see the crosses on the bottom of their wings every time the ack-acks flashed. They were so close he could smell the aviation fuel as they went over. The planes kept going for a couple of minutes, not dropping anything, and then fires started shooting up in the distance, a soft whump as each new incendiary exploded and the flames shot up into the sky. Looked like the shipyards at Clydebank were being hit hard again. Archie pulled at Gunner's arm.

'Come on. If it's anything like last night it'll be an hour or so before they're back. It'll be the real bombers next time now that incendiaries have lit up the way.'

They made their way back down towards the station, the smell of burning wood already starting to drift over from the smoke-covered city centre. People were starting to emerge from the shelters, looking dazed, trying to work out what was going on. A dog was running round and round in circles, howling and barking, driven mad by the noise.

Drummond and Fraser were waiting in front of the station, faces black but for white streaks where the sweat had run through the soot. There were holes peppering Drummond's suit, looked like big cigarette burns. He noticed Gunner looking at them.

'Ashes,' he said. 'Fucking fires everywhere. Where were you? We could have used you two, there's three blocks on fire in Hotspur Street.'

'I took Gunner with me,' said Archie. 'In case the canal went.'

Drummond pulled his jacket sleeve down, caught it in his hand and wiped the soot and sweat from his face.

'You come with me next time, Gunner. We need all the help we can get, no people sightseeing up at the canal.'

'Come on—' started Archie.

Drummond cut across him. 'Shut it, Archie!'

Gunner had had enough. He stepped up to Drummond.

'You know what, Drummond? Fuck off. You wanted me with you, you should have said, I'm no a fucking mindreader.'

Drummond spat sooty phlegm on the ground. 'I need a drink,' he said, and walked into the station.

'Fuck's up with him?' Gunner asked Fraser.

Fraser looked terrible, his hands were shaking, eyes darting round.

'We went up to one of the buildings that got hit in Hotspur Street,' said Fraser. 'A direct hit from an incendiary. A woman said there were people inside. We tried, but we couldn't get the front door open in time. We had to wait for a fireman coming with his axe.' He rubbed at his face, kept his eyes on the ground. 'When he smashed the door in, four wee kids were piled behind it. All dead from breathing in the smoke. The father had locked them in and gone on the piss.'

A tear ran down his face cutting a white path through the grime. He wiped at it and another one came. Archie put his arm round his shoulder, guided him into the station.

'Come on, son, we'll get you cleaned up, eh?'

15

Gunner thought he'd stay out the station for a while, let things cool off. It was strangely peaceful out on the street, dark, not many people around. Even the fires still burning down in the city centre looked beautiful against the night sky. He sat on the kerb and lit up a cigarette. The air in front of him was full of little bits of grey ash swirling around in the wind, looked like snow. The station door behind him banged open and Drummond appeared, half-bottle of whisky in his hand.

'You were right, it wasnae your fault,' he said, holding the bottle out, looking sheepish.

Gunner took it and chucked down a decent-sized slug. It burnt all the way down, some gut rot in a Dewar's bottle, but it felt good. Drummond sat down on the kerb beside him, and they passed the bottle back and forth, neither of them saying much. It wasn't long until the gates of the barracks down the road swung open and trucks started to rumble out, headlights down to slits of light shining through their covers. All of them turned left on Maryhill Road, heading west towards Clydebank and the shipyards.

'Heard it was bad,' said Gunner. 'The kids.'

Drummond nodded.

'If I ever find that cunt of a father, I'm going to beat him to fuck, wait until he comes round and then beat him to fuck again.'

Wasn't much to say to that, Gunner knew he would, knew he would too. Needed to change the subject.

'Meant to ask you, am I getting paid for this?'

'For what?'

'Running about after you, trying to fix what you've fucked up.'

Drummond smiled.

'Always did have a high opinion of yourself, Gunner. Fuck knows, I'll see if I can find some money from somewhere, not much of it around. All the spare money goes to the war, it's bad enough trying to get them to pay me. Lorna's going spare, barely enough to run the bloody house.'

'How is she since . . . ?'

Drummond shrugged.

'Not great. Good days and bad days. Only son killed in the first few months of the war. Takes a lot of getting over. If you ever can.'

'How about you?' Gunner lit up, stared straight ahead.

'I think about him every day. The big stupid lump was still my wee boy. If I could have got killed instead of him I would, no hesitation.'

'I'm sorry, Drummond,' said Gunner.

'I know you are. If you hadn't kept an eye on me when it happened, God knows what I would have done.'

'Saw too many young boys killed out there. I thought I would get immune to it, but I didn't, don't think you can.'

'There'll be a lot more of them before it's over,' said Drummond. 'More mothers and fathers spending evey night just looking at each other, wondering how they got there, trying not to talk about it.'

He held the bottle up.

'To Harry,' he said. 'And all the rest of them. May they rest in peace.'

They were still sitting there when the low noise of planes started up again. The deep rumble brought Archie and Fraser back out. They stood outside the station and watched them come in from the east, a vast grid of planes flying just above the barrage balloons and the range of the ack-acks.

'Heading for the shipyards again,' said Archie. 'Looks like they're going to miss us out.'

Gunner turned to ask him if they should try and get out to Clydebank when they heard the whistling.

'Down!' shouted Drummond. 'Get down!'

They all dropped, started scrabbling towards the entrance of a close and its protecting baffle. They almost made it before the bomb hit. Gunner felt the air move against his chest, so strong it pushed him over, and then there was a bang so loud it felt physical. Suddenly he felt like he was underwater, everything muffled and distant. His ears popped and he could hear the rain of stones and bricks coming down, hitting the pavement with such force they were bouncing back up again. He tried to look round, see where the others were. Archie was lying on the pavement across the way, a plank of smoking wood across his back, not moving.

Drummond and Fraser were half in, half out the close, trying to crawl their way in. The air was full of burning wood and ash fizzing down, trails of spinning smoke in their wake. Gunner felt a burning on his back, rolled over, rubbed his back against the pavement, trying to put the smouldering out. He tried to stand up but everything seemed to be wobbling, he stumbled, fell. Gave up. Tucked himself up into a ball, put his arms over his head and tried to ride it out.

A rain of stones, bricks, bits of wood rattling down on the cobbles kept falling. Gunner looked out from between his hands just in time to see a dog fly through the air and hit a bread van on the other side of the street. A chest of drawers landed by him and burst on impact. There were dead birds everywhere, some still on fire, some just smoking. He buried his head in his hands when he saw a leg land by the grocer's across the street. He didn't want to see any more. It was like being back in France, lying in a ditch hoping and praying he wouldn't get hit.

Then, just as fast as it began, it was over. As fast as a tap being turned off, debris stopped falling from the sky, the last few things, birds and masonry, rattled down and then it was over. Gunner waited for a minute, made sure it was really finished before he got up. He stood up, slapped at the smouldering holes on his trousers and tried to make his way over to Archie. He could hear water running, someone shouting, a bell going on and off. He had to pick his way across the road, it was covered in all sorts, clothes, bits of furniture, half a sink; eventually got to where Archie was lying. He knelt down, pulled the wood off his back and turned him over. His face was dirty, arms were bruised. He was dazed and half deafened, but there didn't seem to be any real damage done.

Gunner helped him up and they struggled back through the debris and made it to Drummond and Fraser. They were standing propped against the close wall checking themselves over. Apart from a big dent in Fraser's tin helmet, a gash across Drummond's nose and a couple of burns on his leg, they seemed to be OK.

Gunner sat Archie down, leant him against the close wall. He winced as his back touched the wall, but he waved Gunner away, said he was OK.

'So much for them no dropping anything on us,' said Drummond. 'That's the last time I listen to you, ya stupit old bugger.'

Archie tried to smile, bright false teeth shining in his blackened face. Gunner took the half-bottle out his pocket and handed it to him. He drank it down quickly, cocked his head. Looked up.

'Fucking hell. There's no more of them, is there?' said Drummond.

There were. All they could do was sit in the close and wait as the planes droned overhead. There was another huge bang and they all ducked before they could stop themselves.

'What was that?' asked Fraser.

'Another bomb, by the sound of it,' said Drummond. 'Not that far either.' He crawled to the entrance to the close and looked out, peered up at the sky, 'Think they've gone over now.' He pulled himself up and walked out into the street, trying to see where he was going through the smoke and the dust.

Fraser and Gunner watched as he made for an ash-covered car, hauled himself up onto the roof, looked around. He shouted, pointed to a jagged tenement roof, flames starting to emerge for the top of it.

'Over there!' he said. 'C'mon!'

16

They were standing in what was left of Duncruin Street. The sun was coming up, but it was losing the battle with the dust and smoke in the air, was hardly making a difference. Water was flowing down the street towards them from a ruptured main, gradually filling a ten-foot crater in the middle of the road. Just next to where they were standing a whole tenement end was exposed. One half of it had collapsed leaving a cross-section of rooms, different patterned wallpapers in each, pictures still hanging on the walls. There was even an open door in one of the flats two flights up, a woman standing in the doorway peering out, baby in her arms.

Drummond coughed, spat black phlegm onto the cobbles. It was hard to breathe, the air was clogged with dust. Burning ash was drifting down around them. Gunner absent-mindedly slapped at a burning hole in the arm of his suit. It was hard not to just stand and stare. The cobbled street was covered in people's things blown out of their flats. A twisted pram, broken plates, clothes, books. There was an armchair sitting proud on a pile of rubble smouldering away.

And everywhere there was blood. Blood, bodies and bits of bodies. Gunner was trying not to look but there was a hand on the pavement beside him, what looked like a woman's arm still wearing a watch lying torn and mangled beside it. A parked car across the street had a teenage boy lying across it, head facing the wrong way. He could hear someone being sick behind him, Fraser he imagined. He didn't blame him, it was more like a vision of hell than a Glasgow street. Slowly people began to emerge from their houses, out from under the debris, pale with ash, wounded, not sure where they even were.

Gunner suddenly thought, shouldn't have taken him so long to remember. They needed to do what they did in France when a building with people in it got hit.

Gunner dug his badge out his pocket, marched towards the centre of the street, badge held high above his head.

'Quiet!' he shouted. 'Everyone needs to be quiet. Now!'

It took a few moments for the noise to die down. Eventually, all that was left was the gurgle of water running down the street and the occasional piece of masonry falling off the damaged tenements. And then they heard it. Someone calling.

Gunner held his hands up, keeping everyone quiet. The noise seemed to be coming from his left. He pointed, and Drummond and two ARP men followed him over, stood by the pile of rubble. They stood stock-still, straining to hear, waiting for it to come again. For a couple of minutes there was nothing, then it came again, fainter this time.

'C'mon,' said Gunner. 'There's someone under there.'

They started to climb the pile of rubble heading to where the noise had come from. Gunner was highest up, he took another step and the pile started to shift under his feet, a mini-avalanche of stones and bricks started tumbling down. They froze. Nobody moving, hoping the pile would stabilise itself.

Gunner looked down to see if there was a bigger bit of stone he could stand on and saw fingers poking out between two broken sandstone blocks. He knelt down gingerly, reached out and touched them, the fingers curled around his like a baby's.

'Drummond,' he whispered. 'Up here.'

It took them over an hour to get the woman out. Them and ten or so soldiers from the barracks that had been sent to help. The pile of masonry she was under wasn't stable, just a nightmare jigsaw of shifting rubble, constantly threatening to move and crush her. They formed a line from her down to the street, passing each brick or lump of stone to each other separately, trying desperately not to disturb the pile.

It was hellish work, fear and strain written on their faces; shirts soaked with sweat. By the time they managed to move enough rubble to pull her out she'd lost consciousness. Her legs just trailed behind her as they lifted her, one of them broken and flattened. They got her down off the pile and onto the street and the medics laid her out on a fruit barrow they'd found somewhere and ran her down to the temporary infirmary at Gaven's pub.

Gunner and Drummond watched her go, then sat down on the kerb taking drinks from one of the canteens the soldiers were passing around. The sun was starting to come up, most of the dust and ash had settled, the air was starting to clear. An ARP man was washing the blood from his hands in the water from the cracked main, a line of others behind him waiting to do the same.

Four bodies were lined up outside Lipton's grocery across from them. Two big ones and two little ones, dark blood spotting the sheets they were wrapped in. Drummond took out his cigarettes and Gunner took one, both coughing as they lit up, throats raw with the dust. They were down to braces and vests now, shirts that hadn't been burnt by the ash had been gathered up to use as temporary bandages. The morning sun was warm on their shoulders, the promise of another sunny day ahead. Drummond watched a couple of soldiers dipping buckets into the water in the crater and using it to sluice down the bloodiest bits of the street.

'At least it's no as bad as last night,' he said. 'Last night was ten times worse, a big bit of Govan went. There's only this street and a couple over in Tradeston tonight.'

'It's bad enough,' said Gunner.

Drummond nodded. 'And Christ only knows what it's like in Clydebank.' He yawned and looked at his watch. Half five. 'I need to get to Central, tell them how many we're down.' He stood up, stretched. 'You coming?'

Gunner shook his head. 'I'm gonnae try and get a couple of hours' sleep at the station, long as that wee cot's still there.'

Drummond turned, made his way down towards Maryhill Road, Fraser appearing out of nowhere to fall in behind. It was only then Gunner remembered he hadn't told him about Nickerson and the order to go back to the regiment. Two soldiers appeared, looked about fifteen, and picked up one of the bodies from the line outside Lipton's, the one at the back struggling to keep all the pieces together in the sheet.

Gunner took another slug of warm water from the canteen. Talking to Drummond could wait. He checked his trouser pocket. The last syrette was still there. He stood up. Time to go back to the station and sleep. Christ knows he needed it.

17

Gunner walked down the street, the sun starting to feel hot on his back, realised he was going to pass Gaven's on the way. As he got nearer the pub he could see a row of bodies laid out on stretchers and wooden doors outside. They were wrapped in blankets, curtains, what looked like a bit of carpet. A group of the walking wounded were being herded down towards where the medics had set themselves up by an ambulance parked on Maryhill Road. That was as near as the vehicles could get, the street completely blocked by debris from the bombing.

He eased his way through the crowd of relatives and crying kids and pushed the big pub doors open, thought he'd see if the woman they'd got out from under the rubble had made it. Took a few seconds for his eyes to adjust to the gloom. The pub was more like a hospital waiting room now.

The long wooden bar at the back had been turned into a makeshift examination table. A man was lying on it, clothes half torn off, a hole the size of a fist in his side, two desperate-looking nurses trying to stuff what looked like a couple of blood-soaked bar towels into it. The doctor from the Kelvin Hall was bent over him, one hand on top of the other, furiously pumping his chest. He still had the same pyjama top on, stripes hardly visible through the bloodstains. Gunner kept his head down and dived into the lounge before he saw him.

The seats and tables in the lounge had been pushed along the sides of the walls, the cleared floor now covered by the wounded and the dying. Some were moaning, a couple were screaming and writhing in agony, some just lay there silently, eyes empty and staring, relatives crouched down beside them. The lounge still had its usual smell of beer and fags, the smell of shite and bleach not quite covering it.

Gunner picked his way across the room, being careful not to stand on anyone, looking for the woman from the rubble. He couldn't see her anywhere. A man in the corner by a pile of chairs was moaning, a horrible, lonely sound. Gunner edged his way over. Most of the back of the man's head was gone, he couldn't be long for this world. He'd nobody by him, his hand kept reaching out trying to grab at something or somebody.

Gunner knelt down and took it. The man's fingers immediately curled around his in a tight grip, some change in his wild eyes. Whatever was wrong with him, he could still sense human touch. They sat like that for forty minutes or so, Gunner holding his hand and telling him it was going to be OK, holding his hand until the grip loosened and the man was gone.

Gunner put his hand down and wiped at his eyes. Crying over a man he didn't know. In all this mess, in France, it was always the little things that got to you. An Air Force pilot trapped in a crashed plane trying to remember the Lord's Prayer as the life went out from his eyes. A German soldier, couldn't have been more than eighteen, trying to give a photo of his mum and dad to a medic as the life seeped out of him. That was what

Gunner's war was, not a story of glorious battles and defeats, just a handful of memories like those. Ordinary people caught up in the nightmare they were living through. Trying to make some kind of contact rather than dying alone.

He looked round for a nurse or a doctor but they were all frantic, another wave of the wounded had just come in. Some Anderson shelter had collapsed, they said. The guy he'd sat with was dead, probably best to leave them to deal with the ones that still had a chance.

Gunner leant forward to raise the sheet over the man's face and dislodged a morphine syrette sticking out of his arm. He lifted his arm to put it across the one on his chest. Stopped. There was an open box tucked in beside the man's torso, six or seven of the wee tubes still in it. Before he could think about it Gunner picked up the box, stuffed it into his trouser pocket and made for the pub door. He'd pushed the door open, was just about to step out into the light when he felt a tap on his shoulder. He turned round, heart racing, excuses for what he'd done rushing through his mind.

'How's you, big boy?'

'Nan?' he said, surprised. He was staring into the face of his brother's girlfriend. 'That you?'

The girl smiled. 'Bet your bottom dollar it is.'

She stepped forward and hugged him, the scent of violets on her, as always. He let her go, stood back, looked at her. Even covered in dust she was quite something. Big red lipstick smile on her face, blonde hair tied up with a scarf, blue eyes shining.

'Nan, fuck sake! What are you doing here?'

She waved back into the pub.

'It's a stupid bloody story. I was visiting my old landlady when the sirens went off. Just my luck. She's in there now, she's got a broken arm, the stupid cow slipped on the lino getting us a cup of tea when the sirens finished. Told her to say she was hit by flying shrapnel, might look at her quicker.'

'What about you?' asked Gunner. 'You OK?'

Nan nodded 'Me? Aye, I'm fine, I stayed under the kitchen table the whole time, smoked my way through a whole bloody packet of Black Cat. Safer than the bloody shelter.'

She stepped back and looked at him.

'What are you doing here anyway?' she asked. 'I thought you were away being a soldier.'

'I was.' He tapped the eyepatch. 'Fucked my eye up.'

'I quite like it,' she smiled. 'Makes you look like a villain.'

He smiled back, a brief silence between them, and then he asked: 'Have you seen Victor? I need to speak to him soon as. It's important.'

She bit at her bottom lip, lipstick coming off on her teeth.

'Hold on,' she said. 'Wait here.'

She walked back towards the bar, stretched over and pulled a bottle of whisky from the shelf underneath. The doctor started to object but she put her fingers to his mouth to shush him and carried on back towards the door. She put her arm through Gunner's.

'Come on, before the moaning-faced bastard really starts complaining.'

18

Outside the pub, the dawn had brought Maryhill Road back to life. Gawpers, reporters, concerned relatives, people trying to get on with their daily jobs; the street was packed. Gunner and Nan waited for a long convoy of army trucks to go by, crossed the road and walked down the path to where the canal looped down from the hill and formed a basin.

The water in the basin was filthy, coated in a film of oil and petrol, an occasional dead pigeon floating by, but the wee brightly painted puffers and barges were almost picturesque in the sunshine. They walked down past the locks and sat down on a pile of apple crates lying on the grass. Nan took the bottle from the pocket of her raincoat and wiped the dust from it.

Gunner shook his head. 'You always could get away with murder.'

She looked mock indignant.

'What? I could have been killed by the bloody Jerries, I deserve a wee reward.'

She took a swig, shuddered and handed the bottle to him.

'Christ, that is grim,' she said. 'I don't know what they put in these bottles but it's definitely no whisky any more.'

Gunner took a long draught and winced. She was right. Still, it did the trick. Things were getting back to normal on the canal. A queue of barges was forming at the basin, a long line of horse and carts waiting at the bank to pick up their deliveries. Gunner watched a coal merchant and his boy start lifting up sacks from the side of the bank and said the inevitable:

'So Nan, where is he?'

She'd taken a tortoiseshell compact out, was looking in the wee mirror, tidying up her hair. 'What makes you think I know?'

'Come on, Nan, you're his girlfriend, you must know,' said Gunner.

'Ex-girlfriend,' she said quickly.

'OK, so it's all off again for this week, is it? Pardon me. Stop mucking me about, Nan, I need to know where he is.'

She stopped fixing her hair, snapped the compact shut and took the bottle out his hand just as he was going for another swig.

'You just cannae help yourself, can you? Sounding like a polis, bossing people round. Always the fucking same. I'm no one of your suspects, Joe, don't treat me like one.'

Gunner held his hand up in apology.

'Look, Nan, Victor needs to come in. If he does I can sort it. If he doesn't and they catch him he'll be fucked. Prison for years. You know what that's like,' he said, and immediately wished he hadn't.

'Well, it didn't take you long to mention that, did it?' Nan said flatly.

A wee puffer sounded its whistle, pulled in at the side of the basin. They watched a boy jump off, tie the boat up to a bollard.

'It wasn't my fault, Nan,' he said. 'I'm a polis, but I'm no the polis that took you in.'

'No but you're the one that made it perfectly clear I wasn't good enough for your precious wee brother. A jailbird. And a leopard doesn't change its spots. That not what you said?'

Gunner couldn't say anything. He had; wished he hadn't, but he had.

Nan stood up, brushed some of the ash and soot off her skirt.

'Tell you what, why don't you tell me where you'll be and if I by chance run into him I'll let him know.'

Gunner nodded. 'One o'clock today. George's Cross. You'll tell him?'

'If I see him I will, but that's a big if.'

Gunner stood up, yawned, stretched. The long night was starting to take its toll.

'Thanks, Nan, I owe you. You still working at the Morvern?'

She snorted. 'That dump? Nope. I've come up in the world, I'm working round the corner. Dancing at the Tower now.'

Gunner looked surprised. 'What, you're working for Con McGill?'

She took another swig of the bottle. 'Front page news. The Tower Ballroom's no Con McGill any more, it belongs to Sellars. I work for him now. Just like everyone else.'

'What's that like?'

Nan shrugged.

'I've worked for worse. He's all right, until he gets angry that is, and then he's a fucking monster.'

Gunner said his goodbyes, carried on down the hill heading for the Maryhill station and the cot in the back room. Drummond was right enough, Sellars was taking over. He yawned. The German, Moore, Nickerson, Victor. All of it was swirling around in his head but he was too tired to make any sense of it. He stopped by the side of the road for a minute, his leg was killing him. He ran his fingers over the wee box in his pocket, checking it was still there. He was exhausted, badly needed a few hours' kip to clear his head, and thanks to the wee box in his pocket he was going to get it.

19

Maybe the contents of the wee syrette Gunner had stuck into his leg were still floating through his system or maybe he was just out of practice; either way, he didn't see them coming. One minute he was walking up Maryhill Road heading to George's Cross to meet Victor, and the next he was doubled over, arm bent up his back and winded from a punch in the stomach.

The two blokes that had a hold of him hadn't said much, just the occasional grunt as they pushed him into the back of the waiting car. One of them pulled a cloth bag over his head, punched him in the stomach a few more times for luck, and that was that.

There wasn't much Gunner could do but sit there in the back of the car and worry about where he was going. His hands were tied behind his back, one of the blokes had his arm across his chest pinning him to the seat. He'd tried to ask what was going on, but all he'd got for his trouble was a punch in the kidneys and a growled 'Shut the fuck up'.

In the darkness of the hood he listened to them striking matches and lighting up, to the steady throb of the engine, and wondered who it was that had taken him. Moore? Had he decided he knew too much about the German? Seemed a bit heavy-handed for him, and besides the two gorillas who'd grabbed him had sounded as Glaswegian as he had. There was only one other possibility, the one that made his stomach roll over in fear. Sellars.

Half an hour or so of low-level panic later the car pulled over to the left, slowed down and stopped. He heard the doors opening, a few mumbled greetings and then he was dragged out the car, felt gravel beneath his feet. He was just about to try again, ask what the fuck was going on, when he felt something heavy come down on the back of his head; pain exploded for a second, and then darkness.

'Wakey-wakey.'

He could hear laughing, seemed to be coming from far away, then the shock as the cold water hit him. He opened his eyes, shook his head and looked into the boyish face of Malky Sellars. He was sitting on a chair opposite him, smiling, cigarette hanging from the corner of his mouth. Malky had been inside for a couple of years, but that would still only make him twenty-five or so. He'd a smart suit on, polished shoes, tie and hanky in his breast pocket. With his reddish side-parted hair and open smile, he looked more like a film star than a gangster.

'Mr Gunner,' he said. 'Nice of you to drop in.'

Gunner rubbed at his nose. His hand came away covered in blood.

'Aye, sorry about that,' said Sellars.

Gunner looked around, tried to work out where he was. It was a large room, wood-panelled, a herringbone floor, leather chesterfields and some paintings of misty hills on the walls. It looked like a gentlemen's club or a posh lawyer's office. The last place he expected to be. He had imagined some cellar or warehouse with dried blood on the floor. Sellars nodded to the corner of the room where the heavy was leaning against the wall.

'Bingo's no very good at the subtle approach.' He smiled. 'Still, to be honest, that's not really what he's here for.'

He took a silver cigarette case out of his pocket, flicked it open, and held it out.

Gunner leant forward and took one. He needed it. Sellars lit it for him and sat back on his chair.

'What the fuck are you about, Sellars?' said Gunner, with more front than he felt. 'Think you can get away with shite like this?'

Sellars smiled.

'Glasgow's a changed place, Gunner. There's only your fat pal Drummond and his wee boys left now. Seems like I get away with most things.'

Gunner cleared his throat, spat a blob of bloody phlegm onto the floor next to Sellars' shoe.

'That right?' he said. 'Well, if you've finished congratulating yourself I'm off.'

He stood up, started walking towards the door. Sellars nodded at Bingo. A couple of hard punches under his ribs later and Gunner was sitting in his seat again and Bingo was back against the wall rubbing at his jaw where Gunner had managed to get one on him.

Sellars sat forward, elbows on knees. 'You and me have to have a wee chat. You gonnae behave yourself?'

'Fuck off, Sellars,' said Gunner. 'I've nothing to say to you.'

Sellars was out of his chair before Gunner could even react.

Had his hand round his neck, thumb pressing hard into his windpipe, cutting off his breathing.

'You just sit there and you fucking listen,' he hissed into his ear. 'Or so help me I'll lose my temper.'

He pushed Gunner away from him. The chair tipped over and Gunner was back on the floor again gasping for a breath. He flinched as Bingo walked over, expecting another kicking, but all he did was sit the chair upright and sit him back down on it.

'Let's start again, shall we?' said Sellars.

Gunner nodded, he'd no fight left in him. Whatever he did, had the feeling it would end with Bingo punching him stupid and him back in the chair. Decided to play along.

'The reason you're here,' said Sellars, 'is my brother wants a word.'

The last thing Gunner was expecting. Nobody met Sellars' brother Matthew. He stayed so far back in the shadows he'd never been arrested, never even been interviewed. There was a rumour he didn't even exist, that he was just a ruse to put the polis off.

'Your brother?' asked Gunner.

Sellars nodded. 'My brother's not like me. He likes a quiet life. You're the only person he's ever asked me to bring here, so think yourself honoured. So, no monkey business, no fucking about, or you'll have me to answer to. Got me?'

Gunner didn't know what else to do but nod.

Sellars stood up, nodded to Bingo. 'He'll be here in a minute. Just sit there and wait. And remember he's my big brother. Show respect or I'll go through you like a fucking hot knife through butter.'

Gunner watched them go, still no real idea why he was here. Sellars hadn't even mentioned Gunner getting him put away, and apart from kidnapping him and having his heavy knock him about a bit he'd been pleasant enough. The whole thing didn't make any sense. He looked about the room again, noticed a decanter full of whisky with some crystal tumblers next to it on a sideboard. Was just about to get up and help himself when the door swung open.

It wasn't Matthew Sellars that came in, it was a woman in her mid-twenties, looked like she'd just stepped out of a fashion magazine. Pale blue suit, high heels, hair held off her very pretty face with a turban sort of thing. She looked at him, took in the burn marks on the dusty suit, the shoes covered in ash, the eyepatch. Didn't look very impressed.

'Matthew is sensitive to the light,' she said, going around the room switching the standard lamps off. She left the reading light on a desk in the far corner on, that was it. The room was practically dark now, took a while for Gunner's eyes to adjust and by the time they had, she was gone and he was alone in the gloom. He reached up, took his eyepatch off, hoped he'd be able to see better for what was to come.

20

Gunner sat in the quiet listening to the sounds of the house. He could hear someone walking about upstairs, creak of floorboards, a dog barking in the garden. He wondered where he was, he thought they'd driven for about half an hour, could be out by Bearsden, or somewhere on the south side by then. Then again they could have just driven round the city centre to disorientate him and he could be two minutes from where he'd been picked up.

'Mr Gunner.'

He looked up, hadn't heard anyone coming in, soon realised why. Matthew Sellars was sat in a wheelchair, rubber tyres silent on the parquet flooring. It was hard to see much of him in the dark but his legs were in calipers, painful-looking iron supports from below his knees to his ankles. He was wearing a pair of dark trousers, a black jumper, the collar of his white shirt just visible beneath it. He was pale, thin, frail-looking, looked like a good wind would blow him away.

'Sorry about the way I got you here, but I don't go out much,' he said.

His voice was softer than Malky's, less of a rough accent, but they were definitely brothers all right. Same reddish hair, same handsome features.

'You could have just asked,' said Gunner.

'Would you have come?'

'No.'

Matthew smiled. 'Drink?' He nodded over at the decanter. 'Would you mind getting it yourself and one for me?'

Gunner poured the drinks, struggling to see what he was doing in the gloom. He carried them over and handed one to Matthew Sellars. He took it in his thin hand, a hand that shook as he raised it to his lips.

'You put my brother in prison,' said Matthew.

'He deserved it,' said Gunner.

'Whether he deserved it or not, you put him away. My brother doesn't forget things like that. He festers on them, lets them eat away at him until things boil over and . . .' He smiled, held his hands open. 'And then people get hurt.'

'What are you telling me this for?' asked Gunner. 'Your brother's nothing special, just another thug. I've dealt with plenty of them before.'

Matthew smiled.

'Come on, you don't believe that, Gunner, and neither do I. My brother is something special. Which brings me to why you are here.' He held his shaky glass up to his lips with both his hands and took another sip. 'When my brother was in prison it gave me time to think, the time I usually waste putting out the fires he has lit. These are different days, Gunner, the war's speeded everything up.'

He tried to put the glass on the arm of his wheelchair but his grip wasn't strong enough; it fell, hit the ground and rolled away.

Gunner went to get it but before he could reach it, Matthew told him to leave it, watched the glass come to a halt by the window. Looked up.

'Do you know what spinal muscular atrophy is, Mr Gunner?' he said.

Gunner shook his head.

'It's a genetic disease. I got it and Malcolm didn't. The luck of the draw. It weakens the body, has no effect on the mind. So, by default, I became the brains and Malcolm became the brawn. However, I would urge you not to underestimate him. He's impetuous but he's far cleverer than people think he is and he likes it that way. Acts the ruffian.'

'He's good at it,' said Gunner.

'Very,' said Matthew. 'And I'm very good at being the brains. Con McGill and his ilk? Idiots. Jumped-up street fighters and debt collectors. Their time is just about up. Your pal Drummond backed the wrong horse, he probably knows that now but it's too late for him to do anything about it. Him and McGill are stuck to each other like shite on a blanket, if you'll pardon my expression.'

'What's this got to do with me?' asked Gunner.

'Everything. When Malcolm was away I had a long time to think, ask questions, learn. That's really what my business is all about, Gunner. Knowledge. The most valuable thing in the world is what you know. And what I know is that when the war's over you'll be back and a couple of years after that you'll be top of the heap just like Drummond was. We're going to be big pals, you and I, do each other good.'

Gunner laughed. 'I don't know how good your eyesight is, but one of my eyes is fucked, may or may not get better. My face is covered in scars and half my leg was blown off in a field in France. Chances are they aren't going to let me back in the polis. Besides, I'm no a gangster's tout. I've never been in anyone's pocket and I never will be.'

Sellars smiled again. 'Exactly. Drummond's a clown, stockpiling nylons in his brother's garage, kickbacks from the shebeens. All small-time stuff. That's his idea of running this town, skimming a bunch of whoors and warehousemen. Not you, you're smart. We're going to be running into each other a lot in the next few years. I'm a reasonable man, you're a reasonable man. We can work together.'

Gunner shook his head. 'I don't shoot people up the arse, Sellars. I'm not your brother. I don't kick people to fuck in wee rooms or nail them to the fucking floor while they scream for their mammies. You think the fact you sit in here all day while your wee brother does it means you're not getting your hands dirty? You're as bad as your brother. Worse, in fact. Go and fuck yourself.'

Again that smile. 'Opposite sides of the coin, Mr Gunner, that's all. You and your pals kick people to fuck in the cells, fit them up, send them away for years. You're no fucking saint, so you think about it. And while you're thinking about it, I'll be kind enough to keep Malcolm's thoughts off any ideas of revenge.'

He pressed a button on the wall.

The door opened and Bingo appeared.

'Bingo,' said Sellars. 'See our guest out.'

Gunner stood up. 'I can find my own way out this pigsty.'

He walked past Sellars and out into the hall. Bingo followed and pulled the door closed. He held up his fist, brass knuckles wrapped around it.

'Get the hood on, get in the car. Don't be a fucking dick and make me use these.'

Gunner knew it was a battle he wasn't going to win. He took the hood from Bingo and pulled it over his head.

21

Half an hour later Bingo said 'Ready?' and pulled the hood off Gunner's head. Gunner blinked in the light, looked out the car window. They were just pulling over at Central Station. The car stopped and Bingo leant over him and pushed the door open.

'Fuck off,' he said amiably.

Gunner did. He got out and looked up at the clock. Just gone half twelve, enough time to get to Victor. He started walking up Hope Street trying to work out what had just happened.

Matthew Sellars was a strange one, right enough. Nothing like he'd imagined. He didn't really know what to make of him. Most of the gangsters he dealt with were like he had said, street fighters who'd battered and slashed their way up the ranks. None of them lasted too long, not smart enough to avoid being replaced by the next young buck on the rise. Not Matthew Sellars. He'd a feeling him and his brother were going to be around for a good while. It was a classic combination; Malky had all the good looks and the front, Matthew more than enough brains for the two of them.

One thing Matthew had said bothered him. *You're no fucking saint.* Didn't know why, but it had sounded like Matthew knew something he didn't. Thought of the farmer, the syrettes stolen from a dead man. Would he have done stuff like that before the war? Didn't think so. Seemed like the horrors of the war were so huge that whatever he did now didn't much matter. God had bigger sins than his to deal with.

He'd worked up a sweat by the time he got to St George's Cross. The weather was turning, clouding over, getting clammy. He stood outside Massey's and looked around for Victor. A queue of wifeys stretched from the big grocer's right down the street, all of them with ration books in hand. Must have had a delivery, news like that spread fast. He crossed the road, dodging the clattering trams, wires overhead thrumming and singing across the big crossroads.

He'd seen a bloke selling fruit from a barrow, wee boy on point looking out for the ARPs. He bought an apple, wee wizened thing from someone's garden by the look of it, but it tasted good enough. He finished it, chucked the core in the gutter and looked at the big clock above the Massey's sign. Twenty past one. Victor was late, assuming Nan had given him the message, that was.

Gunner decided to give it another ten minutes, then head down to Central, give Drummond the news about the boys from MI5 and his orders to go back to his regiment. He watched an *Evening Chronicle* van pull up outside the newsagent's and a boy chuck a bundle of papers wrapped in string out the back. He was just deciding whether to buy one when he finally caught sight of him.

Victor was walking across the street, raincoat flapping behind him, hat stuck on the back of his head, fag in the corner of his mouth. Victor was younger than Gunner by almost five years. Like him he'd got all the Scandinavian genes from their Swedish father, was broad, tall, blond hair. For a conchie on the run, he looked like he hadn't a care in the world. He saw Gunner, waved and strolled over.

'All right, Joey?' he asked.

'Don't call me that.' It was what Gunner always said, and they smiled at each other, unsure what to say next.

Gunner broached the silence first. 'You've got some bloody nerve walking about town in broad daylight!'

Victor shrugged. 'Hide in plain sight, is that not the expression? Besides, there's too many of us, nobody's looking for me.'

Gunner snorted. 'That's what you think, I've got the Chief of Police trying to find you.'

Victor's face fell.

'Don't worry, he's on my side. Drink?'

They headed for Bell's bar just up the road, one of Gunner's regular haunts before he'd shipped out. A busy wee pub, always full. A mixture of people from the offices and shops around, workers from the theatre next door and today about twenty Australian soldiers with tans and big hats complaining good-naturedly about the beer. Gunner got them two beers and Victor found them a seat up the back. Gunner sat down and realised why he'd picked it. Victor wasn't stupid; the angled Red Hackle whisky mirror on the opposite wall gave him a good view of the door, he would see any MPs quick enough.

Victor pointed at his own eye.

'What happened there?'

Gunner couldn't help himself.

'Dunkirk. Happened when I was off fighting the forces of fascism.'

Victor didn't respond, just took a sip of his pint.

Gunner couldn't think of any other way to say it. Blurted it out. 'Look. You need to come in, Victor, come in while I'm here. I can fix it. I'm owed.'

Victor shook his head, eyes still on the mirror above the bar. 'I'm no going back to that fucking farm.'

'You'll no need to go back there, we can get you in somewhere else,' said Gunner. 'There are other farms, hospitals that need people. We'll get you in somewhere half decent.'

Victor looked at him, pulled a face.

'Are you off your heid? That's the way you think it works, is it? That people like me get to pick and choose what happens to them? Do you know what happens to conchies, Joe? We're lower than dogs and everyone wants to have a kick at us. No fucking way I'm going back to that.'

A whoop went up from the Australian soldiers. One of them had climbed up onto the bar, pint in his hand. He downed it within twenty seconds or so and upturned the empty glass on his head. Big cheers all round.

Victor shook his head, smiled. 'Nutters.'

'Where you staying?' asked Gunner.

No reply, just another glance at the mirror.

'You're staying at Nan's, aren't you? That's not fair, you're putting her in it too. She's got a record, if they do her for harbouring you, she'll go back to prison.'

Victor laughed. 'Since when did you give a fuck about Nan? Can't remember the amount of times you told me I could do better.'

They sat there, neither saying anything, sipping their pints, watching the Australians. Gunner didn't want to fight with Victor. He didn't have the time. He tried again.

'It's simple, Victor, if they catch you, they'll put you away. Put you away for a long time. In prison – and prison is no fucking joke. Especially not for someone like you.'

'Like me? What's that supposed to mean?'

'It means you're soft, Victor, always have been. I had to fight your battles for you. There's not going to be a me in prison.'

'Well, thank fuck for that, in that case I might hand myself in.'

That was it for Gunner, he'd had enough. He'd tried. Tried his best.

'Do you know something, Victor? You were the first one warning everyone about the Nazis, standing outside factories with your pals, handing out leaflets, selling your papers. And what are you doing now? Supping an afternoon pint when people are dying over there trying to stop them. All fucking talk and no action, same as always.'

Victor blew out a stream of smoke, kept his eyes on the mirror. 'Don't you worry, I'm doing my bit.'

'How?' asked Gunner, starting to get angry. 'By poncing off Nan and wandering round Glasgow with a big smile on your face acting like there's no a fucking war on?'

Victor shook his head.

'You never could see further than the nose on your face could you, Joe. Everything's black or white, guilty or innocent, and you get to decide which is which. I never asked you to fight my battles. You just couldn't stop yourself. Joe Gunner acting the big man again, no fucking surprise you joined the polis, get to kick fuck out of people and get paid for it.'

Gunner tried to keep calm, not rise to it. Victor knew exactly how to rile him, always had. But this was too important for a brotherly squabble. He needed Victor to do what he was told for once.

'I've got a chance to get you out of this without you going to prison. But it won't last forever, Victor. Come in.'

Victor sat back in his chair. 'I can't,' he said coolly. 'I'm fighting the good fight same as you are.'

'Are you fuck! You're just kidding yourself. Christ, Victor, for once take a telling, eh?'

Gunner went to stand up when he caught sight of Fraser in the mirror above the bar. He was scanning the pub, looking round for someone. Him, no doubt. Gunner stood up and whistled. Fraser saw him, waved and tried to weave his way through the Australians, eventually made it to the table.

'The bloke in the Horseshoe said you might be here,' he said. His face was red, hair slicked down with sweat. 'I've already tried the Steps, couldn't find you anywhere.'

'Well, you've found me now.' Gunner held his pint out. 'Have a drink of this and calm down.'

Fraser gulped at the pint and managed to spill half of it down his front. He wiped his mouth, handed it back and noticed Victor sitting there. Victor looked at him, shuffled in his seat. As far as Gunner was concerned, it served the wee shite right. Young as Fraser was, he was still a kind of a polis with a uniform on. Victor had a right to be worried.

'What is it?' asked Gunner. 'What does Drummond want?'

Another whoop, another young Australian on the bar guzzling a pint. Fraser watched him, amazed, as the whole pint went down.

'Fraser!' said Gunner.

Fraser turned back, was still panting, took him a minute to get it out.

'Sorry. There's another body. Well, not a body, he's still alive.'
'He's what?' asked Gunner. 'Who's alive?'

'There's a German, another one,' said Fraser. 'They took him out one of the warehouses that got bombed in Tradeston last night, they thought he was dead but he's still breathing, they don't think he's got long, that's why Drummond sent me to find you.'

Gunner drained what was left of his pint, banged the empty glass on the table and turned to Victor. Poked him in the chest.

'I'm no finished with you yet,' he said. 'I'll be in here tonight, and you better be here too.'

'Not here,' said Victor. 'The Corbie, I'll be in the Corbie.'

Gunner didn't have time to argue. 'Eight o'clock,' he said, grabbed Fraser, and they pushed their way back through the drunk Australians, out the door and into the sunshine.

22

This time the Kelvin Hall was quiet inside, the crowds had all gone. The only sound was pigeons fluttering up in the roof, cutting across the beams of summer sun coming through the skylights. A few relatives stepped gingerly between the bodies, looking for loved ones, hankies and sleeves held over noses. The smell caught in Gunner's throat as soon as he entered the hall. It wasn't surprising, the bodies had been there for forty-eight hours and the warm weather wasn't helping either. There was a constant low buzz as well, took Gunner a minute to realise what it was. Flies.

Fraser pointed over towards the left-hand side of the hall. Drummond was kneeling over a body, front of his shirt pulled up over his nose and mouth, hairy white belly exposed. The old ARP man was standing next to him looking worried.

'This is Veitch,' said Drummond, standing up as they approached.

The old ARP man nodded a hello.

'He was loading this one into the lorries out the back when he realises the poor bastard is still in the land of the living. Just. That useless posh cunt of a doctor with the pyjamas had certified him dead.' He looked round the hall, raised his voice. 'It's just as well the prick's made himself scarce.'

There was a chorus of tuts and dirty looks from the nearest relatives. Didn't bother Drummond one bit. He turned to Veitch.

'You. Away and find a doctor, and make sure it's anyone but that pyjama cunt.'

Veitch nodded and scuttled off, gas-mask box still neatly strapped across his shoulder.

Drummond slipped his braces off, started tucking his shirt back in. 'Which one was it, then?'

'Bell's bar,' said Fraser.

'You're a creature of habit, Gunner, you should live a little, try stepping into another pub, there's plenty out there to choose from.' He nodded down at the body on the floor. 'This is our man. Bashed-in Jerry number two.'

Gunner moved round to take a look. Like the last time, the man's head was a mess of blood and bone, skull caved in just above the eyebrows. This time the fingertips hadn't been cut off, looked like they had been crushed in a vice. They were flat, a mess of deep cuts. You could see the bone coming through the skin in a couple of them.

'Christ,' said Gunner, looking away. 'Have they no got a doctor to give the poor bastard something?'

'They did,' Drummond said. 'Morphine, it's got rid of the pain. They gave him enough to "ease the passing" as they call it. He's got about half an hour, I reckon. Not that it's going to do us or the poor bugger much good.'

Gunner knelt down beside the man, tried to breathe through his mouth. The man looked about forty odd, the same as the other one. He'd a vest on, pair of suit trousers, socks and no shoes. Trousers and vest deep red and shiny from the drying blood. His chest was rising and falling slowly, his right foot trembling from some twisted nerve. There was a bucket lying across the way, positioned to catch drips from the ceiling. Gunner got a hanky out his pocket, dipped it in the water and started to wipe the blood and dust from the man's face.

He was as careful as he could, but the man's skin was just a thin cover over the broken bones beneath. One of the man's eyes was gone, the socket filled with dark blood, the other was lifeless, staring up at the ceiling. He was still breathing but only just, tiny bubbles in the blood and saliva periodically filling his mouth. His breathing seemed to be getting slower, winding down as the morphine took hold. Wasn't surprising. The man's neck was studded with the familiar syrettes, four of them. One was even sticking out a vein. Whoever put that one in wasn't messing about.

Gunner was wiping the blood away from the man's forehead the best he could when his good eye flickered, seemed to see he was there. He coughed, blood came up out his mouth, ran down his chin, and his lips started to move. He was trying to speak. Gunner shushed Fraser and Drummond blabbing on about shift timetables and leant close in, ear right to the man's mouth. Not much more than a faint whisper and it didn't sound like English.

'Fuck,' said Gunner. 'I don't know what he's saying, it's German.'

'I know some German,' said Fraser. 'We had to do it at school.'

He knelt down by Gunner, trying to turn away from the man's ruined face. He stuck his ear in close, trying to catch it.

'What's he saying?' asked Drummond.

Fraser held up his hand for quiet, blond head inched in closer. Listened.

'He's saying he failed, that he failed them.' He looked up at Gunner. 'It's very faint, I can't get all he's saying.'

'Just try, son,' said Gunner.

Fraser leant in again, listened for a minute or so. Even Gunner could tell the whispering was getting fainter. He didn't know a word of German, but the man seemed to be saying the same thing over and over again.

'*Ich fiel aus. Ich fiel aus.*'

Fraser sat up, still keeping his face turned away from the man. 'It's stopped. I think he's dead.'

Gunner leant forward and felt for a pulse on his neck. There wasn't one. Fraser stood up, face white, blood round his ear and in his hair.

'Well?' said Drummond. 'What did he say?'

'It didn't make much sense,' said Fraser. 'I think he was saying he wasn't close enough, wasn't close enough for them.'

'What the fuck does that mean?' asked Drummond.

'I don't know,' said Gunner. 'You sure that's what he said, Fraser?'

Fraser had just realised he had blood all over the side of his face and was rubbing at it furiously.

'I think so, couldn't swear, but it was definitely something like that.'

Drummond took off his hat, smoothed down his hair.

'Probably didn't know what he was saying. Shouldn't have given him that much bloody morphine. Fucking doctor.'

A pigeon took off from the rafters and flapped around the hall, flying above the bodies and the relatives and priests praying over them. Drummond didn't look up; he had his eyes firmly fixed on the dead man, cigarette jammed in his mouth, hands running through his oily hair.

Gunner knelt back down and started pulling the sheet up over the body. He took the syrettes out of the man's neck and laid them down on the floor, noticed the one that had been in his vein was stronger than the rest. One grain per 1.5 cc rather than the usual half. With that in his vein, the man was as good as dead. Before he could stop himself, he slid it into his pocket.

'You two get out to that camp,' said Drummond. 'Find out what the fuck's been going on there, don't take no for an answer.' He put his hat back on. 'One escaped prisoner is an accident. Two is taking the piss.'

Gunner stood up, knee cracking. 'Away and start the car, Fraser,' he said. 'I'll be out in a minute.'

Fraser sighed, looked at them both. 'I'm working on this case too.'

'Fuck off and don't be so cheeky,' said Drummond.

Fraser started buttoning up his jacket, grumbling all the while.

'I said now!' barked Drummond.

Fraser moved off at double speed. Gunner turned to Drummond, watched him lighting another cigarette off the one in his mouth.

'So how deep are you in?' he asked.

Drummond looked puzzled, almost managed to look convincing.

'Eh? In what?' he said.

'Into Con McGill and his business?' said Gunner. 'How far?'

Drummond blew out a cloud of smoke, waved it away. Looked at Gunner.

'Even if I was, which I'm not, what the fuck's that got to do with you?'

'I'll tell you what it's got to do with me,' said Gunner. 'Sellars and his heavies pulled me in this morning, and they were careful to let me know that Con McGill's days are numbered. So, all I'm saying is you need to make sure you're not in so deep that when they get rid of him they have to get rid of you too. Because they will. I'm warning you. Whatever you've got going on with McGill, get out of it now. Before it's too late.'

Drummond smiled, tilted his head up, watched the pigeon for a minute, then looked at Gunner.

'I was just wondering,' he said, 'exactly how much it is that you charge.'

'What?' asked Gunner.

'How much it is you charge Sellars to deliver his messages for him.'

'Fuck off, Drummond, I'm not delivering a message; I'm just trying to warn you.'

'That right?' Drummond pulled the side of his suit pocket out, pointed in it. 'That the story, eh? Got you in his pocket already, has he?'

Gunner shook his head. 'You don't get it, do—'

'Get out to that camp and do your fucking job,' said Drummond.

He pushed past Gunner, stepped over a row of bodies, and then turned. 'And you can tell your boss I'm big enough and bad enough to look after myself.'

'He's not my boss,' said Gunner, but he was talking to Drummond's back.

23

News must have travelled fast. This time everyone at the POW camp seemed to be expecting them. They were waved through the gates, no security checks. Even Colonel Skinner was waiting for them in the office corridor. He didn't seem quite as in control of things as he had been last time.

'Gentlemen.' He gestured into his office. 'Come in.'

He sat himself down behind the desk and started looking through the papers piled in front of him, shuffling them around with his one good arm. Fraser looked at Gunner and shrugged. Gunner was tired of waiting.

'Two prisoners in as many days,' said Gunner. 'What are you doing, Skinner? Holding the gate open for them and handing them their bus fare into Glasgow?'

Skinner looked up at them, smiled thinly.

'Actually, I was just about to put a call into your superiors in the Glasgow Police Force. One of our prisoners has indeed gone missing.' He picked up a paper, pretended to read it for the first time. 'A Joseph Lenz, I believe. Not familiar with the man myself, too many to keep track of. Apparently, he didn't turn up for roll-call this morning.'

'This morning?' said Gunner. 'It's four o'clock in the afternoon, Skinner. What were you waiting for?'

Skinner bristled. 'We had a search party out; procedures have to be followed, you know.'

'What was his status?' asked Gunner.

'Status?' Skinner tried to look puzzled. 'What do you mean? He was a POW.'

'You know fine well what I fucking mean,' said Gunner. 'Was he a Black prisoner? One of the bad guys?'

Skinner leant forward, pretended to read the paper again, sat back. 'It seems he was.'

'Well, well, there's a coincidence,' said Gunner. 'Was the other prisoner Black as well?'

'We have no other missing prisoner, Mr Gunner. I already told you that.'

Gunner had had about enough. He'd met enough arseholes like Skinner in the Army, and for once he didn't have to listen to them.

'There are two men dead, Skinner. Two men that came from your shambles of a camp, so despite you and your fucking Lord Haw-Haw accent I'm going to find out what happened to them and then I'm going to find out why you're trying to stop me and then I'm going to hang you out to fucking dry.'

Skinner stood up, pushed his chair back. 'Now you listen to me, Sergeant Gunner, I don't have to take that kind—'

'Who told you I was a sergeant?' Gunner said quietly. 'I never mentioned it, never told you I was in the Army. I only ever told you I was a detective.'

Skinner stopped, looked nonplussed. He took out a hanky and wiped at his weeping eye.

'Friends?' said Gunner. 'Someone must have known this Joseph Lenz. Get them in here now.'

Skinner looked at him, then picked up the phone.

Ten awkward and silent minutes later there was a knock on the door and a young guard held the door open for two men. They were both thirty odd, dressed in a mixture of civvies and worn-out German uniforms. They shuffled in, looking wary.

'This is Hans Gerhart,' said the guard, pointing at the taller one. 'And this is Florian Hoffman. Gerhart is the pal, Hoffman is going to translate.'

Hoffman took a pair of small wire-framed glasses from his pocket and put them on. He nodded to Skinner and Gunner. He was ready.

'Ask him when he last saw Lenz,' said Gunner.

Hoffman turned, spoke in German to Gerhart, waited for the answer, and came back.

'He says he saw him last night before bed. When he got up this morning he wasn't there.' The words spoken in perfect cut-glass English.

'Does he have any idea what happened to him?' asked Gunner. 'Had he made any plans to escape?'

Same process. Hoffman glanced over at Skinner before he spoke. 'He never mentioned anything. Although he was friendly with him, he was a solitary man, kept himself to himself.'

Gunner looked at the ceiling and sighed. This charade wasn't getting him anywhere. Gerhart leant forward to Hoffman and mumbled something.

'What did he say?' asked Gunner.

Hoffman shook his head. 'Nothing. He just asked how long I thought this interview would go on.'

Fraser cleared his throat. 'That's not actually what he said.'

Everyone turned.

'You speak German?' Skinner asked. 'Why didn't you say?'

Fraser shrugged. 'You didn't ask.'

'So, what did he say?' asked Gunner.

Fraser looked over at Hoffman, but his head was down, eyes fixed to the floor.

'He said he was sick of answering questions, that he already told the other men everything.'

There was a silence. Gunner turned to Skinner and raised his eyebrows.

'Other men?' he said. 'Now who would they be, Corporal Skinner?'

'I don't know what he's talking about,' Skinner said blandly. 'Most likely your young colleague was mistaken in what he heard. Is he fluent?'

He nodded at Hoffman, and Hoffman rattled off a string of heavily accented German.

Fraser looked confused. 'I couldn't follow all of that, was a bit fast . . .'

Skinner raised his eyebrows. 'There you go. Youthful enthusiasm, trying to impress and managed to overstretch himself. Anything else you want to ask?'

Gunner fought the urge to punch the smug bastard, injuries or not. 'Not much point, is there, Skinner? You've made sure of that.'

Skinner sat back down behind his desk. 'Well in that case . . .'

Gunner and Fraser stood on the steps of the office watching

a group of weary prisoners, shovels over their shoulders, being marched back into camp. Gunner padded his pockets, found his cigarettes.

'That is what he said.' Fraser was defiant. 'I heard him. Honest.'

Gunner exhaled, waved the smoke away from his face.

'Don't worry, son, I believe you. Someone was there before us, made sure he kept shtum.'

Fraser looked puzzled. 'Who?'

They started walking back to the car.

'If I was a betting man, I'd say they got a visit from the men from the Ministry of Food.'

'What? Aren't they on our side?'

'Apparently, there are sides, Fraser. Sides and sides. And there was me playing all nicey-nice.' He stopped, flicked the butt of his cigarette at the perimeter fence. 'Not any more.'

Fraser looked at him. 'Sometimes I've got no idea what you're talking about.'

24

There was no one back at the barracks. Moore he could do without, but he needed to see Nickerson, find out what he was playing at. There were a couple of empty glasses on the table, the crust of a sandwich on a saucer and a folded copy of *The Telegraph*. Looked like he had just missed them. There was a telegram lying on the table too. Addressed to him, marked urgent. Had to be his orders to go back, no way he was opening that. As far as he was concerned, he knew nothing about it. He checked his watch, just past seven. Victor should be in the pub by now, not much point waiting around here.

It was a warm night again, but the clouds were thick overhead; at least there was no chance of another raid tonight. The Corbie was about a mile away, up in Springburn Road. He shook his head. The Corbie, of all fucking places. He hadn't been there since he was a beat polis. Back then, they were called because someone got stabbed in the snug. As it turned out, the whole pub just happened to have been facing the other way at the time. Nobody saw a thing.

The streets were quiet, people still worried about another raid. At least the walk would give him a chance to think, try and sort out in his head what was going on. Drummond and the dying German. Skinner. Nickerson. Moore. He knew they were all connected, just couldn't figure out how and why. Why would someone be murdering escaped POWs? If they were Black prisoners, maybe they were just being executed? Even then there had to be better places to dump the bodies than on the streets of Glasgow. Was Skinner in on it? Was Drummond? And if he was, why had he asked him to help find the murderer?

He was so deep in thought he didn't notice the girl until he almost bumped into her. She asked him for a light, let her coat fall open, tidy body in a thin cotton dress.

'Thanks for that,' she said, lighting up. She looked at him. 'You looking for a good time?' she asked.

Gunner thought about it for a minute, then shook his head, kept walking. He wouldn't have minded, she was a good-looking girl, but a quick shag against a close wall wasn't that tempting. Yet.

He'd already tried that in France. He hadn't even been there that long, couple of weeks. It was the first day it had felt warm, springlike. He was walking down a farm track back to the camp. He'd called at the farm looking for eggs and milk and ended up giving a suspicious farmer a stupid amount of money for a crusty loaf and two bottles of wine. Halfway down the track, a girl emerged from the trees at the side of the road, long dark hair, couldn't have been more than nineteen or twenty. She stood by the tree and slowly pulled up the front of her dress. No underwear, pubic hair shockingly dark against her white skin. She pointed at the loaf in his hand.

He followed her back into the trees. She leant back against a big oak tree and undid the buttons on the front of her dress.

He watched as it fell open and he was hard already. He fucked her against the mossy tree trunk, trousers round his ankles. It didn't last long. All the time he was moving inside her she didn't look at him, just kept her eyes on the loaf lying on the grass. He grunted, finished, and she pushed him aside, ran for the loaf and started stuffing the bread in her mouth. He buttoned up and left her there, dress open, tearing at the loaf, eyes shifting from side to side, terrified someone would appear and take it from her.

The memories of France were like half-remembered dreams, he wasn't really sure if they had happened or not. He'd only been there a couple of months before they started retreating towards Dunkirk. Days and days of walking, not sleeping, running every time you heard a plane. Most days it was easier to get hold of wine than water, wasn't sure where he was most of the time, half drunk, plodding on.

Gunner looked up at the sky, rain starting to fall, the moon still hidden behind the clouds. Looked like they were definitely going to be OK. No raids tonight. He waited to cross the road by the Vogue Cinema at the bottom of Bilsland Drive. There was a crowd of people outside, nothing kept Glasgow folk from their night at the pictures. The big illuminated sign above the entrance was dark, couldn't see what was playing. No neon across the door either.

Gunner crossed over, kept walking. People emerged from the darkness every so often, a round of muttered sorrys as they almost walked into each other. The blackout made everything take longer.

It took him twice as long as he thought it would to get to the Corbie. It was just after half eight when he finally pulled the pub door open, pushed aside the blackout curtain and went in.

The Corbie was one step above a slops joint, the kind of pub that sold the beer collected under the taps when a drink overflowed. One very small step. It was a long thin pub, canvas-covered benches along the walls, wee round tables in the middle, angled mirror on the wall with HAIG WHISKY written on it. Between the two broken overhead globes and the fug of cigarette smoke, it was near enough a blackout inside as well.

Gunner scanned the clientele looking for Victor. They were a fine lot, old jakeys nursing pints, young neds who should have been in the forces, and the occasional cauliflower-eared hard man past his prime. He walked up to the bar and ordered a pint, tried not to notice the filthy glass the barman poured it into.

He handed over a bob and took a sip. Rank.

'Over here.'

He turned. Victor was sitting in the gloom of a corner with a half-empty pint glass in front of him. Gunner ordered him another and carried them over.

'What you drinking in this dump for?' asked Gunner, sitting down.

'Nobody gives a fuck who you are in here,' said Victor. 'It's safe. Even the polis don't like coming in.' He gestured to a copy of *The Telegraph* lying on the table. 'You seen the paper?'

Gunner shook his head. Had to be the first time someone had brought a *Telegraph* into the Corbie. Reading anything other than the *Racing News* in here was asking for trouble.

'What's happened?' he asked.

'Rumblings. We're fighting this war on two fronts, you know.'

'We?' said Gunner, raising his eyebrows.

Victor ignored him and carried on. 'Fighting the fascists in Europe and cunts like the Anglo-German Friendship Society at home. Upper-class English wankers who'd be quite happy to have Hitler in Britain as long as he keeps the servants in line. Makes me bloody sick.'

'Then why don't you do something about it, rather than sitting on your arse bellyaching?'

'I am doing something . . .'

Victor stopped, shook his head, didn't go on.

Gunner wasn't letting him off that easy.

'You and your commie mates were all gung-ho for Joe Stalin, and then he goes and signs up with Adolf. Must have been a hard one to swallow.'

Victor shrugged, didn't seem bothered. 'Tactical. There's a long game being played, things will change.'

'Oh, aye? And how would you know?' asked Gunner. 'You and your conchie pals got a hotline to Uncle Joe do they?'

Victor didn't say anything, took a sip of his pint.

'Thought as much,' said Gunner. 'Load of shite.'

The two of them ended up sitting there saying nothing. It was Victor's usual trick, retreat into a pitying silence, as if Gunner were too stupid to even try to explain things to. It drove him up the wall, had done since they were boys. Gunner drained the last of his pint and got up to get another. He felt like getting pished. Victor could fuck himself if he didn't want to come in. He'd tried his best. What else could he do? He was halfway to the bar when the door opened and the blackout curtain was wrenched half off its rail.

'Good grief,' said Nickerson as he stumbled into the pub. 'Fancy meeting you here.'

25

Nickerson was drunk. Not just everyday drunk, he was royally guttered. His tie was undone, pale blue shirt hanging out his trousers, tweed suit crumpled and dusty. Blood ran down the side of his face from a cut over his eyebrow. He took a hanky from his pocket and dabbed at it. 'Well, Gunner, what are you waiting for? Buy a man a drink won't you?'

The pub had gone silent, everyone turned to watch the new arrival. English, blind drunk, and sounding as posh as the King. Not a good combination if you wanted to get out of the Corbie alive.

Nickerson lurched over to the bar.

'Gin, I think,' he said. 'A treble. Sun's well over the yardarm, eh?'

He grinned at the barman. Didn't go down well.

'What the fuck are you doing here?' hissed Gunner. Nickerson had to be the very last person he'd expect to see in the Corbie.

Nickerson grinned, caught sight of his reflection in the mirror behind the bar and started trying to straighten up his tie.

'Well?' asked Gunner.

He looked down, to see blood dripping from Nickerson's chin onto the bar. 'Jesus, what happened to your face?'

Nickerson fished the hanky back out of his pocket and wiped at his face, then tried, vainly, to light a cigarette.

'No idea really,' said Nickerson. 'I met a fellow traveller in the public conveniences by the station. I slipped getting up and bashed my bloody head on the sink.' He smiled. 'Hazards of the game, eh?'

He finally managed to get the cigarette lit as the barman plonked the gin down in front of him. He knocked it back in one.

'Another, I think,' he said. 'And then I got in a cab and asked the driver to take me to a pub where working men drink. An old foible, I'm afraid. Opposites attract. There's nothing quite like the smell of sweat on a working man. Spice of life. Consequently, the taxi driver dropped me in this charming establishment.'

He looked round, eyes fixing on a table of young neds staring at him with contempt.

'Delightful clientele,' he muttered to himself. The fact Gunner was there too suddenly seemed to dawn. Nickerson turned to him. 'And what are you doing here?' he asked. 'Is this your local?'

'Having a word with my brother.'

'Your brother?' said Nickerson. 'You must introduce me.'

Gunner got another round of drinks, Nickerson looking round and beaming at everyone as they waited. Took it over to the table and sat down.

'Victor, Nickerson, Nickerson, Victor,' said Gunner still wondering how he'd got himself into this mess.

Victor nodded over, looking wary. Gunner didn't blame him. There was no way Nickerson was getting out the pub without a doing, and Victor wouldn't want to be with him when it happened. Introductions met, they sat there, not quite knowing what to say. Nickerson alternated between slumping against the bench and gazing across at the table of neds.

'You have to get him out of here,' said Victor. 'He's gonnae get his head kicked in otherwise.'

'No,' said Gunner. '*We've* got to get him out of here. I need to speak to this clown, get him sobered up. I'm going for a piss, then we'll get him up the road to the station. Just keep him quiet and don't let him start any trouble while I'm gone.'

Gunner walked across the bar and out to the toilets in the back yard, feeling eyes on his back the whole way. A bloke was finishing up at the urinal, Gunner could see the handle of an open razor in his inside pocket as he bent forward to button up.

'That queer a pal of yours, then?' he asked amicably.

'No. An acquaintance.'

'A what? Naw, he's a cunt's what he is.'

Gunner nodded in agreement. 'You know what, pal? You're not wrong there.'

The bloke pushed past him and out the toilets. Victor was right, they needed to get out of here, and quick. Gunner was walking back into the bar when he realised his shoelace was undone. He bent down to tie it and, looking up, saw Victor and Nickerson reflected in the angled mirror above the bar. Deep in conversation. Somehow Nickerson didn't look so pissed any more. He looked alert, hands waving as he spelled something out to Victor. Victor was nodding, concentrating hard, making notes in a wee jotter. From the way they were talking, there was no way they had only just met.

Gunner stood up, about to ask them both what the fuck was going on, when the front door burst open and two uniformed polis ran into the pub. Victor took one look at them and vaulted across the bar, a tray of glasses exploding as his legs caught them and they hit the ground. He pushed the barman aside and was off through the back shop before the polis knew what was happening.

One of the polis cursed, went over the bar after him. The other scanned the crowd, looking for someone, and then saw him. Nickerson. He ran at him and bundled him onto the floor. Nickerson protested at the top of his voice but his drunken indignation was getting him nowhere. The big polis gave him a couple of jabs in the kidneys and he soon quietened down. The polis took the handcuffs off his belt and clicked them shut around his wrists.

The other polis came back in from behind the bar shaking his head and they hustled Nickerson out the door, arms pushed up his back. The door closed behind them and the pub sat in stunned silence. The whole thing had taken less than a minute. The police weren't messing about, they knew exactly who they were looking for and where to find them. They hadn't been interested in anyone else.

Gunner stepped out of the shadows of the corridor. There was nothing he could do for Nickerson, and as far as he could tell, Victor had managed to get away. He hadn't recognised the two polis, must be out-of-town boys. He waited a couple of minutes, then stepped outside, just in time to see a Black Maria driving off. Gunner was pretty sure they would be taking

Nickerson to Central. Whatever he had done, Nickerson was a big fish. One for the bosses to deal with.

He stood outside the pub and lit up. Clearly Nickerson and his brother were mixed up in something together, but what that was he didn't know. Only one way to find out. He buttoned his jacket up against the rain, hailed a taxi, and headed for town.

26

Central Station was down by the Clyde, an imposing red sandstone building that took up a whole block. It housed the main police offices and cells, even had stables and a garage at the back. Gunner stopped just up the street, decided to wait before going in. He wanted a drink and he wanted to give them enough time to get Nickerson processed and in the cells.

The Moray Arms was the nearest pub he could think of that wouldn't be full of off-duty polis. The place was quiet when he went in; quick scan round, no polis in sight. He ordered a pint and sat at a table in the corner, tried to think things through.

It seemed like Drummond was where everything began. He'd been waiting for him at the train station, got him into all this, desperate for him to find out who killed the first German. Since then he'd been taking a back seat. He'd been a bit shifty about the second German; he wouldn't be surprised if he had something to do with the morphine in the poor guy's jugular. Then Nickerson wanted him to find out what had happened to the Germans too, claimed he'd been frozen out by Moore. Seemed like everyone wanted to know about the Germans and they all wanted him to do their digging for them. And God knows where his brother fitted in. What did he have to do with Nickerson? How did Victor even *know* someone like Nickerson?

He rubbed at his eyes, lit a cigarette. He was tired and he wasn't getting anywhere. Had an uneasy feeling he was being set up for something, and there was no way he was going to be the fall guy for whatever Drummond or Nickerson were up to. He didn't owe either of them anything, all he'd done was try to help, and it felt like he was being fucked over. Big time.

He fingered the syrette box in his pocket. His leg was killing him again, a dull ache that he knew was going to develop into crippling pain in an hour or so. He smiled to himself. Maybe he was done trying to solve everyone's problems. Maybe he should just fuck them all off. Do what he wanted to do, for a change.

Nothing was stopping him from checking into one of the wee boarding houses down by the river for the night. No one would know who he was or where to find him. His fingers went to the box again. Ten minutes from now he'd be lying on a bed, empty syrette beside him. He'd be warm, floating, no worries and no pain.

Mind made up, he finished his pint and walked out of the pub. He looked down the street at the station. Two beat officers were coming out the front door, looked like they were starting the night shift. He turned, started walking towards the river, hand round the box in his pocket, comforting thoughts of the oblivion to come on his mind.

The Broomielaw was quiet for once, no boats loading or unloading, the only sound the clanking of the tied-up boats bumping off each other as they moved in the current. He leant across the rail and looked down at the river. Filthy, same as it always was. Full of broken wooden crates from the warehouses and slicks of oil. Across the river, in the Gorbals, there was a row of boarding houses, catered for the lads off the boats.

He'd been in the one at the end of the row once when he was in uniform, called there when one of the residents had done a runner. As far as he could remember it was clean, woman who ran it seemed nice, not the nosy type. He peered over, could just make out the sign in the window. VACANCIES. An omen; he smiled, started walking towards the bridge.

'Identity card, sir.'

He turned. Two ARP men stood there, blackout torches shining in his face.

He fumbled in his jacket looking for his card.

'What you are doing down here, sir?'

No card to be found, but he fished out his police badge, showed them that.

'Just on my way up to Central, having a cigarette before my shift starts.'

The ARP smiled. 'Fair play. Come on, we'll walk you up. It's a bugger to see anything in this blackout without a torch.'

Gunner shook his head and fell in beside them as they walked back up to Low Central Street, torch beams leading the way. Omens my arse, it seemed.

He left them at the station entrance and watched the two ARPs walk up the road. He finished his cigarette, dropped the butt on the pavement, and hoped he would know the duty sergeant. If not, he was going to have a lot of explaining to do to get to Nickerson.

He pulled the station door open and stepped inside. It turned out he did know the desk sergeant. Jack Lang. A miserable old bastard, been there for years. Any other time he'd be cursing the useless old bugger, but tonight he was delighted. Being useless and not giving a fuck was exactly what he needed. Lang was leant over the desk, *Evening Citizen* spread out in front of him, meaty finger tracing the words.

'Y'all right, Jack?' said Gunner.

Lang looked up from his paper with disinterest. 'You back, then?'

Gunner nodded.

'Need to check on someone they brought in an hour or so ago. An English bloke apparently?'

'What?' said Lang, screwing his face up. 'That posh queer?'

Gunner nodded. 'That's him.'

'Thomson!' shouted Lang, and the turnkey appeared from the back office. Gunner didn't recognise him, but they were all of a type. Wee retired men making some extra on their pension. This one was no different. Missing front teeth, what was left of his hair Brylcreemed over his bald spot, and a cardigan with a hole in it.

'Number 22,' said Lang. 'Let Gunner here in.'

Gunner went to say thanks, but Lang had already gone back to his paper. He followed the wee turnkey down the corridor, remembering the smell of bleach and unwashed bodies that always hung about the cells. Thomson stopped outside number 22. Started unlocking the door.

'Best keep your back to the wall.' He grinned, and pushed the door open.

Nickerson was sitting on the bench, head in hands, braces gone, brogues without laces sitting on the stone floor beside him. He looked up.

'Gunner!' he said surprised. 'We meet again.'

Gunner pulled the door closed behind him, looked round the dismal, green-tiled cell. It consisted, like they all did, of a stone bench, a slop bucket, a threadbare blanket, and a wee barred window near the ceiling. It was always cold in these cells, no matter what the weather was like outside. Tonight was no different.

'You want to tell me what the fuck you've been playing at?' he said. 'And make it quick, I'm not supposed to be in here.'

Nickerson sighed. 'Have you got a cigarette by any chance? I'm in deadly need.'

Gunner handed the packet over and Nickerson lit up, inhaled with relish. 'That little shit of a turnkey took mine.'

'What have they arrested you for?' asked Gunner.

Nickerson sighed, looked sheepish.

'All my fault, I'm afraid. I gave them the excuse on a plate. My friend from the station toilets turned up here. Rather more than a coincidence. Think they might have been following me.'

'Must have been, that's how they knew you were at the pub.'

Nickerson nodded.

'Anyway, the poor man looked scared shitless, hardly surprising, you can get two years' heavy labour for . . . you know. Apparently, he's a schoolmaster. And of course, the police had coached him through the whole story. How I propositioned him, made a lewd and horrifying suggestion. So distressed that he felt the need to go to the police.' He smiled. 'As you can imagine, that's not quite what happened, but you can hardly blame him. His job's on the line. They even had some fat old copper standing behind him the whole time, making sure he got his story right.'

'What did he look like, this copper?' asked Gunner.

'Broad, black greasy hair swept back, smoking for Scotland. Looked a nasty piece of work.'

Drummond.

'What happens to you now?' asked Gunner.

Nickerson dropped his cigarette on the floor, picked up one of his shoes and stamped it out.

'That, Gunner, is the question. Who knows? They're coming to get me, should be here any minute, taking me back to London.' He thought for a minute. 'What happens rather depends on how much they know. Either I'll be charged with importuning in a public lavatory or, somewhat more drastically, with high treason.'

'Jesus, you can get hanged for that.'

Nickerson smiled.

'Come on, don't look so grim, Gunner. It will never happen. Old school tie and all that, I'll get through it. One of the advantages of Eton and Cambridge and a father in the House of Lords. They don't like prosecuting their own. Besides, whatever happens, MI5 don't want one of their operatives standing in the dock, very bad form, don't you know.'

'Before you go, can you tell me what's going on with these Germans?' asked Gunner. 'What do you know?'

'Germans, plural?'

Gunner nodded. 'We found another one. The same scenario, body dumped amongst the bombing casualties. Fingerprints gone; face destroyed.'

Nickerson stood up, started padding around the cell in his red socks.

'This is a difficult situation, Gunner, I'm not sure I should be telling you this, but needs must. Can I trust you?'

Gunner laughed. 'Doesn't look like you've got much choice, and besides, I'm not sure I should be trusting *you*. You've been lying to me since day one. What's to say I don't just say goodbye, walk out this cell, pretend you never existed?'

Nickerson stopped, smiled. 'I rather asked for that, didn't I? I'm sorry, but it's habit, as much to protect you as to protect me. Never tell anyone anything other than that which is absolutely necessary.'

Gunner shrugged. 'Got the feeling you want to tell me, more than I want to hear it.'

Nickerson looked like he was making up his mind, sat back down on the bench and looked at Gunner.

'The British Secret Service is a broad church, allows for a variety of views, that's one of its great strengths. Normally I can live with that, but not this time. This time the stakes are too high. There are people in the organisation planning a great change, a change that will turn the war on its head. Some of the more conservative elements see a different way to end the war. They'd like nothing more than some cosy tête-à-têtes with the Nazi leaders. Work out how to divide the spoils. Some of us don't want that to happen, it's a path of no return, do you follow me?'

'I think so. Are you sure about this though, that these people want to betray the country?'

'That's not how they see it. They see it as the way forward. Two Aryan races together. Hitler and the King shaking hands at Buckingham Palace, and fuck the Russians or anyone else the Nazis want rid of. These people need to be stopped, it's of paramount importance. That's what we are working to make happen,' said Nickerson.

'Who's we? My brother?'

Nickerson smiled. 'The Germans that were killed were lookalikes, failed lookalikes.'

'What?'

'The two bodies you found, they looked the same, yes?' said Nickerson.

Gunner nodded. It was true. Both tall and thin, middle-aged, balding.

'They were POWs,' said Nickerson. 'Hand-picked because of their resemblance to Rudolf Hess.'

'Hess?' said Gunner. 'What's he got to do with it?'

'Do you know much about Hess?' Nickerson asked.

Gunner shrugged. 'Same as anyone else. Hitler's second-in-command. Some kind of an aristocrat I think . . .'

Nickerson nodded.

'And a very strange man indeed. Believes in astrology, ley lines, secret histories of the Aryan peoples, all sorts. And he believes very strongly in the power of the aristocracy, in their God-given right to rule.' He smiled. 'He's a bit like my father in that respect, but that's by the by. Hess has been in touch with Lord Glancaird and his cronies, the Anglo-German Friendship lot. The rumour is he's trying to broker a kind of deal and certain elements in the Secret Service are happy to help him do it.'

'What kind of deal?'

'Appeasement by any other name. He's coming to the UK, secretly, of course, to make it final. The Germans and the Anglo-German fuckers want the same thing. Britain run by the aristocracy under the Nazis. That, of course, would leave Germany free to attack Russia and that simply cannot be allowed to happen.'

'I don't get it,' said Gunner. 'Why are the lookalikes here? Why were they killed?'

'Insurance.'

'What? You need to go slower, Nickerson, I'm trying to take all this in.'

'OK, say Hess's plane goes down and he gets killed. Or he gets here and he gets troublesome. He's something of a loose cannon, might go off the rails at any point, so they need a puppet at hand to step in in case he does.'

'That they control.'

'Precisely. The men you found were being groomed for the role, to be kept in the background, kept ready to replace Hess. They won't let anything stop the plan; if the real Hess doesn't play ball they'll just replace him with a fake Hess who will. The ones they've tried so far didn't make the grade. Didn't look enough like him, couldn't do his accent, asked too many questions.'

'So who killed them?' asked Gunner. 'You?'

Nickerson didn't answer. Sat back on the bench. He looked tired all of a sudden, rubbed at his eyes.

'Nickerson? Who killed them?'

'Moore, I think. Not personally of course, wouldn't get his hands dirty.' He looked up at Gunner. 'What happened to them is done, nothing anyone can do about it now. What's important is what's about to happen.'

'Which is?'

'Another candidate is coming in soon. A Gunther Troz. He's coming up from some POW camp in Yorkshire, he's coming in through the Internment Centre they've set up in some football ground. Hampden, is it?'

Gunner nodded.

'He arrives tomorrow morning and, unfortunately, they think he's ideal. If they approve him the plan goes forward immediately. You have to stop them picking him up. If they have a decent replacement that's the missing part of the jigsaw. They'll go ahead with the plan.'

Nickerson leant over. Put his hands on Gunner's shoulders. Stared right into his eyes.

'You have to stop that happening, Gunner. I trusted you enough to tell you this, don't let me down. The fate of millions of Russian citizens could depend on it. We need to buy time to derail the plan, I can't do that while I'm locked up in here. You have to help us. You simply have to.'

Gunner looked at him.

'No,' he said. 'You and Moore have been fucking me about for days. Then suddenly Moore's the bad guy and I'm your big pal and we're going to save the world. I don't buy it.'

Nickerson sat back, looked like he was about to cry.

'How can I convince you?' he asked.

'That's your problem,' said Gunner. 'All I'm going to do is get my brother to hand himself in, tell Drummond to go fuck himself, and forget being a polis again. I've had enough of it.'

Nickerson looked straight ahead, started reciting.

'Victor Thomas Gunner, born 25th of September 1918. Went to Colston Secondary. Two years at Glasgow University studying history and politics, union organiser at various works in north Glasgow. Joined the Communist Party in 1936. Joined Friends of the Soviet Union in 1937. First mentioned in a report by a filed officer in 1938. Possibility of recruitment by the Soviet intelligence agency, placed on an awareness list, checked every two months. Brother Joseph James Gunner, born 3rd of May 1915. Currently on medical leave from serving as a sergeant in the Highland Fusiliers. Injured in Dunkirk, unlikely to return to active duty, ligaments and muscles of left leg irreparably damaged.'

Nickerson turned and looked at him.

'This isn't a game, Gunner. I'm deadly fucking serious. If you want me to get down on my knees and beg you, I will. You have to help us.'

'Last thing I want is you down on your knees in front of me, Nickerson. I've seen where that goes. Is Victor in danger?'

'Probably,' said Nickerson.

Gunner sighed. 'You're not making this up, are you?'

Nickerson shook his head. 'No. I'm not. I've never been more serious. Will you help us?'

Gunner did what he knew he shouldn't and nodded. What real choice did he have?

'So, if the lookalikes are here in Glasgow, that means Hess is coming here.'

Nickerson nodded. 'We weren't sure where he was coming in, but it would make sense now.'

'Rudolf Hess in Glasgow?' said Gunner. 'Who'd believe it?'

'Nobody,' said Nickerson. 'That's probably the point.' He stopped, looked worried. 'What time is it? That little turnkey shit took my watch as well.'

Gunner looked at his wrist. 'Just after eleven.'

'Fuck. They'll be here any minute. You have to go, you can't get caught in here. If they know I've been talking to you they'll take you too.'

'I don't get it, Nickerson, how am I supposed to . . . ?'

But it was no use, Nickerson was practically pushing him out the door.

'Speak to Victor, tell him what I told you. And Christ, Gunner, don't get caught before you do! Now go!'

Gunner stepped out of the cell, heard voices and marching feet echoing down the corridor. He tried the cell next door, rattled the handle; no use, it was locked. The feet were getting nearer. He tried the next one, locked as well. He swore, slipped back into Nickerson's cell, and eased the door shut behind him.

Nickerson looked horrified. 'What are you doing, Gunner? I told you, you have to go!'

'Too late.'

Gunner looked round the cell, nowhere to hide. 'Stand by the window and don't say anything when they open the door.'

'What are you going to do?'

Gunner shushed him, the boots were practically outside the door now. He peered out the spyhole just in time to see two well-dressed men talking in English accents standing in the corridor. He pressed himself hard against the side wall, felt something digging into his side. He put his hand in his pocket. The blackout torch he'd taken from the station. He grasped it hard, waited.

Soon as the door opened he swung his arm round and hit the first bloke square in the face with the torch. His nose gave way and he dropped to the floor. Gunner stepped over him and kicked the other one in the balls before he had a chance to react. He pushed him to the side as he fell and ran down the corridor making for the back door of the station. He could hear shouts behind him, but he didn't look back, just kept running.

The back door key was where it always was, hanging on a

hook beside the door. Gunner grabbed it, unlocked the door and burst out into the yard. It was raining hard now, sheets of it coming down. He weaved his way through the parked Morrises and Alvises and rolled under one just as the back door of the station flew open behind him. He lay there, panting, trying not to make any noise. Three sets of feet came out the door, the shiny black shoes of two English blokes and a pair of worn brown leather shoes he'd recognise anywhere. They stopped.

'Where does that lead?' an English voice said.

Then the familiar voice. 'That gate? Out to the street, then down to the Broomielaw. Could be anywhere by now.'

'Fuck,' the English voice said, and he came towards the car Gunner was under and booted the tyre hard. 'Fucking hell.'

After they went back into the station Gunner waited under the car for a good ten minutes or so, watching the rain pelting down. It wasn't too bad under the car; dry, warm as well, must have been driven not that long ago. He was still thinking about what Nickerson had told him. It seemed completely far-fetched but Nickerson couldn't have known all that stuff about him and Victor if he was making it up, and the bodies of the dead Germans were real. So now he had to get a hold of Victor and tell him about the new German or all hell would break loose. Some part of him wished he had just gone down to the boarding house after all.

The back door opened again and the wee turnkey appeared and lit up. One of Nickerson's fags, no doubt. The fact Drummond was involved in all this somehow was no surprise. He'd do anything to preserve his wee money-making schemes. But Victor? That's what he really couldn't believe. His conchie brother was really involved with MI5? He supposed it made some sense, explained his protests that he was doing as much as he had to fight the fascists.

He watched the turnkey drop the last of his cigarette on the cobblestones and grind it out before he went back in. Gunner gave it another few minutes for safety's sake and rolled out from under the car. He dusted himself down, looked around; seemed quiet enough, so he walked out the back gate into Turnbull Street and started hobbling up the road, leg on fire with pain.

Five minutes later he was standing at Glasgow Cross sipping a tea he'd bought from a stall to warm up. He was just draining the last of it, about to put it back on the counter, when a black van drew up, stopped at the lights across the road. One of the English blokes was driving, the other was in the passenger seat peering at a map, bloodstained hanky to his face. The lights changed and the van set off down the London Road. Whatever happened was up to him now. Nickerson was gone.

27

Gunner trudged up the stairs of the close, stopped outside the door of the top floor flat and knocked on the door. After a couple of minutes and the sounds of some fumbling there was a voice at the door.

'Who is it?'

'It's me, Gunner. Joe. Open the door.'

He knew he had to find Victor and this was the only place he could think of to look. The flat door opened a crack and a sleepy-faced Nan peered out.

'Joe, what you doing here?' she asked stepping out onto the landing and pulling the door shut behind her. She'd a nightie on, low cut, showed off her curves. She noticed him looking and pulled her dressing gown round her.

'I'm looking for Victor.'

'Victor?' she said. 'He's not here. I've not seen him for a couple of days. maybe he's—'

'I don't have time for this, Nan,' said Gunner. 'I have to speak to him.'

She shook her head again.

'Look, Nan, he'll want to speak to me. Believe me.'

'He's not here!' she said.

'Oh for fuck sake!' Gunner reached round her and pushed the door open.

'What do you think you're doing!' Nan tried to pull him back, but he shrugged her off and stepped inside.

The flat was warm, smelt of sleep, beer, and lavender perfume. It was a room and kitchen like most of the flats in the street. One room with a kitchen at one end, a bed in an alcove in the other, toilet outside by the stairs. The table sitting in the middle covered in empty beer bottles, a full ashtray sitting on a copy of *Picturegoer*. For a minute Gunner thought Victor wasn't there at all, then his head appeared from under the bed.

'Jesus Christ, Joe!' he said. 'You gave me the fright of my life, I thought it was the bloody MPs.'

Victor pulled himself out, stood there in his skivvies and vest.

'Get dressed,' snapped Gunner. 'You've got a lot of fucking explaining to do.'

Victor took his shirt from the back of the chair, slipped it on. He sat down on the bed, looked around for his socks.

'Does she know?' asked Gunner.

'Does she know what?' said Nan indignantly. 'Fuck's going on, Victor?'

That was a conversation Gunner didn't want to be around for.

'I'll meet you downstairs,' he said. 'Hurry up.'

Gunner was leaning against the baffle wall at the entrance of the close watching a fox cross the road when Victor appeared down the stairs, still buttoning up his shirt.

'What'd you tell her?' he asked.

Victor shrugged, pulled his braces up over his shoulders. 'Not much.'

'Well I've just had a chat with your pal Nickerson,' said Gunner. 'The one you don't know, he—'

Victor held up his hands. 'Not here.'

They ended up at a mobile canteen at the bottom of Balgray Hill. Victor bought a couple of teas and they sat down on a bench in the playground opposite. Springburn was famous for locomotives but the big works weren't making those any more. They'd all been converted to make tanks and heavy artillery. The demand was so high the works were running round the clock. Soon as one set of workers finished, another lot started. The noise of the factories never stopped now.

Victor sipped at his tea and made a face.

'What the fuck are you playing at, Victor?' asked Gunner. 'You're going to tell me everything or I'm going to fucking well beat it out of you. You hear me?'

Victor at least had the decency to look sheepish.

'Right here, right now. Everything. Nickerson will do for a start. How come you two know each other?'

'Nickerson and I share some mutual friends,' Victor said carefully. 'Some friends that are concerned about the fate of the Russian people.'

Gunner looked at him. Couldn't believe what he was hearing.

'What, so you're a Russian spy now?' he said.

Victor shook his head, waited until two women, hands yellow from the munitions work, moaning about the shift getting out late, walked past.

'No. I'm not a spy,' said Victor. 'I'm just trying to do my bit. I'm a communist, Joe, you know that. You've known that for years.'

'Aye, but I didn't know you bloody worked for them.'

'I don't. People like me and Nickerson just want two things. Russia to be allowed to fulfil its destiny and the evil of fascism to be stopped. What's so wrong with that?'

Gunner didn't say anything. It made sense to him, but he wasn't going to give Victor the satisfaction.

'We all want the same thing. You joined up, Joe, but there are more ways to win the war than being in the Army. So, I'll do what needs to be done,' said Victor. 'It's my duty.'

'And Hess?' asked Gunner. 'What's that all about?'

Victor looked at him, amazed. A little victory. 'Nickerson told you about that?'

Gunner nodded, put his tea down on the ground, and lit up.

'I don't think he wanted to, but he was desperate. They managed to arrest him for being a queer, were about to cart him off to London. He needed to tell someone.'

'Christ,' said Victor, looking worried. 'Nickerson's gone? That's the last thing we need.'

'So it's true then? Hess is coming here?'

Victor nodded. 'On the invite of the Anglo-German Society. And the Duke of fucking Windsor.'

'But why all the lookalikes? I still don't get it,' said Gunner.

'Hess is unpredictable, believes in all sorts,' said Victor. 'Movements of the moon, fuck knows what. He's a nutter. They're insurance. Soon as he goes too far off his trolley one of them gets put in his place.'

Gunner hesitated, didn't want to ask it.

'What happened to them? Did you kill them?'

'Me?' Victor laughed. 'No. I think that was Moore or one of his cronies. Tidying up, getting rid of loose ends.'

'Aye well, another candidate is coming in, apparently.'

Victor nodded. 'I know.'

'This morning, I mean,' said Gunner.

Victor turned. 'What?'

'He's coming in to Hampden stadium.'

Victor looked worried.

'Christ, I didn't realise it was so soon. How are we going to get to him?'

'We?' Gunner shook his head. 'Not me, pal. I've done my bit, passed the message on. You and your commie mates can get on with this one. I've got my own battles to fight.'

'What battles?'

'That's my business, Victor. I'm an ex-polis with a fucked-up leg that can only see out of one eye, not a bloody Russian spy.'

Victor shook his head in disgust. 'Thanks, Joe, thanks a fucking lot.'

Gunner couldn't help himself. He'd had enough of Victor and Nickerson keeping him in the dark and ordering him about.

'So, let me get this straight. You want me to get into Hampden somehow, find some bloke amongst fuck knows how many hundred prisoners, shoot him dead, and then walk away? And do all this on the word of some drunk cunt I still don't trust as far as I can throw him?' He shook his head. 'I don't think so, Victor. Nickerson could be setting us up, who fucking knows what he's up to? Do you really think you and me are going to save the Russians, change the war? Two Glasgow guys? I don't think so, it doesn't work like that.'

'I have to try,' said Victor quietly.

'No, you don't, Victor! You want to. Lost causes and martyrdom, that was always your game. Too fucking good to just join up like the rest of us. Well, off you go, Victor, now you've got your chance. Away and save the fucking Russians.'

They sat there staring at each other, Gunner realising his fists were clenched and he was breathing hard. Had to keep himself from punching Victor in the face. One thing he hated was being treated like a fool, and that's exactly what had been happening. Wasn't going to happen any more.

Victor shook his head again, got up and walked down the hill towards town. Gunner watched him, half thinking he should go after him. Victor didn't have a hope in hell of getting into Hampden, never mind doing something about it if he did. Then again, that was Victor all over, all talk no action.

He looked up at the sky, it was starting to get light. A hooter sounded and a tide of people started streaming out the works. Shift change. Gunner was tired and he was cold and his leg was agony. All he wanted was to be curled up in a clean bed, morphine letting him sleep.

He started walking; that would have to wait. There was someone else he needed to find, and fast.

28

Gunner didn't have long to wait, the morning shift started at eight and it was ten to when he got to the station. Like the good boy he was, Fraser was early, appeared five minutes later, buttoning up the top button of his uniform as he walked down the street.

'Where is he?' asked Gunner, stepping out from the darkness of a close by the station.

Fraser stopped dead. Terrified.

'Mr Gunner! You gave me the fright of my life. Who? Mr Drummond?'

'The very man,' said Gunner.

'He's down at the Tradeston site,' said Fraser. 'I'm going down there now.'

'Perfect. Let's not tell him I'm coming, eh? Be a nice surprise.'

They turned the corner from the station and suddenly they could see the smoke rising from the warehouses bordering the river spiralling up into the sky. The fires that the incendiary bombs had started two nights before must still be smouldering. It was only when they got down by the bridge that they could tell how bad things were.

They crossed the river in silence, both of them taken aback

by the scale of the damage. There was a fifty-foot gap in the line of warehouses where the bomb had hit and the fire had taken hold. A line of ambulances and fire engines surrounded the gap, one of the engines still spraying water over the blackened and smoking timbers of what had been the warehouse. There was a strange sickly-sweet smell in the air, mixing in with the acrid smell of the burnt timber.

'Who are they?' asked Gunner as they approached. He was pointing at a line of three men in civvies standing in handcuffs beside a police van.

Fraser looked over. 'More bloody looters, it looks like. They were all over this place like rats soon as the fire died down a bit. They weren't just in the warehouse either, arrested a few in the ruins of the houses stripping the bodies. Bastards.'

The wind changed and they both coughed, smoke blowing over towards them. It didn't stop Gunner lighting up though.

'Mr Drummond'll be over at the flats, I think,' said Fraser. 'I've got to help take these bastards down to Central in the van. I'll see you later, eh?'

Gunner nodded and Fraser hurried off towards the line of handcuffed men and the big sergeant watching over them. Gunner crossed the road and made for the flats. The cobbles were sticky beneath his feet, thick with some syrupy substance; whatever had been in the warehouse, he supposed. Jam, honey, fuck knows. Explained the sweet smell though.

He turned the corner and saw there was a Daimler parked at the side of the road, black, polished to a mirror-like shine. Even if Buster hadn't been standing next to it, Gunner would have recognised the car anywhere. Con McGill's car. The only Daimler in Glasgow.

Buster nodded as he approached, and a smile broke across his big, scarred face.

'Mr Gunner, long time no see.'

Gunner held out his hand and they shook. Gunner wasn't a small man but his hand all but disappeared into Buster's massive paw.

'They no called you up yet?'

Buster grinned, pointed down at his feet. 'Fallen insteps, bloody murder they are too.'

Buster was all right far as Gunner was concerned. He was a professional, played the odds. Had always been pretty straight with him. His boss on the other hand was a prize arsehole.

'What's Midget McGill doing here then?' he asked, nodding over at the car.

Buster pretended to wince.

'Now, now, don't let Mr McGill hear you call him that. He'll get all upset. He's having a meeting with someone. They're sitting in the back of the motor.'

'Who's that then?' asked Gunner.

Buster didn't get a chance to answer before the back door of the Daimler swung open and the diminutive McGill stepped out, followed by Drummond. They were saying goodbye, shaking hands like old pals. McGill was wearing his usual cut-off George Raft outfit, even had bloody spats on. No wonder Sellars was taking over, McGill already looked like he was from another age.

Drummond flinched when he saw Gunner, but recovered quickly, patted McGill on the back, said he'd stay in touch. McGill got into the front, Buster stepped into the driver's seat and they were off, tyres whapping on the sticky cobbles as they accelerated away.

Gunner stepped forward, looked Drummond in the eye.

'You shall know them by the company they keep, eh, Drummond?' he said.

Drummond was having none of it.

'Can the shite, Gunner, and grow up. Wait until you try living on a polis pension, you won't be so bloody holier than thou then.'

Despite himself, Gunner smiled. If nothing else, Drummond wasn't one to roll over easily.

'C'mon,' said Drummond. 'Let's go for a walk, get away from here. This bloody smell's giving me the boak.'

They walked further down the riverside, sat on a wall by the railway bridge. The Govan ferry had been converted into a fire tender and was sitting in the middle of the Clyde spraying three jets of river water onto the warehouses. Two firemen were standing at the bank, shouting at the pilot, trying to direct the water onto the last of the flames.

Gunner lit up, waved his match out and dropped it into the river.

'What the fuck is going on, Drummond?' he said. 'I've had a night and a fucking half. Almost got fucking carted away to London in the back of polis van. You got me into this, I think you owe me the truth.'

Drummond sighed, eyes on the ferry spraying water. 'You want the whole sordid story?' he asked. 'You're not the only one that thinks he got fucked over, you know.'

Gunner nodded. Hadn't believed Drummond was going to tell him, but it looked like he needed to get it off his chest.

'It all started off so simple,' said Drummond taking his hat off and pushing his hair back. 'I met you off the train because I needed help. You've seen what the force is like now, full of old men and wee boys like Fraser. All fine for directing traffic, but fuck-all use for anything else. A body with no fingers and a smashed-in face was more than me or them could handle. I heard you were coming back so I thought I'd ask you a favour, get you to help out. Even though you can be a right arse you always were a good polis. Perfect timing.'

'And then?' asked Gunner.

Drummond smiled.

'And then it all went to shite. Even faster than you could imagine.'

He lit another cigarette off the one in his mouth, spat the old one out.

'I got a visit. Your flatmate Mr Moore and the Head of Glasgow Police. You know who Moore is?'

'Think he's Secret Service, something like that.'

'Christ knows who he is, but put it this way. He was the one giving the orders, not the Head. And they've got news for me. Suddenly I'm being told the bloke in the Kelvin Hall isn't a murder victim any more. Now he's a problem they need to disappear soon as. All change. Now the plan is he's never existed, no investigation, forget it happened.'

He grinned.

'And what had muggins here done? Just gone and put our best bloody polis on the job. They weren't happy, not happy at all. Moore decided the easiest way to stop that was to get you sent back to the Army. Made a phone call, told us you'd be gone by the morning.'

'But I didn't get the telegram,' said Gunner.

'Yes, you did,' said Drummond. 'It was delivered. You just didn't bloody open it. Naughty boy, Gunner. They weren't pleased. Weren't pleased at all. That's when they started looking for you. And then they had a special request for me, hush-hush, no questions asked.'

'What was it?' asked Gunner.

Drummond watched the ferry spinning around in the water trying to get closer in to the warehouses.

'The second body, the doctor at the Kelvin Hall realised he was still alive. So he started telling everyone, the hospital, the ARPs. Moore realised they'd fucked it up. The last thing they needed was some half-dead German recovering and telling tales. They didn't want to take any chances, so they sent me back to the Kelvin Hall to help his passage into the great unknown.'

'Murder him, you mean,' said Gunner.

Drummond looked at him.

'Come on, Gunner, I'm no that bad! He was going to die anyway. They just needed me to hurry it up.'

Gunner shook his head. 'Christ, Drummond, what a bloody mess.'

He shrugged.

'And I walked into it with my eyes wide open and a smile on my face. Picture it. I'm sixty-four, sitting on my arse in my hoose trying to stay out from under the wife's feet every day. Then all of a sudden, I'm a polis again and then the next thing is I've got a top-secret mission. I was like a dog with two pricks. Back in the game.'

'So what did you do to him?' asked Gunner.

'Too much morphine, the easiest trick in the book, except

you got there too bloody quickly. That wee bastard Fraser's good, managed to find you, and then when the wee bastard turned out to know German . . .'

He held his hands up.

'What about Nickerson?' asked Gunner. 'How does he fit in to all this?'

Drummond looked puzzled, shook his head.

'That's a weird one. I don't know what happened there. One minute he's in on everything, the next minute Moore comes to me and asks me to set him up. Get him out the picture, out of Glasgow. He tells me Nickerson's queer as a three-bob note, always drunk and not too careful when he goes looking for a pal. It wasnae hard.'

Gunner couldn't help himself, looked up and down the bridge.

'What about me, Drummond? Are they coming for me? Do I need to get out of here?'

Drummond laughed, shook his head, 'Always did have ideas above your station, Gunner. It's no you that they're looking for. It's your brother.'

'What?' said Gunner.

'There's a call going out to the radios in a couple of hours, Chief Inspector authorised it. Victor Gunner. Name, description, everything. Suspected of treason, armed and dangerous. They're no messing about, Gunner. You know what suspected of treason means?'

Gunner did, but Drummond didn't pause.

'It means they can shoot him on sight, and if I know them, they will. I don't know what your brother's done, but they want him out the picture big time, and they're gonnae have every polis and every Military Police helping them do it. If you know where he is, tell him not to even fucking breathe too loud or he's fucked.'

The ferry blew its hooter, set off back down the river to Govan.

'Do you know where Victor is?' asked Drummond.

Gunner nodded.

'Well, don't fucking tell me, I don't want to know. I just hope for his sake he's somewhere quiet and out the way. And if he is, tell him to bloody well stay there.'

Gunner watched Drummond take out his packet of Player's from his pocket, shake one out and light it from the one in his mouth, the same thing he'd done hundreds of times. He looked at his watch. Nine o'clock. Victor would be headed over to Hampden. A football ground full of polis, MPs, even the fucking Army. He hadn't a hope in hell.

'I'm going to go and warn him.'

Drummond exhaled a stream of blue smoke. 'Better hurry,' he said. 'Call goes out at eleven.'

Gunner started to walk away, stopped and turned back. 'I'm only saying this because we're pals.'

Drummond raised his eyebrows.

'Are we?'

Gunner nodded. 'You taught me more about being a polis than anyone else. Without you they wouldn't have been going to make me a detective. I'm grateful for that. Very grateful.'

'Christ, Gunner, calm down, you're making me blush. And that's not becoming in a man of my age or stature.'

'Which is why I'm saying this again. Don't go anywhere near Con McGill. I mean it. He's a dead man walking. Don't be there when it happens because they'll take you down too.'

Drummond didn't say anything, just kept smoking, eyes on the boats in the water. Moved his head slightly, could have been a nod, could just have been him taking a draw from his cigarette. Whatever it was, it was as much as Gunner was going to get.

29

'Fucking bunch of Nazi bastards!'

Gunner turned his head, but he was too late to avoid the spittle flying from the man's mouth. He got his hanky out and wiped it off his chin. He was just about to ask him to move along a bit when the man let fly another mouthful.

'I hope you rot in hell, ya bastards ye!'

He shouted again, then nudged Gunner, pointed at one of the POWs being marched down Cathcart Road.

'He looks a right evil bastard, that one.'

Gunner nodded and managed to step back a few yards before he got spat on again. The shouting man was one of a crowd of about fifty gathered outside Cathcart station to watch the POWs coming off the train and being marched across the road to Hampden stadium. Gunner had got there just as the train pulled in, clouds of smoke rising up from the tracks down in the dip. He looked up and down the street wondering where Victor could be. All he could see were soldiers and MPs, loads of them. Last thing Victor needed.

'I'm here every day,' the shouting man said. 'Waiting in case a train comes in.'

'That right?' said Gunner distracted by the stink of the man and the fact he had newspaper pictures of Winston Churchill stuck all over his coat.

The German POWs were making their way across the street in rows of three. They looked wary, some trying to smile, some content to keep their heads down. Most of them were still dressed in combat gear, grey uniform with the skip cap, a couple in desert uniforms. Gunner scanned them as they marched past, trying to see if any looked like Hess. The shouting man nudged him again. Gunner turned, exasperated, was just about to tell him to fuck off when he said, 'There's a man over the street waving at you.'

'What?' said Gunner looking over.

Victor was standing on the opposite pavement, a picture of the King and Queen on a bit of cardboard held in front of him, shouting abuse at the POWs going past.

Gunner waited for a break in the crocodile and ran over, soldiers marshalling the line throwing him a dirty look.

'Fuck you playing at?' he hissed at Victor.

'Hiding in plain sight. Always works. No one is looking for me amongst these nutters. Especially with this stupid sign. Nan made it. It's good, isn't it.'

Gunner pulled at his arm. 'Always the smart-arse. C'mon. I need to talk to you.'

Gunner half led, half pulled him to the back of the crowd, both still keeping their eyes on the passing POWs.

Victor pulled his arm away. 'What are you doing here anyway? Last I heard this was none of your business.'

'Aye well, let's just say it is my business now. You need to go, Victor. In a couple of hours they're going to charge you with treason, every polis and MP in Glasgow will have a description.

They'll be after you, Victor, and they'll find you and they'll kill you.'

Victor's face fell, no longer his usual cocky self. 'What?'

'You heard. Drummond told me this morning. You've got to get out of here, Victor, find somewhere, lie low for a couple of days until I find out what's going on.'

A huge grin spread over Victor's face.

'I told you! You know what that means? Hess is definitely coming. I knew it! I fucking knew it. You believe me now?'

Gunner nodded wearily. 'Maybe he is, not that it's gonnae do either of us any good.'

'Oh yes, it is. We've got to get into the stadium, Joe, get a hold of the lookalike.'

Gunner held up his hand. 'You're no going anywhere. Are you not listening to me? They can shoot you on sight, Victor. No repercussions. It's no a game any more. I'm serious, you need to go quick.'

He shook his head. 'I can't. I've got to try.'

'You haven't got a hope in hell!' said Gunner. 'Where would you even start? Eh? How are you going to get to him?'

Victor said nothing.

'You need to disappear. I fucking mean it, Victor. Tell Nan where you are if you can, but just go.'

Gunner hesitated, couldn't quite believe what he was going to say.

'If you do that, I'll go. I'll get in somehow, I promise.'

Victor looked doubtful. Paused, then nodded, looked around.

'OK. There's one of us in there already. Murray Barr, he works for the Civil Defence, sorts out what prisoners go where. All you have to do is find him, tell him the prisoner's name, he'll get him transferred straight back out of Glasgow before they get to him, that'll buy us a few days at least.'

The crocodile was tapering off, the prisoners trailing down the hill to the open gates of the stadium.

Gunner nodded. 'I'll find him. Now go, for fuck's sake.'

Victor turned, started walking towards the train station. Whistles started to blow as the last of the crocodile disappeared through the gates. Gunner swore under his breath and started running. He made it about halfway down the hill before his knee was screaming so much he had to pull up. All he could do was stand there, hopping on one leg, swearing and watching the big wooden gates of the stadium rumble shut.

30

Hampden stadium was vast, the biggest in the world, they said. Certainly seemed like it as Gunner made his way round the perimeter looking for some way in. It took him a good half an hour to do it. Fact he had to hobble didn't help, his knee was in agony. And after all that, no luck. Every gate or door was guarded, vast brick walls unclimbable, even if his knee had been up to it. He'd told Victor he'd get in, but he'd no idea how he was supposed to do it.

He ended up back where he started, opposite the big gates in the west stand. He sat down on the grass, rested his leg, and stared at the high walls. The occasional shout or whistle drifted over the top. Not like match days. On those days you could hear the roar miles away, all the way to the city centre, 150,000 men all shouting in unison at the top of their voices; it was something else.

The sun was climbing in the sky now, getting warm. He yawned, realised how tired he was, hadn't slept properly for days. He lit a cigarette and lay back on the wee bit of grass that was left amongst the Dig for Victory allotments that now surrounded the stadium. Closed his eyes for a minute, tried to think.

When he woke up the cigarette had burnt out, the butt beside him in the grass. He lifted his arm, looked at his watch: he'd only been out twenty minutes or so. He yawned, stretched. Even the twenty minutes seemed to have done some good. He sat up, stopped, rubbed at his eyes, not quite believing what he was seeing. A German POW was coming towards him, ambling through the huts and vegetable plots of the allotments, as if he were on a Sunday stroll to check his cabbages.

The POW stopped for a minute, took off his peaked cap, wiped the sweat from his forehead, then kept coming. Gunner stood up, not sure what to do. He looked around; there were no soldiers or MPs in sight. The prisoner kept coming, heading straight for him. Gunner padded his pockets looking for anything to defend himself. Nothing. The prisoner stopped about ten yards away and peered at him.

'I fucking knew it,' he said in a broad Glaswegian accent. 'Joe bloody Gunner.'

'Billy Nairn?' said Gunner, 'Is that you?'

He nodded. 'Who'd you think it was, the fucking Panzer Corps invading Mount Florida?'

They shook hands, Gunner still not quite sure what was going on. Billy Nairn had been in his class at school, they'd played in the same football team, been at the same station for a while.

Gunner stood back, tried to take in the fact Billy Nairn was now a German POW.

'What's with the get-up?' Gunner asked. 'Last thing I heard you were down south, Aldershot or somewhere like that.'

'I was,' said Billy. 'Was sent there straight after I joined up, left Maryhill station a couple of weeks after you, and now I'm back up here dressed as a fucking Nazi. You wouldnae believe it if I made it up.'

Gunner just looked at him. The expression on his face must have said it all.

'Don't ask,' said Billy. 'It's the latest brainwave of they useless cunts in Intelligence. My maw was German, Dad was half Polish. They spoke German in the hoose, it was the only way they could understand each other. So when the cunts in charge find out I speak fluent German I get sent back up here. Next thing I'm given this uniform and told to go in there and mingle aboot the prisoners, keep my ears open, find out if anything's afoot. Total waste of time. There's me and three German teachers frae Edinburgh wandering about listening to those buggers. They're no talking about escaping or giving away Army secrets. All they bloody talk aboot is when their bloody dinner's coming and what it'll be.'

He coughed up a gobbet of phlegm and spat it onto the grass, rubbed at it with his foot.

'These army cigarettes are pure pish.' He looked up. 'That's my tale of bloody woe. So what are you doing here anyway?'

'Leave. Back for a while. Need to get my eye better.'

'Too right you do, you look like Long John bloody Silver.'

'Listen, Billy, I need you to do me a favour, I need to get in there. Can you sort it?'

'Aye, no problems,' said Billy. 'But why do you want to get in there? It's bloody miserable, moaning-faced Germans and civil servants with specs on, with their bundles of bloody forms.'

Gunner tapped the side of his nose.

'Got to deliver a wee message for Drummond. Apparently there's an opportunity for some supplies to go missing.'

'Ah get you,' said Billy. 'By the way, tell him if he's looking for more army petrol I can sort him out. C'mon.'

31

They walked back towards the stadium, Billy heading for the door cut into the big wooden gate. He tapped it with his knuckle and a young soldier sporting a face full of acne opened it.

'Mate's wi' me,' said Billy. 'He's a polis.'

Gunner held out his badge, but the soldier didn't even look, just swung the door open and let them in. They ducked down, stepped through the door and into the stadium. Gunner couldn't believe how easy it turned out to be to get in; maybe sometimes luck was just on your side.

They climbed up the steep back stairs and eventually came out at the top of the west stand. The trains must have been coming in all through the night. The football field below was covered in German and Italian prisoners. There were temporary showers set up, a medical tent, even a delousing station. The prisoners were lined up in neat rows, single file, all facing a long row of desks along the far side of the pitch. They were shuffling forward slowly, the man at the front of each line being interviewed, then having a set of papers stamped.

'I better get down and start listening in,' said Billy. 'Waste of fucking time, but needs must.'

Gunner nodded. 'I'll come with you. I need to find someone.'

They walked down the narrow passage between the stands and onto the pitch. Billy wandered off into the crowd leaving Gunner standing uncertainly at the back of the line of desks. The soldiers didn't seem interested in him, barely interested in the prisoners either. They were young, bored, standing in groups smoking and yawning, shoving wandering prisoners back into the lines every so often.

Gunner approached the man at the first desk with his police badge out.

'Murray Barr?' he asked. 'Looking for Murray Barr.'

The bloke behind the desk didn't even look up, just kept stamping at an ink pad and then a pile of papers.

'Tenth desk along,' he said.

Murray Barr turned out to be a fat bloke with wavy red hair plastered onto his skull with hair oil. The morning sun was already starting to make him sweat, trails of it running down his big florid face. The prisoner in front of his desk was getting agitated, started shouting something at him in German. Murray snapped something back, didn't seem to do much good, just provoked more shouts. The prisoner was leaning over the desk now, finger in Murray's face. That was the final straw. He'd had enough; he stood up and whistled. A couple of nearby soldiers came rushing over. No questions, no explanations, one of them hit the prisoner in the kidneys with the butt of his rifle and he bent over in agony. The soldiers grabbed him and they hustled him off.

Murray pushed his chair back, stood up and stretched, indicated to the bloke at the next desk he was off for a piss. Gunner fell in behind him as he walked towards the stand.

'Murray Barr?' he asked.

Murray stopped, turned. 'Who's asking?'

'I'm a friend of Victor's,' Gunner said.

Murray shrugged. 'No idea what you're on about, pal.' He walked on.

Gunner cursed and followed him; maybe it wasn't going to be as easy as he thought.

Murray walked through the doors and into the stand, the segs on his shoes hitting the concrete floor, echoing in the vast empty space ahead of him. He pushed the door of the gents and went in. Gunner followed.

For a fat bloke, Murray was surprisingly strong. Within seconds he had Gunner pushed up against the wall of the toilets, forearm across his neck.

'Who the fuck are you, pal?' asked Murray. 'And why the fuck are you following me?'

'Joe. Victor's brother,' said Gunner, trying to breathe.

'Prove it,' said Murray, unconvinced.

Gunner managed to point down to his pocket. Murray delved in and pulled out his wallet, eyebrows rising at the sight of the police badge. He read it, let go of Gunner and stepped back. Gunner slumped down against the wall, rubbing at his sore neck.

'I didn't know Victor had a brother,' said Murray. 'Where is he anyway?'

'Lying low. That's why I'm here. They've brought another one in, that's what I've come to tell you.'

'What? The double?' Murray said, excitement in his voice. 'The double's here?'

Gunner nodded, still rubbing at his sore neck.

'What's the name?' asked Murray. 'Don't worry, I'll get him sent to the back arse of nowhere soon as.'

'Troz. He's called Gunther Troz,' said Gunner.

'Fuck, we're at the S's already. C'mon.'

He turned and started running back through the empty building, heels echoing, Gunner following behind.

Murray sat back down at his table, sweat pouring off him now, and barked 'Name!' at the first prisoner.

'Tisten,' the man said hesitantly and held his papers out.

Murray looked back at Gunner. They were just in time. Gunner tried to look down the line, checking if he could see anyone who looked like the two bodies they'd found. The prisoners all looked much the same, hard to make out any real difference with the caps and uniforms. Then shouts started coming from his left, a couple of lines further down. Prisoners were getting pulled out of the queue, papers looked at, then shoved back in. He couldn't make out what was going on. He looked down at Murray. He shrugged, no idea either.

The next prisoner approached the table. 'Topp,' he said.

The commotion had moved to the next line now, Gunner could see a couple of soldiers walking up and down the line, shouting something. As they moved up the line towards the desks, Gunner made out what it was.

'Troz! Gunther Troz!'

Murray looked up, he'd heard it too. They looked at each other, unsure what to do next. The shouts rang out again.

'Troz! Gunther Troz!'

Halfway down Murray's line, a soldier stepped out with his hand up. He was tall, thin, balding.

'I am Troz,' he said, put his hands above his head and waited for the soldiers to come to him.

Nothing Gunner and Murray could do now but watch as the

soldiers gathered around Troz and checked his papers. Some nods, and one of the soldiers stepped out, shouted down the line. Two burly men emerged from the crowd, a slighter one walking beside them. Moore. Gunner swore under his breath.

'Better get out of here,' said Murray.

Gunner nodded, tried to move back into the shadow of the stand. Moore and the two big lads approached Troz, all smiles and back slaps. Moore held out his hand and Troz shook it. Looked like they had their man and there was nothing Gunner could do about it now.

He saw a flash of movement out the corner of his eye. Realised Murray was running. They didn't see him until he was right on them. He ran straight at Troz, weight and momentum sending the German flying; he landed on his back and Murray was on him. Raised his hand, knife held high. Just as he went to plunge it down, one of the burly men pulled a revolver from his belt, put it to Murray's head and pulled the trigger. A crack and a flash and Murray's head disappeared in a red mist.

Gunner groaned, looked away for a minute. When he looked back, Murray was on the ground, blood pouring from what was left of his head. Troz looked shell-shocked, covered in Murray's blood.

Moore turned, pointed to where Murray had come from, and one of the burly guys started trotting over. Moore was just about to turn back to Troz when he stopped, looked back, looked directly at him.

Gunner turned and ran across the football field. The shouts and whistles started before he even made it to the bottom of the stand. He ran up the first few steps, knee sending out warning signals already. Boots clattering behind him, he turned, three soldiers a lot younger and fitter than he was after him.

He heard one of the soldiers behind fall, cursing as he went down. The other two were getting closer, they were only a few yards away now. Gunner pushed on, lungs bursting with the effort of sprinting up the steep stand. He was only a couple of steps from the top when he heard the sound of a breech being pulled back, and then a shout: 'Stop! Or I'll shoot!'

Gunner kept going, heard the sharp crack of the gun, then the whistle of the bullet above him as he vaulted over the iron barrier and launched himself into space.

32

However long it had taken to build the wee hut, it only took Gunner a second to smash it. He landed half on it and half on the big compost pile of clippings and cut grass beside it. He lay there for a second trying to work out how badly damaged he was. A chicken appeared, looked at him curiously, clucked a few times and wandered off.

Gunner rolled off the pile, tried to stand up. He was doing pretty well, seemed like his knee was still the sorest part in spite of the fall. There were a few cuts and scratches across his hands from where he'd hit the shed, and a pain in his shoulder, but other than that he seemed surprisingly OK. He pulled the little shards of wood from his hands, dusted himself down and started running again, as fast as his damned knee would let him.

He'd almost made it across the allotments and back onto Cathcart Road when the big stadium gates started to open. He got up onto the road, ducked into one of the closes and started sprinting up the stairs looking for a well-kept door. He'd learned that when he was first on the beat: a well-kept door was always the sign of an old biddy. And more often than not, they were eager to help a policeman. He found one on the third floor, neat black paint, brass knocker shining. He knocked. The door opened a crack and a teenage boy, fourteen or fifteen, peered out.

Gunner groaned inwardly. Not enough time to find another one now, he'd just have to wing it. He held out his badge.

'Can I ask you a few questions?'

The boy looked glum.

'I told Mac we'd get done for this, I bloody knew it.'

Gunner could hear trucks drawing up in the street below, doors slamming, men jumping down onto the pavement.

'That's right. Need to come in and interview you.'

Gunner stepped into the flat. He'd been half right, the place was as neat as a pin.

'It's my granny's,' said the boy. 'My maw told me to stay here for a while, lie low.'

'That right?' said Gunner. 'Need you to do me a favour. When the Army knock on the door, you stay quiet and don't answer. Got it?'

The boy looked puzzled.

'You a deserter? Running away from the soldiers?' It dawned. 'You're no looking for me or Mac at all, are you?'

Gunner could hear footsteps on the stair, doors being knocked.

'Just stay fucking quiet,' hissed Gunner. 'OK?'

The boy smiled. 'Sure thing.' He held his hand out. 'Ten bob.'

'What?' asked Gunner.

'Ten bob,' said the boy. 'Or I start screaming my head off.'

'For fuck sake!' Gunner started digging in his pockets, found a ten-bob note and handed it over.

They both jumped as the door was battered. 'Army! Open up!'

The two of them stood there, hardly breathing. The knocking came again, harder this time. 'Open up!'

Sound of another set of boots on the landing.

'Nobody home, then?' said a cockney voice.

'Doesn't look like it, sir.'

The cockney voice again. 'Fuck it. C'mon.'

They waited until the footsteps had gone and crawled through to the front room, pulled the dirty net curtain to the side and peered out. The street below was swarming with army boys, a couple of folk from the street standing staring, wondering what was going on. Gunner crawled over to an old armchair and sat down. The boy sat opposite him, a huge grin on his face.

They heard whistles and looked out the window again. The soldiers were climbing back into the trucks, heading back to the stadium. He watched them go, thought he'd sit tight for another wee while, make sure he was definitely in the clear. Was pretty sure Murray was a goner: he'd looked pretty bad lying on the ground, blood pumping out of him.

Drummond had been right. These people had stopped messing about, they were serious now, really serious. The gloves were well and truly off. They had Troz, they had their double. The plan was about to go into action. No way were they going to let him or his brother derail it. If that meant shooting them like they had Murray, then it looked like they were more than happy to do so.

33

Gunner waited an hour or so in the flat, cleaned himself up as well he could. Let the boy make him a cup of tea.

'You are a wee shite,' Gunner told him as he handed the cup over.

'Maybe,' said the boy 'but the army boys are gone and you're in the clear. Well worth ten bob I'd say.'

Gunner drank his tea, waited another wee while, made sure they had definitely gone.

'Could make you a cheese sandwich for two bob?' said the boy, taking his empty cup.

'If I wasn't fucking starving I'd boot your arse,' said Gunner digging into his pocket.

The boy came back a couple of minutes later, substantial sandwich in hand. Gunner devoured it quickly and left, closed the door behind him and slipped down the stairs and out onto the street. He looked up and down. Seemed quiet enough; no soldiers to be seen. He walked up Cathcart Road towards town.

If things were still the same as they had been before the war, it meant Nan would start work about nine. He looked at his watch. Only three o'clock. He needed somewhere to disappear for a few hours, somewhere out the way of Moore, Drummond or whoever else was looking for him. He couldn't go to the barracks or the station, they'd probably already alerted the hotels and B & Bs. Couldn't think of anywhere else to go.

By the time he'd walked a couple of hundred yards his knee was too sore to go on. He got on a tram into town, sat upstairs at the back, kept his head down. A couple of Canadian officers got on and sat in front of him; one of them had an address written on a piece of paper. He turned around. Smiled.

'Excuse me, sir, does this trolley car take us to this address?'

Gunner looked at the bit of paper. *The Overseas Club, St George's Place*. He passed it back with a smile.

'Aye, it does, and funnily enough, that's where I'm headed myself.'

Twenty minutes and a boring conversation about the weather in Alberta later, they were there. The woman behind the desk at Reception waved the two Canadians in with a smile, held her hand up in front of Gunner when he went to follow them.

'Overseas officers only,' she said.

Gunner held out his badge.

'Police business. Need to go in.'

She looked down her nose at the badge and then at him, but she relented and let him pass.

The Overseas Club had a dining room, a smoking room, and a couple of lounges filled with leather chesterfields and sagging armchairs. It was full of odds and sods; Canadians, Poles, Australians, even a couple of Yanks with their peaked caps on the table in front of them. The two Canadians headed off to the dining room; Gunner told them he'd be in later and slipped down the stairs to the gents, hand cradling the box of syrettes in his pocket. For his knee, he told himself. For the pain in his knee.

He got into the cubicle, opened the box and took a syrette out. Looked at it. Wasn't much doubt now, he really needed the syrettes. Needed them big time. He sat for a minute, tried to convince himself he should try and stop, but his heart wasn't in it. He knew he was kidding himself. But now wasn't the time. He took the cap off and stuck the syrette into his thigh. Only a few seconds, and he felt the warmth spread through his body.

When Gunner opened his eyes, a middle-aged woman in a black dress and lace pinny was standing in front of him. She smiled at him.

'I thought I'd leave you sleeping, son, you looked like you needed it. How's about a cup of tea?'

Gunner nodded, still a bit dazed, 'That be great. Cheers.'

She nodded and wandered off to the counter. He looked around. He was in one of the lounges, four Yanks playing poker at a table in the corner. The last thing he could remember was being downstairs in the cubicle, but he must have made it up here before he flaked out. He looked at his watch, half eight. He'd been asleep in one of the armchairs for a good four or five hours. He yawned, stretched, felt better for it. He pushed his foot out experimentally, stretching his leg. A dull twinge, nothing else. The last of the morphine in his system no doubt helping.

The waitress brought his tea over just as a group of Polish officers came in, twenty or so of them all laughing and joking, well on the way already. They settled on the chesterfields and ordered teas and Coca-Colas, filling the drinks up from their flasks when the woman wasn't looking, or more accurately when she was pretending not to see. One of them, a big lad with silvery hair, held his flask up to him. Gunner nodded and he poured a large slug into his mug. He sipped at it, enjoying the warmth as the vodka-laced tea went down.

He watched the Poles getting steadily drunker, morphine still making him happy to just sit for a while. The big lad offered him another drink, but he smiled, put his hand over his cup. He'd had enough. He went back down to the gents and stuck his head under the cold tap for a couple of minutes, tried to clear his mind. He combed his hair back, took his eyepatch off and looked at himself in the mirror. Still had the cuts on his hands from the shed, but other than that he didn't look too bad.

Troz was in Glasgow, there was nothing he could do about that, all he could do was warn Victor, get him to disappear. The door burst open and one of the Poles staggered in, just made it into the cubicle before being sick. Gunner put his comb back in his pocket and straightened up his tie. Time to get going. The Tower Ballroom was only a couple of streets away and Nan should have started by now.

34

Gunner was leaning over the balcony of the Tower Ballroom looking down through the haze of cigarette smoke at the dancers below. The place was rammed, war was obviously good for trade. Crowds of foreign soldiers were standing around, Canadians and Australians mostly, girls flocking around them. Gunner didn't blame them, they all looked healthy, well fed, with good teeth and money to spend.

Glasgow lads didn't look too happy about it, though; they were standing in groups at the back throwing the soldiers dirty looks. Although Gunner hadn't been here for years, nothing much had changed. The band was louder, the crowd was younger, but other than that it was the same old cattle market.

He scanned the dance floor looking for Nan but he couldn't see her. She was listed on a card by the door with some guy called Willie Manson as 'third exhibition couple'. Gunner wasn't sure if that meant third on or third best. A girl with auburn hair and a figure that would stop a clock walked up the stairs and along the balcony. Gunner, like most of the other men in the vicinity, couldn't help but follow her with his eyes.

She walked up to the big booth in the corner and waited for two heavies to get up and let her in to sit down. She took a cigarette out of her bag and sat waiting for it to be lit. One of the heavies eventually caught on and took out a box of matches. She lit up and settled back on her seat. She caught Gunner looking at her and she smiled over, French inhaled like a film star. Whoever she was waiting for was a very lucky man.

'She's as good a ride as she looks.'

Gunner turned to find Malky Sellars standing there grinning. He was dressed up tonight, Prince of Wales suit, new haircut, even smelt of some kind of cologne. He leant into him.

'You can have her if you want,' he said. 'I'll sort it. No bother. She'll let you do whatever you want. Get her to suck you off, believe you me she's very good at it.'

Gunner stepped back, shaking his head.

Sellars shrugged. 'Don't say I didn't offer. Seems my big brother is quite taken with you, Gunner. That doesn't happen very often. You should be honoured.'

Gunner shook his head. 'I told your brother and I'll tell you now, I'm not interested.'

Sellars smiled his movie-star smile. 'You will be. My brother always gets what he wants. One way or another.'

He took a silver cigarette case from his pocket, flipped it open and held it out. Gunner took one and Sellars lit it for him.

'How's your pal Drummond?' he asked.

'Drummond's Drummond,' he said. 'Con McGill's the man you want, Sellars. Just leave Drummond alone.'

'I'd love to,' said Sellars. 'But my big brother has told him three times to keep away from McGill and he doesn't seem to be listening. Fact I heard they had a wee chat down at the Clyde this morning. That right?'

Gunner nodded, didn't seem any point in lying.

'Your Drummond is a lucky man. Three times he asked him, that's two more chances than my brother normally gives anyone. No way he's going to give him a fourth, not after that chat today. That's just taking the piss, and no one takes the piss out my brother.'

'Just leave him, Malky, he's not a threat to you. It's just nylons and petrol coupons, small stuff.'

Malky leered at him. 'That what he told you, was it? You really think my brother would be angry about that shite?'

'What is it, then?' asked Gunner.

Sellars shrugged.

'Him and Con started a nasty wee sideline, taking money off Jewish folk, telling them they could get their relatives out of Germany or Poland or wherever the fuck they are. Never happens and they just keep the money. Our next-door neighbours when we were growing up were the Shapiros. Jews. My mum and dad loved them; they had no kids, so they helped a lot with my brother when he was young, when he was ill. Matthew never forgot that. Has always been a big friend of the Jews in Glasgow. He asked Con and Drummond both to stop. Politely. Three times he asked but they still haven't. They've run out of chances.'

'Maybe I can talk to him?' said Gunner. Soon as he said it he realised how feeble it sounded.

'Not my decision to make, Gunner, I just do what my brother tells me, stood me right so far. You know as well as I do, they're both history. Or they will be soon. Anyway, neither of them is worth worrying about. Things are changing.'

He dropped his cigarette on the floor and stepped on it with his shiny patent shoes.

'Toodle-oo,' he said. 'See you around.'

Sellars walked off in the direction of the redhead's table. The heavies jumped this time, let him in beside the girl. He'd his tongue down her throat in seconds, hand pushed up the front of her dress. He looked over at Gunner and winked.

Gunner made his way along the dimly lit balcony and down onto the main floor. He flashed his badge, told a group of pissed-up lads round a table at the edge of the dance floor to move on. Ten minutes later the bandleader wiped the sweat from his shiny forehead with a big white hanky and made an announcement.

'Ladies and gentlemen, please welcome our third exhibition couple! Willie Manson and Nan Taylor!'

Some scattered applause and the crowd parted, started lining up around the walls as Nan and her partner stepped out onto the dance floor. She was all dressed up in some sort of white number with sequins on it, body twinkling in the spotlight as she moved. Gunner had no idea whether she was a good dancer or not, but the crowd clapped appreciatively when they finished their number. The couple stood in the spotlight for a minute or so, milking the applause. They bowed, the spotlight went off and the band started up again. Business as usual.

Gunner made his way to the bar at the back of the hall, avoiding the crowd surrounding the two dancers. Nan saw him out the corner of her eye, waved over. Gunner stood at the bar and waited. Five minutes later she was there. She kissed him, a light sheen of sweat on her cheek, the smell of perfume.

'You were good,' he said.

She smiled. 'Thank you. Is Sellars here? Have you seen him?'

Gunner nodded.

'He's upstairs. Why?'

'Hope he saw me dancing, need more work.'

'Might have been busy.'

'The redhead?'

Gunner nodded again.

'Thought that would have run its course by now. Anyway, what brings you to this temple of sin?'

'You seen Victor?'

She nodded, began to speak, but he held his hand up.

'Don't tell me where he is, Nan, I don't want to know, but you have to tell him to stay hidden, they're not fucking about any more . . .'

Gunner was suddenly aware of her partner hovering at her shoulder, trying to pull her away.

'Why?' said Nan, looking scared. 'What's happened, Joe?'

Her partner tugged at her again and she turned around, told him to fuck off.

'Look, I've only got another two dances, then I'm done. I'll see you out the front after. OK?'

Gunner nodded and watched as she walked away and stepped into the circle of light on the dance floor to a ripple of applause. The couple spun round and round a few times before Gunner went off in search of a drink.

The gents in the Tower Ballroom were enormous, rows and rows of pale green sinks, mirrors and wooden stalls. The noise inside was worse than out the front with the band. Groups of lads were combing their hair in the mirrors, shouting friendly abuse at each other, two drunk guys sitting down against the wall singing 'Fools Rush In'.

Gunner gave a young bloke a tanner to pour a slug of his half-bottle into his drink, knocked it back, paid him for another and knocked that back too. He stood in front of one of the sinks, combed his hair in the mirror. He looked tired, needed a bath and a shave, a new shirt and a good night's sleep, in a bed, not just a morphine slump in a chair. Didn't think he was going to get any of them soon.

Twenty minutes later Gunner was waiting outside the entrance to the dance hall. He'd smoked a couple of cigarettes, wished he'd bought a few more slugs of whatever that boy had in his bottle. He was just about to go back in and find him when Nan appeared, face still flushed from the dancing. She'd only a wee fur stole thing, she was shivering as soon as they started walking. Gunner gave her his jacket and she pulled it round her shoulders. They didn't say much; he tried but she'd waved him quiet. Told him they'd be back at the flat in ten minutes, they could talk there. It was hard to walk quickly with the blackout in full effect. They stumbled a good few times, missing cobbles not helping.

They were just about to cross Garscube Road when he heard it. He stopped. Nan kept walking, then realised he wasn't beside her. She turned.

'What is it?' she asked.

Gunner stood quietly, didn't hear it again.

'Thought I heard a Bren gun,' he said, shaking his head.

'What's a Bren gun?'

'Rifle that shoots multiple shots. Must have been imaging it. Thought I was back in France for a minute.'

'Nope,' said Nan. 'Last time I checked we were still in shitey Glasgow.' She blew into her hands, rubbed them together. 'Hurry up, I'm freezing.'

Gunner fell in beside her and they kept walking.

35

They had just walked under the bridge at Possil Road when Gunner saw the ambulance and the police van parked in the front yard of the Whisky Bond building on Dawson Street. There was a police car there as well, the mortuary van off at the side.

'Christ, what's happened now?' asked Nan.

Gunner shook his head. Whatever it was, it wasn't anything he needed to get involved with.

'Probably tried to rob the Bond warehouse and something went wrong,' he said. 'How much further?'

'Just up to Kepochhill Road, five minutes.'

Gunner nodded and they started walking again.

Had only gone a couple of steps when he heard his name being called.

'Mr Gunner!'

He stopped, looked up at the warehouse, couldn't make out who was calling him.

'You go on, I'll be ten minutes, be some polis that needs a hand. OK?'

She nodded and Gunner hurried up Dawson Road. He'd just got up to where the vans were parked when he heard a voice.

'Mr Gunner.'

He turned, and Fraser was sitting on a pile of old sacks, WHISKY BOND printed on each one.

'Fraser? What are you doing here? Has there been a robbery?'

Fraser shook his head, tried to speak, but all that happened was he started crying. Gunner sat down on the sacks, cursed Drummond under his breath, put his arm around the boy's shoulders and let him cry.

36

Turned out he had been right, he had heard a Bren gun. It was the only thing that could have done damage like this. Gunner stood by the Daimler and tried to work out how many bullet holes there were. It was impossible to count, they were everywhere, all over the bodywork, the tyres, windscreen and windows gone. Con McGill's pride and joy was no more. And neither was Con McGill. He was half out the car, body, head and shoulders on the ground, as riddled with bullets as the car.

Buster Lang had made it out the car, was lying a couple of yards away, back of his head now just a pulpy mess, body not much better.

Funny thing was, Drummond didn't look too bad. He was still propped up in the back seat. The bullets hadn't hit his head, all body shots. His head was thrown back, half a smile on his face. As if knew it was going to happen. Gunner reached into the car and patted Drummond's pockets. Fished his Zippo out his jacket pocket, wiped the blood off it with his hanky and put it in his pocket.

Typical Drummond. Died the same way he had lived. Always knew best, listening to no one, juggling his multiple schemes and deals, always one step ahead of the game. Not this time though, this time his luck had finally run out.

Gunner sat down on the kerb and watched the police and the ambulance guys do what they had to do. Flicked the Zippo lid open and ran his thumb down the wheel. Flame jumped up and the smell of petrol immediately reminded him of sitting in the car with Drummond. Cigarette after cigarette. He blew the flame out and put the Zippo in his pocket. Looked up and Fraser was standing there; then he sat down on the kerb beside him. The boy looked shaken, tears still coming down his face.

'He thought you were great, Fraser,' said Gunner. 'Thought you had the makings of a real cop. Of course, he'd never tell you that, you know what he was like, but he told me. Told me a good few times.'

Fraser nodded his head. Wiped the tears and snot away with the back of his hand.

'How did it happen?' asked Gunner. 'You weren't here, were you?'

Fraser shook his head, pointed over to a tall man in a black raincoat, with moustache. Kenny Strand. He'd been retired like Drummond, must have come back to help out.

'He knows.'

Gunner stood up, walked over to Strand, shook hands.

'What a fucking mess,' said Strand. 'How do I explain to the Chief of Police that Drummond was sitting in a car with Con bloody McGill when he died?'

Gunner shrugged.

'Not much you can say. Going to be pretty obvious Drummond was up to his neck in it with McGill. What happened?'

Strand pointed over to the Bond. A man in a boiler suit, face pure white, was standing in the doorway. Even from here Gunner could see his hand shaking as he raised his cigarette up to his lips.

'Nightwatchman came out to empty the bins round the back, said that the car was parked there, the three of them in it. He was just about to walk over and ask them what they were doing there when another car drove up, gun barrels poking out the window, started firing before they even pulled over. Stopped the car and got out, still firing. Brens. They just stood around the car and emptied the magazines, drove off. Said it was like a bloody gangster film in Chicago.'

'Christ,' said Gunner. 'He give any description of them?'

Strand shook his head. 'Too dark. Better go and make sure these guys are doing what they're supposed to do. Most of them have never even seen a murder scene, never mind this mess.'

Gunner nodded, watched Strand walk over to the car. Wasn't sure why he'd bothered asking about identification. If the nightwatchman had identified them then the chances were he would be dead the next day too. No way was he going to risk that for two quid a week.

He took out his fags and lit up. It was Sellars all right, who else would it be? He'd made it pretty clear that McGill and Drummond's days were numbered. He'd tried as hard as he could to get Drummond to stay away from McGill but he hadn't. Why the fuck not? Pride, he supposed. Money. Being back in the game. And where had all that got him? Dead in the back of a car.

He walked over to Fraser. The boy was looking a bit less tearful.

'You go for a drink with Strand and the other lads when

they're done. Remember Drummond in beer and whisky and war stories. He would have liked that.'

Fraser nodded.

Gunner dug in his pocket, took out the Zippo, gave it to him.

'He'd have wanted you to have it. Off you go.'

Fraser took it and walked back towards the car.

Gunner wasn't sure what it was but something had changed in Fraser. Maybe he was just being forced to grow up, face the realities of life. Whatever it was, he was less of a frightened boy, more of a young cop.

37

Gunner started to walk back down the hill heading for Nan's when he saw them. Sellars and Bingo and some of his lads looking over the wall that ran along by the canal. Passing a bottle back and forth, laughing, enjoying the view of the crime scene. Sellars looked down at him, paused a moment, then smiled and raised his bottle. That was when all the anger Gunner had been trying to keep down burst all over him like a tidal wave.

He ran round the front yard, leg screaming in agony, and down the path to the canal. They all turned as they saw him coming. Gunner ran at Sellars, determined to get him down and kick the fuck out him. Sellars just stood there, didn't move an inch, smiling as Bingo stepped into Gunner's path and punched him hard in the stomach. The speed he was going and the force of Bingo's fist knocked all the air out of him. He bent over, tried to catch his breath, managed to suck some air into his lungs, just in time for Bingo to get a kick in at the side of his head. He groaned, collapsed onto his knees, thought he was going to pass out before Bingo grabbed him by the collar, pulled him up, dragged him over to Sellars, pushed him down onto the ground and rested a heavy boot on his chest.

Sellars walked over and peered down at him. Bottle of whisky in one hand, cigarette in the other.

'You need to calm down, Gunner,' he said.

Gunner struggled to get up but Bingo just put more of his weight down on his chest. Had a feeling Bingo would have no hesitation in pressing harder and breaking a few of his ribs if he didn't stop.

'Three times he was told. And him and fucking McGill kept at it. Took sixty quid off some woman in Stonyhurst Street this morning, told her they could get her brother out of Berlin. Now I don't give much of a shit about some stupid woman handing over sixty pounds, but my brother heard about it and he did. What you call the final straw.'

'Since when was your brother such a fucking saint?' Gunner managed to get out.

Sellars knelt down beside him, took a drag of his cigarette and flicked the ash into Gunner's face.

'You need to start thinking straight. You've got a choice. End up like that stupid cunt Drummond or wise up. I'm not sure my brother's patience with you is going to last much longer.'

'Fuck off, Sellars. If you think I'm going to work with you or your brother you're stupider than I thought.'

Sellars grinned.

'Now a wee birdie told me that apart from fucking your eye up, you managed to fuck your leg up too. That right, is it?'

Gunner didn't say anything, too fearful to speak. His leg was agony, never mind anything more Sellars planned to do to it.

Sellars lifted his hand, bunched it into a fist. Held it over one leg, then the other as he spoke.

'Eeny, meeny, miny, moe, catch a—'

Then he battered it down onto Gunner's left leg.

The pain was immediate and total, he thought he was going to pass out, hoped he was going to pass out, but he didn't, just rode wave after wave of pain. He bit down, tried not to scream out or cry. Stared into Sellars' grinning face and swore that, whatever happened, one day he would kill the fucker.

'Seems the wee birdie was right,' Sellars said.

Sellars stood up, walked towards the canal, motioned to Bingo.

Bingo grabbed him under the arms, dragged him over to the side of the canal, dumped him down, foot on his chest.

Sellars peered over the edge into the dark, oily water, then turned and squatted down by Gunner.

'Plan was to get Bingo here to drop you into the canal just to ram the point home, but now that I've had a look and realised just how fucked up your leg is, I've got a feeling you wouldn't be able to get yourself out. That right?'

Gunner looked over. The surface of the water was three or four feet down and the walls of the canal were slimy brick. Knew he hadn't a fucking chance of getting himself out.

'I asked you a question,' said Sellars.

Gunner nodded.

'Now I wouldn't do something that rotten, leave a man to drown in all that sewage and fucking rat's piss. Not as long as someone asked me nicely not to. So, Gunner, why don't you ask me.'

Looked up at Bingo.

'What should he say?'

Bingo grinned.

'How about, "Please don't put me in the canal, Mr Sellars"?'

'Perfect,' said Sellars. 'Off you go, Gunner.'

Gunner could feel tears in his eyes, tears of humiliation and frustration as much as anything else. Felt Bingo press his boot down. Told himself that he didn't have a choice, he had to say it if he was going to get out of this alive.

'Please don't put me in the canal, Sellars.'

'*Mr* Sellars,' said Bingo.

'Please don't put me in the canal, Mr Sellars.'

A big smile broke on Sellars' face.

'There, that wasn't so hard, was it.' He leant into Gunner's face. 'Not sure if you've realised it, but you're a fucking prick.'

He stood up.

'Right, boys, let's go,' he said. 'We've got more celebrating to do.'

Gunner lay there, felt the tears run down his cheeks, and listened to their steps crunching on the gravel path. Waited until he heard a couple of cars start up before he tried to sit up. Soon as he moved his leg, he doubled in pain. More than he could stand.

He lay there, watched the stars above. Could hear Strand telling everyone to pack up. Watched a rat run along the canal bank and told himself he was alive, that was what mattered. That he would live to fight another day, and no matter what he did, he would wipe the fucking grin off Malky Sellars' face.

38

By the time Gunner got to Nan's flat he was exhausted. This was the most he had walked for a long while. His leg was killing him, Sellars battering his fist down on it hadn't helped either. He managed to make it up the stairs and knocked on the door. Had a feeling she might be asleep but the door opened immediately. Nan's worried face in the doorway.

'What happened to you?' she asked. 'You look like you're about to pass out.'

'Nothing, was a break-in at the Bond, just wanted me to have a look.'

Not quite sure why he'd lied, but he had. Just didn't want to relive it again. Drummond's dead eyes staring up at nothing, the humiliation at the hands of a cunt like Sellars.

'Can I sit down?' he asked. 'My leg's killing me.'

Nan nodded, pointed at a table with two chairs.

'Sit there, I'll be back in a minute.'

He did. Nan's flat was warm, smelt of stewed tea and the bunch of sweet peas in a jam jar on the table. She disappeared behind a curtain strung across the corner of the wee room, reappeared in a dressing gown, a scarf tied in her hair.

'Tea?' she asked.

Gunner nodded and she picked up the kettle, lit the burner. He watched her, the way she moved. She'd had a tough life, Nan, but she had an elegance about her, a way of doing things. He picked up her cigarettes, lit one. She took it out his mouth, took a drag, and put it back, smiled. He asked what he had to ask.

'Where is he, Nan?'

She looked at him. 'Like you said, Joe, it's better you don't know. He's nowhere near here, he's at some pal's outside Glasgow. I don't even know where it is.'

'He has to stay there,' said Gunner. 'He's in real trouble. They shot someone today in broad daylight, someone who'd done a lot less than him.'

She nodded.

'There's a number, I can call it in the morning, ten o'clock. He'll answer it. I'll tell him.'

She turned back to the tea things, not before Gunner saw the tears welling in her eyes. He got up, stood beside her, put his arm around her shoulders.

'He'll be OK, Nan, you know what Victor's like, the bugger could lose a fiver and he'd find a tenner the next day.'

She turned and looked at him, took his hand in hers.

'You're staying.'

He wasn't sure if it was a question or a statement. He nodded.

'That OK?'

She kissed him. Knew then he was staying for sure. He put his hand into the gap in her dressing gown. She felt warm, soft.

'I'll get us something to drink,' she said. 'Get in bed.'

Gunner sat on the end of the bed, took his shoes off, was unbuttoning his shirt when she reappeared, a half-bottle of whisky and two glasses in her hand. Dressing gown gone, skin pale and luminescent in the glow of the wee lamp by the bed. He pulled her to him, wrapped his arms around her. She batted him off, climbed over him, and got in beneath the clothes.

'Hurry up and get undressed,' she said. 'It's bloody freezing.'

Afterward, they lay there listening to some dance band on the radio, only light the two orange tips of their cigarettes. Nan moved her hand down his leg, settled on the scar by his knee.

'What happened there then?'

'Bomb,' he said. 'Shrapnel.'

She found his hand under the covers, held it.

'I don't love Victor, you know,' she said. 'I used to . . .' She tailed off.

'It doesn't matter.'

She smiled. 'Might do to him. Where did it happen?'

'Dunkirk, couple of miles outside. We were in a farmhouse, what was left of a farmhouse. Been there for a day or so, trying to avoid the bombers, thought we had.' He took a drag of his cigarette, light illuminating Nan's face lying next to his. 'I remember hearing them coming over, they were low, lower than usual. You could hear the noise in your chest, the thumping of the engines. One hit close by, you could feel the shock in the earth. Billy, the guy I was with, turned to me and he said, "Fuck sake, they're close now." And that was it, the last thing I remember.'

She pulled him close, told him everything was going to be all right. And he wanted to believe her, because sometimes that's your best hope and the only hope you have. The belief that everything is going to be all right.

39

Gunner was running along a road in France, bombs whistling down behind him, feeling like his lungs would burst any second. Could hear the planes above him closing in, some guy screaming. A truck up ahead of him exploded, body flying up into the air. Didn't know how much longer he could keep running, leg felt like it was going to give way any second. Couldn't see anywhere to take shelter, had to keep going, he had to. A bomb exploded beside the road, felt the blast hit him and he tumbled forward, ended up sprawled out on the road, blood from somewhere running into his eyes.

Then he felt his arm being shaken. Woke up to find Nan standing by the bed with a cup of tea. He sat up, blinking at the sunlight flooding the wee room, trying to get back to the here and now.

'Breakfast in bed?' he asked, sitting up.

'Aye well, don't get used to it,' said Nan. 'It'll no happen again.' She was dressed, pulling her coat on. 'The wee woman across the street's got a phone. If I give her a tanner she lets me use it. I'll call Victor and tell him to stay put.'

Gunner sipped his tea, nodded. 'Make sure he gets it, Nan, it's serious. He can't come back to Glasgow.'

She came over, sat on the bed. Started fiddling with a loose thread from the candlewick bedspread. Looked at him.

'Last night, Joe, it was nice and all, but we're ships in the night, eh?'

Gunner nodded. Told her what she wanted to hear. 'Ships in the night.'

She smiled and stood up. Put a scarf on her head, tied it and started tucking her hair under it.

'I'll be back in ten minutes or so,' she smiled. 'Get your arse out of bed pronto, I've got to get to work.'

He saluted. 'Roger.'

He watched her go, pulling the door behind her. He lay back in the warmth of the bed for a few minutes, the smell of her perfume still on the sheets. He could hear a coal cart outside, the sound of the horse's hoofs on the street, the driver shouting he was here. All he really wanted to do was close his eyes and go back to sleep, to lie there until Nan came back, persuade her to come in beside him. Tell her they could be more than ships in the night.

When Nan got back, Gunner was shaving at the kitchen sink. Victor's soap and razor. She came in, sat down at the table, took her scarf off and lit up.

'Go OK?' he asked.

She nodded. 'I told him, he seemed to get it. He asked if you were OK.'

Gunner wiped the last of the soap off his face, took his shirt off the back of the chair, and then he heard it. The clatter of boots on the stair.

He looked over at Nan. She was staring down at the table.

'Nan?'

She didn't move, didn't take her eyes off the table, didn't speak.

'Nan?'

She looked up, eyes wet with tears. 'I'm sorry,' she said.

He stood there listening to the footsteps getting louder and louder.

'Who'd you phone, Nan? Who?'

She shook her head. 'I had to, Joe. I had to.'

There was a loud banging at the door.

She stood up, wiped her eyes and pulled the door open. Two Military Police walked in, followed by Moore, suited and booted as always. He looked around, seemed surprised at how small the flat was. He looked over at Gunner. Smiled.

'Get dressed,' he said and walked back out the flat.

'Why?' asked Gunner, looking at Nan. She didn't answer.

'Hurry up!' barked one of the MPs, handing Gunner his shoes.

He started putting them on and Nan started crying, proper crying.

'Joe I . . .'

He finished tying his shoelaces, put his jacket on. The MPs were standing at the door waiting on him.

He took his tie from the mantelpiece, bent over and kissed her on the top of the head.

'It's OK,' he said. 'Ships in the night, eh?'

40

Gunner was sat in the back of the car, wedged between the two MPs. He'd thought they would take him to the barracks or Central, but now he'd the feeling they were heading to the camp at Thornliebank. If that was the case then it wasn't good; two bodies had come out of there already and he didn't want to be the third.

The car swung over towards the George V Bridge. The row of warehouses on the docks was still smouldering, smoke still drifting over the boats banked up along the side of the Clyde. Yesterday morning and his chat with Drummond seemed a long time ago now. They drove onto the bridge, crossed the river and headed south down Pollokshaws Road. Gunner's heart sank; it was the way to the camp.

'Where we going?' he asked.

No response from the MPs or Moore. He leant forward, pretended he was shifting his weight, tried to see if he could lunge over, open the doors and roll out the car.

'Don't even think about it.' A bored tone to the MP's voice.

Moore turned round from the front seat, looked at him with pity.

'How'd you get Nan to do it?' Gunner asked.

Moore yawned, took out his cigarettes.

'Easily,' he said. 'She has a criminal record and she's working as a prostitute.'

'She's not a prostitute, she's a dancer.' He realised how weak it sounded as he said it.

'She works for Malcolm Sellars. So, I told her I'd let Sellars know she was passing information back to the police unless—'

'Was she?' asked Gunner.

Moore shook his head, blew out a stream of smoke.

'But Sellars doesn't know that and, probably rightly, she's far more scared of him than she is of us.'

Gunner shook his head. 'You really are a prick, Moore.'

'I wouldn't be too concerned about her, Gunner. Sorry to disappoint you, but you weren't our first choice. We wanted Victor but she wouldn't give him up, not even with the threat of Sellars. But she gave you up pretty easy.' He turned round in the seat. 'So where is he, Gunner?'

'I don't know.'

Moore turned back, sighed, rubbed at the condensation on the window.

'You're not an idiot, Gunner. You will change your mind, tell us where he is. How long that takes is up to you.'

Twenty minutes later they were heading up the dirt road to the camp. They stopped briefly at the security gate and after the guard saw it was Moore, he waved them through. They drove round the side of the main camp and pulled up outside the hut where the Black prisoners were kept. The two MPs hustled Gunner out of the car and dragged him up the steps to the door. A couple of good hard punches to the kidneys and they pushed him in, locked the door behind him.

He stayed down on the floor for a while, letting the pain subside, feeling sorry for himself. He waited until he heard the car drive off and pushed himself up to his feet, looked around. The hut was about the size of a classroom, marks still on the floor where the cots and lockers had been laid out. Apart from a German newspaper lying under one of the barred windows, it was empty, everything gone. Gunner sat down against the wall. Looked like the move had been done in a hurry, no trace of the Black prisoners left, was as if they'd never been there. Didn't give him much hope.

It was dark when they came back. He was half asleep when the door burst open and the two MPs were on him before he'd a chance to get up. They rained down boots and fists, he felt his nose go, warm blood pouring down his face. He saw a boot draw back before it hit him square in the head, hurt like anything. He gave up, curled into a ball and tried to protect himself. It didn't do much good, blows and kicks kept coming, raining down until he let go and plunged into the welcoming darkness.

He was wet, spluttering, he opened his eyes and then shut them again as the pain hit. He was upright now, tied to a chair, hands behind his back, rope pulled tight enough to make his wrists bleed. He ran his tongue round the inside of his mouth, tasted blood.

'Are you with us, Gunner?'

He tried to focus, eyes bleary, head spinning. He recognised the voice. Moore. Another bucket of water. He coughed, shook his head, blinked, tried to get the water out of his eyes. The room slowly came into focus. It was small, only light a bare overhead bulb. He guessed he was still in the camp but he had no real way of telling. It was still dark outside, just the noise of the wind blowing through trees.

Moore stood in front of him flicking through a file. The MPs had gone, replaced by two bruisers stripped down to vests and trousers, braces dangling. He was pretty sure one of them was the driver. They stood behind Moore, smoking and looking bored. No uniforms this time, no identification. Not a good sign.

Moore snapped the file shut and stared at him. 'Where is he?'

'Who?' said Gunner.

Moore sighed. 'Your brother. The traitor.'

'He's not a traitor,' said Gunner.

Moore raised an eyebrow.

'Really? What's he been telling you then? Let me guess. He's just a friend of the Soviet people, only in this to fight fascism, the real war is against poverty and injustice.' He smiled. 'You look guilty, Gunner. Hit the nail, did I?'

He nodded to one of the heavies. He came towards Gunner. He was young, didn't look much more than a teenager, but his arms were thick, roped with muscle. He grinned. Looked like he was going to enjoy himself. He punched Gunner in the stomach. Hard.

Gunner jerked back, then fell forward, was sick down his front. Moore stepped back sharply, a disapproving look on his face.

'Where. Is. He?'

'I don't know,' said Gunner. 'And even if I did, I wouldn't tell you, you cunt.'

Moore looked bored, nodded. Another punch, this time in his kidneys. Gunner closed his eyes, tried to ride out the pain. Wasn't easy.

Moore leant in close.

'Gunner, I don't have time for this. You are going to tell me where he is, we both know that. Unless you start talking, these too will work you over, and every time you pass out from the pain they'll bring you round so they can do it again. They won't kill you, Gunner, they'll just make it go on and on and on. That what you want, is it?'

Gunner shook his head. 'What I want is for you to kiss my fucking arse.'

Moore tutted. 'Nothing more tedious than bravado. Always such a waste of time.' He gathered up his papers. 'Boys, I'll be back in a couple of hours.'

It took a good half an hour before Gunner passed out for the second time. They'd taken him off the chair and taken turns kicking him around the floor. Then they brought him round and started again. At some point he pissed himself and at some point one of his teeth came out. It was only when one of the bruisers kicked him in the side of the head that he passed out again. Another couple of buckets of water and he came round. Immediately wished he hadn't, pain was hitting him from everywhere, whole body screaming in agony. He stuck a shaking finger in his mouth, felt the space where his tooth had been.

He lay there, watched the two of them wiping the blood off their hands with an old towel. The older one came over and undid his fly, pissed on him while the other one laughed. He finished, buttoned his fly up and knelt down beside him.

'We're taking a little break. Gonnae go for a beer in the mess hall.' He sounded east coast, Fife, somewhere like that. 'Then we're going to go to the stores, see if they've got any bolt cutters.'

He leant forward, grabbed Gunner's balls, squeezed them hard. Gunner hardly noticed. Just more pain.

'So why don't you lie here for a while and have a wee think about what we're going to do with those bolt cutters when we get back.'

41

Gunner lay there, listened to them laughing, locking the door behind them when they went. They knew what they were doing, all right. Leaving him there imagining what was going to happen to him was worse than the reality. He'd done it himself often enough, left someone stewing in the cells with the promise of a beating to come. He had to stop thinking about it, to try and use this time when they were gone.

He dragged himself over to the wall and propped himself up. He sat there looking at his finger sticking out the wrong way and wondered what the hell he was going to do. Even if he wanted to tell them, he had no idea where Victor was. They weren't going to believe that. They were just going to keep at him until he passed out permanently.

Gunner wondered how Victor was doing, could only hope he was keeping his head down. Knew one thing about his brother: Victor wouldn't survive a beating like he'd just had. He'd talk, and if he did that, Nickerson was finished. Maybe he was already. They had Troz, they were all set to go. Weren't going to let someone like Nickerson stop them.

There was a noise at the door. Gunner tried to stand up, looked round the empty room, desperately trying to see something he could use as a weapon. Nothing. He stood behind the chair, leaning on the back for support. The door swung open.

'Fuck sake. They've made a right fucking mess of you.'

'Paolo?' asked Gunner. 'Is that you?'

He'd never been so happy to see the wee tout in his life.

Paolo came into the room, usual cardigan and trousers with a white P painted on them. He eased the door shut behind him.

'Jesus,' he said, looking Gunner up and down. 'They did you over good and proper. Cannae say I blame them. I'd have joined in if they'd asked me.'

'What you doing here, Paolo?' asked Gunner, hope rising. 'Can you get me out?'

The ratty wee Italian looked him up and down, noticed the dark stain on his trousers. Laughed.

'Pissed yourself, did you? Clatty bastard. I'll remember that.'

He walked over to the window, looked out.

'If it was up to me I'd leave you in here to get kicked to fuck some more, but somebody wants you out.'

'Who?' asked Gunner, not really following what was going on.

'Seems Matthew Sellars has taken a wee fancy to you, wants you out of here.'

'What?'

'You heard,' said Paolo. 'And what Matthew Sellars wants, Matthew Sellars gets. Can you walk?'

Gunner let go of the chair, took a few wobbly steps. Paolo swore, put Gunner's arm round his shoulders.

'C'mon, before those cunts get back.'

They stood at the door and Paolo opened it a crack. 'There's a hut across the way, we're gonnae make for that first. OK?'

Gunner nodded, hoped he could make it.

They stepped out the door and into the rainy night. Gunner could hear the noise of a piano from the mess, could see the lights of the main camp over to the left. They scuttled across the yard, Paolo half dragging Gunner, and made it to the shadows of the hut. Paolo leant him against the hut wall and looked up and down the camp. All quiet.

Paolo pointed at the perimeter fence. 'Can you get over there?' he asked.

Gunner nodded. He wasn't sure he could, but he was going to try. Anything was better than being in that hut. He put his arm back round Paolo's shoulders, let him take some of the weight, and they headed for the perimeter fence. Gunner was in real pain, leg and everything else crying out with each step, but he knew he had to keep going. Bit down on his lip to stop moaning.

Up ahead, one of the hut doors opened and a guard stepped out, the flash of a match as he lit his cigarette. They froze, pushed themselves back into the shadows. They were so close they could hear him humming 'Danny Boy' under his breath. They stood there willing him back in. Two agonising minutes later he finished his cigarette and flicked it away in a shower of sparks. The door creaked, then banged, and he was gone. Time to go.

By the time they got to the fence Paolo was wilting under the strain, both of them doused in sweat. They collapsed on the ground, both breathing heavily.

'You OK?' Gunner managed to get out.

Paolo nodded. 'You weigh a fucking ton.'

They sat there for a minute or so, getting their breath back. The camp was quiet but they both knew the two bruisers could come back any minute. Gunner looked up at the fence. It was about twelve feet high, wooden supports ringed with barbed wire. His heart sank.

'How do we get out?' he asked. 'I can't get over that.'

'We? You're joking, aren't you? I'm going nowhere, pal,' said Paolo. 'It's you Sellars wants, no me.'

He nodded into the darkness.

'About twenty yards down there there's a pole with a white paint mark on it, wire at the bottom's only held on wi' tacks, just pull it and it'll come away. Remember and put it back when you go through, we need that way in and out.'

Sudden noise of piano music and people talking; someone had opened the mess door. Paolo looked back. Light was spilling from the open door.

'Go now! Fucking move!'

'Thanks, Paolo,' said Gunner.

'Aye, don't thank me. Far as I'm concerned, you're a cunt, always were, always will be. Thank your pal Sellars, and you make sure and tell him how I saved your life. Now beat it!'

Gunner crawled along by the perimeter fence, hurt a bit less than walking, until he came to the pole with the white mark. He pulled at the wire, thanked God when it came away easily. He lay down on his front, snaked his way under it, and got through to the other side. He turned and pulled the wire back into position the best he could. Pulled himself up with help from the wooden fence post and tried to make out where he could go in the dark.

The ground in front seemed to fall away after a few yards so he made for that. A few painful steps later he was standing on a ridge. Was sure he could hear the noise of a river in the gorge below. That had to lead to another river, maybe the Clyde? It seemed as good an idea as any. He started to edge his way down, being careful. Hoping he wouldn't fall, hoping the bruisers wouldn't come after him.

Twenty minutes later Gunner stopped, sat down by some trees. He knew he should keep going, put as much distance between him and the camp as he could, but he just wasn't able. He was exhausted, his body hurt too much. He searched in his pockets for cigarettes, couldn't find any. He tried the back pocket of his trousers, found a packet, and pulled it out. He looked at it. It wasn't cigarettes, it was the packet of morphine syrettes. He opened it, two were empty, squashed and burst but there was one left, one full one.

He looked across the hills towards the camp, didn't see any torches, car headlights. Maybe they were still in the mess, supping at their pints. He stood up, managed to walk a couple of hundred yards, found a tree that had been blown over. He settled into the sandy hollow beneath it, climbed in between the big roots. He tried to cover himself in leaves and took the syrette out of his pocket. He stopped, looked at the little grey metal tube. Knew he'd be better keeping going, trying to get to Glasgow before dawn, but he knew he wasn't going to.

He took the cap off with a shaky hand and stuck the needle into the skin of his stomach. Whatever was going to happen to him could wait. He settled down against the roots, the earth felt soft underneath him, a beetle crawled across his hand and he watched it. It stopped, stuck its antenna in the air as if it were listening for something. The trees around him creaked, swaying slightly in the wind. He ran his tongue across his lips, wished he'd some water. The syrette fell to the ground, he smiled, watched a drop of blood rise from the little hole in his skin until his eyes flickered and closed.

42

The rain woke Gunner up. The hollow under the tree roots was sheltered but not sheltered enough, he was getting wet. He sat up and looked around, couldn't see much; was still dark but the moon was bright in the sky. He looked at his watch. The face was smashed, stopped at half seven, must have been the time when they started kicking him around the room last night. He yawned, still drowsy. The morphine would usually knock him out for a couple of hours. By his best estimate that made it about two in the morning. He shivered. It was cold, time to get going.

Gunner stood up, tried the weight on his leg, not too bad. He took a piss and even in the gloom could see it was dark with blood. Still, the morphine was doing its job, the pain was still constant but it was in the background now, bearable.

Happy as he was to be out of that room and away from the two bruisers, he knew it came with a price. Matthew Sellars would be looking for something in return, something big. Was getting a bit too involved with the Sellars brothers for his liking. One rescuing him and one taking great delight in kicking him around. Dealing with them would have to wait. He had to get back to Glasgow, and quick.

He'd gone about half a mile when he stepped out the trees and onto the edge of a ploughed field. There was a road over to the left. He recognised it. It was the field where he'd met Walter and the rest of the conchies. The moon had disappeared, rain was coming down harder now, the distant rumble of thunder. That made his mind up, he'd go to the barn where they slept, find Walter and stay there for the night, head for Glasgow as soon as it got light.

He peered into the slanting rain, trying to get his bearings. There were shadows at the far end of the field. Had to be the farm buildings. He set off, tripping over the ridges of turned earth more than once. As he got nearer the buildings he stopped, hoping the farm dogs were all asleep for the night. The barn was off to the left, a tall black shape outlined against the grey sky.

Gunner pulled the wee door set in the big barn doors open and stepped inside, stood for a minute, shook the water off. As his eyes adjusted to the dark, he made out some cows tied up by the side wall. They looked at him, shuffled around, one gave out a low moo. He eased around their warm bodies heading for the ladder up to the loft. He was halfway up when he heard the click and rasp of a Zippo and a face appeared over the edge of the loft above him. Features illuminated by the lighter's yellow flame.

'Who's there?' the man said uncertainly.

Gunner kept climbing. 'Sergeant Gunner,' he said, hauling himself up with some difficulty. 'Is Walter here?'

The man shook his head. Around him the other conchies were groaning, waking up, a few shouts of 'Go back to sleep!'

He lowered his voice. 'Walter's gone.'

'Gone?' asked Gunner. 'Gone where?'

'I don't know. He went with the other policeman; they came for him a couple of hours ago.'

Gunner couldn't work out what was going on. 'What other policeman?'

'I was half asleep,' said the man apologetically. 'I didn't hear his name. It was the one that was here with you before, the one that sat in the car.'

'Fraser?' said Gunner, amazed. Couldn't be.

'I don't know his name,' said the man. 'He was tall, blond hair, younger than you.'

Had to be Fraser. Gunner sat back on the hay. What the fuck was Fraser doing here? And why had he taken Walter?

'Where did they go?' he asked.

The man shook his head again. 'I don't know. He showed Walter some papers and they went off.' He peered at him. 'Are you OK?'

'Not really,' said Gunner. 'Why?'

'Non-com medic.' he said. 'Served for a while then I couldn't stand it any longer. Let me have a look at your hand.'

Ten minutes later Gunner had a tight bandage torn from a sheet round his ribs to keep the broken ones steady, iodine in his cuts and a makeshift splint round his broken finger. Between all that and the hunk of bread and pint of milk he wolfed down, he felt a hundred times better. Good enough to try and head for Glasgow.

'What time is it?' he asked.

'Don't know,' said the man. 'I had a watch, but the farmer's son broke it.'

Gunner held his wrist up, showed him the smashed face.

'I know how you feel.'

The man grinned.

'It's probably about two, maybe three.'

'How do I get to Glasgow from here?' asked Gunner.

The man stood up and walked over to the wee window set in the thick stone wall of the barn. They looked out. The man pointed. Wasn't much use, Gunner couldn't see where he meant.

'Down that way, half a mile or so, there's a back road, will take you down into Clarkston and then into town. Then a couple of hours' walk you'll be back in Glasgow.'

'Must be strange being this close?' asked Gunner.

The man nodded. 'I used to live a couple of miles from here. Cambuslang. Seems a lot further than that now. We're cut off here, no newspapers, no radio. Couldn't believe the bombs the other night. We were worried that was it, that an invasion had started. You were overseas?'

Gunner nodded.

'France. Funny thing is, it looked a lot like here, green fields, farmhouses, wee roads. And we had no real idea what was going on either. Just had to keep moving towards the coast no matter what happened, that's all they told us.'

Gunner stuck his good hand out. 'Thank you. I don't even know your name.'

The man smiled: 'It's not important.' He reached into his trouser pocket, brought out a little leaflet with a picture of Christ on the front, a beatific expression, hands aloft. 'If you want to thank me, read this.' He pressed it into Gunner's hand 'Good luck.'

43

Gunner made his way down the ladder, crossed by the shuffling cows, opened the door, and stepped out into the night. Looked up at the sky. At least the rain had stopped. He started walking, decided to stick to the fields until he got to the road, stay out the way in case they were looking for him. Once he got to the main road he could hitch a lift.

He still had no idea what Fraser was doing up here picking up Walter. Had they guessed he might head for the conchies? No, they would have been waiting for him there. But nobody knew that he knew Walter. Nobody but Fraser, that is; he'd seen him from the car that day they came up. Didn't make any sense.

The road was visible in the distance, not far to go now. Then he heard it. Heard it before he saw it, a lone truck coming back up the road, heading towards the camp. The headlights were covered, just little slits of light in the darkness. It was still enough to identify it as an army Bedford. God knows he'd seen and heard enough of them this past couple of years. He looked around, saw a little copse of bushes and trees off to his left. Better safe than sorry. He climbed over the dry-stone wall and dropped over the other side.

The morphine was wearing off now; his leg was starting to

hurt again, it was easier to crawl than walk. He was just about there when a fox jumped out of the bushes into his path. It stood there for a minute, frozen. There was fresh red blood on its snout, he must have disturbed it eating a rabbit or something. It moved away, the white tip of its tail slowly disappearing into the darkness. The lorry was getting nearer, he could hear the engine straining as it climbed the hill. He scuttled into the bushes and settled himself down to wait for it to go by.

What would they do with Walter? They were probably hoping he knew where Victor was, but Gunner couldn't see that. Victor had been gone from the conchie farm for weeks; how would Walter know where he was? Unless Walter was caught up in it all too, that was. Nothing would surprise him now. They wouldn't take him back to Glasgow if they wanted to find out what he knew, they would do it somewhere around here.

The headlights swung round the corner, then the truck turned and kept going, heading past him and up the hill towards the camp. Gunner waited another couple of minutes before he stood up; being careful. Was hard to see anything much in the gloom. He started walking in what he hoped was the direction of Glasgow; was getting hard to tell. Had only gone a few hundred yards when he smelt it. Manure and something sharper under it like rotten eggs. He kept walking and it got stronger. Took a while to work out where he'd smelt it before. It had been in France on one of the farms they had stayed in; it was the smell of a slurry pit.

He kept walking in the direction of the smell, knew he had to look, even if he didn't want to, was scared of what he might see. Wasn't long until he could see the outline of a broken-down fence surrounding a concrete pit, stink of animal waste and whatever else the farmer had dumped in there getting stronger the closer he got.

Smell got so bad he covered his mouth and nose with his sleeve and edged forward. He climbed over the fence, made sure he didn't get too near to the edge, and looked over the pool of stinking mud. Thought he saw a lump over at the other side, a flash of white. He edged round until he could see properly.

Walter's shoulders and arms were on the edge of the pool, rest of his body trapped in the stinking heavy mud. Gunner edged closer. They must have had a go at getting him to tell them where Victor was before they pushed him in. His nose was bloody and broken, one eye dark and swollen shut, two front teeth missing. Finger joints at funny angles.

Gunner looked away and threw up. Wasn't sure if it was the smell of the slurry or what had happened to Walter. He couldn't have been dead when they pushed him in, maybe just unconscious, came round and tried to crawl out. Too weak from the beating to make it. Gunner made himself take another look, bright moonlight illuminating the scene, tried not to see the fear etched on what was left of Walter's battered face. He said the Lord's Prayer for him under his breath, then walked away into the night.

44

He managed another half a mile or so before he had to stop and rest again. He sat down on the grass, patting his suit looking for cigarettes he knew he didn't have. Tried not to think about poor harmless Walter slowly sinking down into the dark slurry. By the time the sun came up no one would even know he had been there. And all because of Fraser bloody Lockhart. Fraser was the only one who knew about the connection between Walter and Victor. Fraser who could speak German maybe better than he had let on. Fraser who had been with him every step of this investigation, sticking close, saying nothing, taking it all in. Was hard to believe it, but it looked like Fraser was playing a different game.

So Fraser had to be working for Moore somehow. But *how* could Fraser be working for Moore? He was a nineteen-year-old police cadet from bloody Perth. It didn't make sense, but then nothing much had since he'd come back to Glasgow. Nothing to do but keep going, he got up, started walking, ignoring the pain. Hoped he'd be back in Glasgow for first light.

Was just about to start walking when he heard something behind him. Probably another fox or a badger. A few minutes further down the path he heard it again, definitely footsteps this time. He was being followed.

He walked faster, trying to put some distance between him and whoever it was, then ducked off the path and into the trees. Found a fallen branch, held it in his hand ready to batter his follower.

Footsteps. He edged closer to the path. Held the branch above his head, ready to strike. As the steps approached, he moved forwards, was just about to bring the branch down when he realised who it was.

'Victor! For fuck sake! I almost killed you!'

Victor looked as surprised as he did.

'Joe, is that you?'

'Course it's me. What the fuck are you doing here?'

'I went up to see Walter and that Christian guy told me he'd gone off with the polis and then you'd come looking for him. Told me you were making for Glasgow, showed me the way he showed you.' He peered at Gunner, at the cuts and bruises on his face. 'What happened to you? And why were you looking for Walter? I thought your boys had taken him?'

'We need to talk,' said Gunner. 'I need to show you something.'

Victor didn't move. 'I can't. I've got to wait here.'

'Wait for what?'

'The plane,' he said quietly. 'The plane.'

'What plane?' asked Gunner, getting exasperated, and then he realised. 'Hang on, are you telling me Hess is coming here?'

Victor nodded, looked at his watch.

'In about an hour. He's going to bail over here, ditch the plane.'

They sat in silence for a minute or so, Gunner trying to take it all in and not get angry with Victor. Less than ten or so miles from Glasgow and not a sound to be heard.

'Why here?' asked Gunner.

'He's come to meet some arsehole duke with an estate around here. He believes in astrology and the master race as well. All the shite Hess does. This duke's friends from the Anglo-German Friendship Society are running out of time. They want Hess to meet the King as soon as. Start talking about carving up Europe. They need this settled before the Russian front opens up.'

'Jesus Christ. You got any fags?' Gunner asked.

They sat down on the bank of a wee burn; Gunner lit up, drew the smoke deep into his lungs. Felt dizzy, then felt better.

'What's all this got to do with Walter?' Gunner asked. 'I thought he was a bloody devout Christian as well, showed me the cross around his neck.'

'He's a friend of the Soviet people. Christianity was his cover story.'

Gunner breathed in, tried to keep his temper in check.

'Victor. I swear if you don't stop this shite and tell me what's really going on I'm going to fucking kill you. I got kicked halfway to fuck tonight because of your "friendship with the Soviet people" shite. Either you come clean, or I swear I am going to fucking kill you.'

Victor looked at him. Seemed to make up his mind.

'Walter and I were put in that farm to be in place when the plane came, so we'd be close. The trouble was, I couldnae stick it, that's why I left for Glasgow. Walter's made of sterner stuff.'

Victor stood up, start walking back and forward.

'Trouble is, the messages from our comrades are coming in

to Walter, he's a radio hidden in that barn. I haven't heard from him for forty-eight hours, no update. So this information could all be out of date by now. Might not be coming at all or he might be landing somewhere else. Need to find Walter and find out what he knows. Why did they take him anyway?'

'They didn't,' said Gunner. 'He's been beaten up and chucked in a fucking slurry pit. He's dead.'

Victor turned 'What? Are you serious?'

Gunner nodded.

'Saw it myself. Poor fucker.'

Victor looked dumbstruck.

'Walter? Who'd do that to Walter?'

'I think a bloke called Fraser Lockhart did it. Drummond's boy.'

'Your Drummond?' asked Victor.

'Not any more. Drummond's dead too.'

'What?'

'Nothing to do with all this, he got warnings from the Sellars boys, chose to ignore them. We need to get to Glasgow soon as.'

Victor nodded.

'I know but I can't believe Walter's dead. It's not . . .'

He broke off, cocked his head.

'Oh Christ, can you hear that?'

Gunner listened. Heard nothing. 'What?'

'That noise,' said Victor. 'I think it's a plane.'

Gunner could hear the engine now, sounded like a Messerschmitt. He knew that sound from France. They looked at each other.

'Hess!'

They ran out the shade of the woods onto a field of young potato plants, trampling them as they went. They could still hear the noise, but there was no sign of the plane. They scanned the sky, first rays of sun just starting to light it up, trying to pinpoint exactly where the noise was coming from.

'There!' shouted Victor. 'Over there!'

Gunner looked up. Sure enough, off in the distance, there was a Messerschmitt coming over the Cathkin hills. It was flying low, wings swinging up and down, looked like the pilot had lost control. Then the engine sound stopped. They could hear the pilot trying to start it again. It spluttered a few times, then came back to life.

'Christ, I thought he was a goner then,' said Victor.

'So did I,' said Gunner. 'Looks like he's got . . .'

He stopped. The engine noise had cut out again. They watched; the pilot must be struggling to start it again, but it wouldn't catch. The plane began to lose height quickly.

'It's crashing!' shouted Victor. 'He's going to crash!'

All they could do was watch as the nose of the plane started to tip forward. It looked like it was about to go into a nosedive when a parachute suddenly flowered above it and was tugged up into the sky.

'He's bailed, the bastard's bailed!' shouted Gunner.

The parachute drifted along in the wind as the plane below it accelerated downwards, heading towards the hills. It was swaying wildly from side to side now. The strain was too much, one of the wings flew off and started spinning towards the ground. The plane passed it, disappeared behind the line of the hills. For a moment there was silence, and then there was a bright light, and the boom of the explosion hit them.

They shielded their eyes, both of them swearing as dust and bits of grass were blown into their faces. Gunner wiped his eyes with his sleeve, blinked. Through the haze he could see the parachute drifting closer to the ground. It was so close they could see the figure under it now, frantically pulling the strings to steer himself away from the fiery wreckage. He managed to pull it left and the parachute drifted away and disappeared behind a line of trees.

Victor grabbed Gunner. 'Come on. We have to get to him before anyone else does. Run!'

45

The plane must have landed further away than they thought; they had been walking for a mile at least. Nothing to do but keep going, making their way across the fields and woods towards the smoke drifting up into the sky. Gunner was doing a kind of lopsided trot, trying to keep the weight off his left leg. Victor kept running on ahead, then waiting exasperated as Gunner struggled to keep up. He was trying, but the beating back at the camp had taken it out of him, even with the bandages his ribs were in agony; he'd started coughing up blood as well.

'Over here!' shouted Victor.

Gunner caught up, saw what he was looking at. The field in front of them was covered in scraps of wreckage shining in the grass. Little bits of engine casing, half a wooden seat, a metal panel with a number 6 on it. There was a smell of burning in the misty air, engine fuel and rubber. The smoke they had seen up ahead was tailing off now, just a thin stream emerging from behind the hills up ahead rather than the gutting, oily clouds of before.

Gunner looked up at the hills, cursed, and started climbing; Victor was way ahead of him in minutes, disappearing over the top, leaving Gunner to struggle upwards through the thick heather. He stopped for a minute, tried to catch his breath, felt like he couldn't get enough air into his lungs, shallow breaths making him dizzy. Eventually, he made it to the top. Victor was standing there, breathing heavily, steam coming off him like a horse.

'He's here, Joe, he's really fucking here.'

They looked down at the crash site, neither of them saying anything, just trying to take it in. There were ten or so little oily fires dotted around the field, sooty flames lighting up the area around them. The main body of the plane was over to the left. It had broken up into several large pieces: the cockpit area, a wing with a swastika on it, a strip of fuselage burnt black. The pieces were stretched in a line of fifty yards or so, half buried amongst the scorched and blackened grass of the field.

The little fires lit up a figure standing off to the side. The man was tall, thin, balding, dressed in a Luftwaffe uniform and a flying jacket; the right leg of his trousers was ripped, blood staining the grey cloth.

Gunner nudged Victor and pointed. 'That him?'

Victor nodded, 'Looks like it.'

Gunner stared down at him, trying to get a clear view through the smoke and flickering lights from the fires. Whoever he was, he definitely looked like the two murdered Germans. Same height, same build. There was a pop and the fire next to him flared up. Hess stepped back and Gunner saw another man. He'd an old tweed jacket on, cords and boots, looked like a farmer. He was standing about ten feet from Hess, shotgun pointed squarely at the German's chest. The two men weren't moving, just standing staring at each other, stuck in a stand-off.

'C'mon,' said Victor, grabbing at Gunner. 'Let's get down there.'

Gunner didn't move. 'And do what exactly?'

Victor looked at him as if he were mad. 'Get Hess.'

'Victor, there's a farmer down there with a shotgun. What are we going to do, wrestle it off him and shoot the fucker?'

'I don't know but we've got to do . . .' He turned, looked down the hill. 'What's that?'

They stopped, listened. It was faint but it sounded like the rumble of car engines. No blackout headlights this time, three sets of bright headlights emerged from behind the trees and lit up the field. They pulled off the road and started bumping their way across the field towards the wreckage. Hess turned to watch, went to walk towards them, but the farmer barked something, raised his rifle. Hess held his hands up to placate him, stayed where he was as the three cars pulled up beside them.

'Who are they?' asked Victor.

Gunner shook his head. 'No idea.'

The car doors opened and a couple of men in suits got out, followed by some MPs from the car behind. They stood there looking at Hess and the farmer and the burning wreckage, not quite sure what they should be doing. The passenger door of the third car opened and a figure emerged and walked straight towards Hess.

Gunner squinted, trying to make out who it was. The figure stepped into the car headlights and Gunner saw the familiar grey suit. It was Moore. He took his hat off and walked towards Hess, hand held out. They shook hands and smiled at each other. Moore took a packet of cigarettes out of his pocket, offered

Hess one. He took it, and the two of them stood there smoking and chatting, for all the world like two old pals who'd met on a railway platform.

As they watched, a second figure got out the back of the third car, wandered off a couple of yards, fumbled with his flies, and started to pee.

'Who's that?' asked Victor.

'It's Fraser,' said Gunner, still not quite believing it himself. For some reason the sight of Fraser made him feel more sad than angry. He felt betrayed.

Fraser buttoned up his fly, walked back to the car, nodded to the MPs and got back in. Moore finished his cigarette and dropped it, pointed over to the car and started walking Hess off towards it, Hess limping heavily. The two suits moved towards the farmer, beckoning him towards their car. The farmer shook his head and they kept coming. They were a couple of yards away when the farmer raised his gun again and pointed it at them. They put their hands up, backed off towards the cars.

Moore closed the car door on Hess, walked back and approached the farmer. Gunner could see he was talking, couldn't hear what he was saying. No doubt giving him some speech about how they were taking the prisoner away to be dealt with. The farmer didn't seem to be buying it. He kept the rifle up, shook his head. He wasn't going anywhere. Moore seemed to give up, walked off looking angry. He spoke to the suits, pointed at the farmer, then got in the car with Hess.

'Fuck,' said Victor. 'They've got him.' He sat down on the slope.

'What do we do now?' asked Gunner.

'Get down there quick,' said Victor. 'C'mon!'

They half crawled, half tumbled down the side of the hill, trying to stay down and out of sight. They veered off to the right and ended up in a clump of bushes twenty yards to the left of the cars. Victor sat up, hair thick with grass and face covered in mud.

Gunner stayed down low, pulled Victor down beside him. The car with Hess and Moore started up, the engine failing a couple of times, then catching. This car moved off, the other one following, headlights swinging round, casting bright light and shadows on the wreckage of the plane. It bumped its way across the muddy field heading for the road back into Glasgow. The car sat there, the two suits standing ten yards from the farmer looking down the barrel of his gun, trying to talk to him.

Gunner looked at the farmer, looked at the two suits. Had an idea.

'The other car,' he said. 'We'll take it.'

Victor looked at him like he was mad. 'We'll what? Are you nuts?'

'Just follow me,' said Gunner. 'And keep the fuck down.'

They crawled towards the car, trying to keep an eye on the farmer and the two suits. The car was between them, hopefully blocking any view of Victor and Gunner crawling up behind it. Victor got there first, eased the driver's door open. Gunner got in, crawled over, tried to fold himself down into the footwell of the passenger seat. Victor got in slumped as low in the seat as he could while still being able to see out the windscreen.

'We've only got one shot at this,' said Gunner.

Victor nodded. He peered over the dashboard; the two suits were still facing away. 'Wish me luck,' he said, sat up in the seat and turned the key in the ignition. The noise sounded unbelievably loud in the quiet morning. The two suits turned just as the engine coughed and didn't catch.

'Fuck sake!' said Gunner.

Victor tried again. This time it caught.

'Go!' shouted Gunner.

The car lurched forward, heading straight for the two suits. Gunner eased up into the seat in time to see one of them draw his gun and point it straight at them.

'Keep going, Victor!' he shouted.

Victor stepped hard on the accelerator; the car bumped across the field, a burst of flames and sparks as it ran over one of the small fires and sent the wreckage flying. The windscreen cracked before Gunner heard the shot, he felt a shudder and a soft whup as the bullet just missed his shoulder and burst into the leather seat behind him.

Victor punched at the windscreen trying to knock the glass out so he could see. He hit it hard with the heel of his hand and half the windscreen fell away to reveal the two suits a couple of yards ahead, guns pointed straight at them.

'Faster!' shouted Gunner.

Victor stood on the accelerator again, a crack and a burst of light from one of the guns, a loud clang as the bullet hit the side of the Alvis. The two suits jumped out the way at the last minute, but the car clipped one of them, knocked him sprawling. Victor kept going, the car bouncing and lurching its way across the crash site towards the road.

Gunner looked back. One of the suits was on the ground, his mate kneeling beside him, the farmer still pointing his rifle at both of them. The car swerved to avoid a bit of fuselage and suddenly they were on the dirt road heading towards the gate and the road to Glasgow.

Victor sat back in the seat, started laughing.

'Fuck sake, Joe. Are you OK?'

Gunner nodded. 'Where'd you learn to bloody drive?'

'Uncle Jimmy taught me,' said Victor, a big smile on his face.

'That explains it,' said Gunner. 'He couldnae drive for shite either.'

He nodded down the hill; the headlights of the cars were just disappearing into the valley.

'Better get going, we don't want to lose them.'

46

They'd only gone a quarter of a mile or so before they started to see them. People started appearing on the road. There were little kids with torches, couples with dogs. A car drove past with a family in it, kids in the back pointing at the fires up the hill.

'Who are all these people?' asked Victor.

Gunner shrugged. 'Fuck knows. Sightseers, I think. Looks like we weren't the only ones who saw the plane crash.'

A couple of fast black cars passed them going the other way, backs of them full of lights, cameras and tripods. Gunner caught a glimpse of a fat bald man in the passenger seat of one.

'Press boys here as well. That was Archie Sweeney from the *Citizen*. It's not going to be much of a secret now. It'll be all over the papers tomorrow, no way they can news blackout this.'

Victor looked at him. 'You think so?'

Gunner shrugged. 'Don't know, might just stop them.' An open farm truck went past with five or six Home Guard in the back.

Victor shook his head. 'I wouldnae be so sure. Hess isn't there, could say any fucker came down in the plane.'

'Suppose it depends how much that farmer saw and how much he opens his mouth to the press,' said Gunner.

'He didnae look the type to be hushed up,' said Victor. 'He's probably shot they two by now for trespassing on his land.'

They'd caught up to the car now, were keeping a good couple of hundred yards behind.

'Where do you reckon they are going?' asked Victor.

Gunner shrugged. 'Central probably. Or the train station, maybe the airfield, you'd think they'd be trying to get him down to London.'

Gunner opened the glove compartment. Smiled as he brought out a packet of Black Cat and a box of matches. He lit up, pulled the smoke deep into his lungs. Still couldn't believe Fraser was caught up in all this. Mind you, he had been working for Drummond so maybe they were all in it. Drummond, Moore, Fraser. Wondered how Nickerson was getting on, hoped he was doing OK. Even if he was a drunk toff, he'd met worse.

They kept behind as the car ahead drove through the outskirts of Glasgow. They crossed the George V Bridge and instead of turning right to go to Central, the car kept going, heading for the north of the city. It was still too early for many people to be out and about. The city was quiet, no drunks singing their way home. Like a ghost town. Gunner had an inkling where the car in front was heading, but it was only when the car turned into Garscube Road that he was certain.

'They're taking him to the Maryhill Barracks,' he said.

'You sure?' Victor asked.

Gunner pulled his suit around him, stuck his hands in his pockets, car was freezing with no windscreen. 'Looks like it.'

He was right. Ten minutes later the car ahead indicated and turned into the barracks' entrance.

'Pull up here,' said Gunner.

Victor steered the car into the side of the road by the police station, a hundred yards or so up ahead. They both turned and looked out the back windscreen. A soldier was leaning over the passenger window of the car. He stood up, the barrier went up, and he waved them through. They watched as the barrier came down again. Victor turned the key in the ignition and the engine died.

'What do we do now?' he asked.

'I don't know, Victor,' said Gunner. 'This might be the end of the road.'

'It can't be,' said Victor. 'You know what's at stake.'

'Look, Archie Sweeney and the lads from the *Record* and the *Herald* will be up there now snapping away, asking the farmer all about what Hess said to him. There's no way they can keep it secret. They're no gonnae let Hess go and have a cosy chat with the Anglo-German Society now. It's over.'

'I wish I could believe that,' said Victor. 'You don't know what these people are like, Joe, they'll find a way to make it happen. We still need to get rid of Hess.'

'We?' asked Gunner.

'OK, me, I need to get rid of Hess. It's my duty, it's what I was put in the conchie camp for, took months of planning. I can't just walk away now.'

'So what are you going to do?' asked Gunner.

Victor reached into his inside jacket pocket, took out an old decrepit-looking revolver.

'Kill him,' he said. 'I'm going to kill Hess.'

'Not with that you're not, you're more likely to blow your bloody hand off.'

'I need to try, Joe.'

He looked half determined and half terrified.

'Victor,' said Gunner, trying to talk slowly, deliberately. 'This has turned into a suicide mission. You think you can get past the barrier, find out where Hess is, then kill him? They'll shoot you if you even manage to get past the barrier. I know this is what you've been working for, planning, but it's over. What use is there in getting yourself killed? You know Hess is here, the press'll know Hess is here, there's no way they can keep it secret.'

Victor nodded.

Gunner breathed a sigh of relief.

'I know all that, Joe, but I still have to try. I have to. There's too much at stake. I don't matter, Russia matters. Ending this war matters. I have to.'

Gunner looked at him, had a feeling he was going to try and do it no matter what he said.

'Sit here,' he said. 'Keep a look out and I'll be back in ten minutes.'

He got out the car before Victor could protest.

47

It was a long shot but it was all he could think of. If Victor was determined to do it, he had to give him a better chance than that useless revolver. Gunner tried to walk as fast as he could but his leg was killing him, could only manage a hobble. He was heading for Ruchill Street; it was only five minutes away but at this point that felt like miles. His leg hurt, his eye hurt, everything hurt. Knew at least half of that was not having a syrette; his body was crying out for the morphine.

By the time he got to the close he was sweating, all he wanted was another morphine syrette and to lie down, but he had to keep going, even if it was going to be a wild goose chase. He climbed up the stairs, more pain, and stood outside the door to the first-floor flat. He put his ear to the door, could hear music, had to be a good sign.

He knocked on the door. All he could do was hope.

A minute or so later it was opened and a big bloke looked him up and down. Gunner could imagine what he was thinking. His suit was ripped, he was covered with mud, dried blood from the beating still on his face. He'd limped up looking like your everyday Glasgow jakey after a night on the meths.

'Sellars here?' asked Gunner.

'Maybe,' the bloke said. 'Maybe not.'

'Can you tell him Gunner's here? He'll want to speak to me.'

The bloke looked at him. Couldn't have looked less impressed if he'd tried.

'You know what this place is, right?' he asked.

Gunner nodded.

'So the chances are, the boss is busy, if you catch my meaning, not sure he'll want to be interrupted.'

Gunner didn't have time for this.

'Just get him,' he said. 'Or I'll tell him you turned me away, and you'll live to regret it, you dumb fucker.'

The bloke looked at him like he wanted to punch him up and down the stairs.

'Wait here,' he said, and closed the door.

A couple of minutes later the door opened again. The bloke held it wide.

'Wait in the kitchen,' he said.

Gunner walked through the flat, headed for the kitchen at the back. He sat at the table, took a drink from a bottle of Red Hackle someone had left and tried not to listen to what was going on next door. Whatever was going on, it sounded like it would come to an end soon. Grunting getting faster, as was the squeaking of the bedsprings. Gunner took another drink. He knew he shouldn't be here, knew he shouldn't be doing what he was about to do, but he couldn't help himself. It was the only way he could think of to help Victor.

A few minutes later Malky Sellars was standing in the kitchen doorway. He'd a pair of suit trousers on, bare feet and chest.

'Been in the wars again, I see,' he said, hooking his braces over his shoulders. 'You should look after yourself better, Mr Gunner.'

Gunner smiled weakly. 'Glad you're still up, Sellars.'

Sellars grinned.

'Well, I was until a few minutes ago. Balls deep in fact.'

He moved to the table and sat down, picked up the bottle and took a swig, grimaced, yawned. Looked at Gunner.

'So, Mr Gunner, why are you knocking at the door looking for me in a whorehouse at this time? Must be something desperate, I would think?'

'I came to say thank you,' Gunner said. 'For getting me out the camp.'

Sellars nodded.

'No problem. My brother's decided you're part of the plan. He wanted you back in Glasgow in one piece. And I just do what my brother tells me.' He grinned again. 'Most of the time, that is.'

Sellars reached for the bottle and took another swig. Gunner could see the scratches on his back and shoulders. Sellars saw him looking.

'Sometimes it's better if they're not that keen,' he said. 'Adds a bit of spice to the proceedings.' Sellars pushed his hair back from his face and yawned again. 'Takes it out of you, though.' He leant back and shouted.

'Tam! Get me a glass of water!'

The bloke from the door appeared and went to the sink, let the tap run for a minute, filled a pint glass, handed it to Sellars, and headed back to his position in the doorway. Sellars took a long drink.

'Now I can't imagine you've come all this way to thank me for getting you out of trouble, have you?'

Gunner sat there; knew he was about to do something that couldn't be undone. Didn't have a choice.

'There's something else I need,' he said.

Sellars looked at him, then back at Tam.

'Besides a new suit?' he asked.

Gunner smiled, and then he shook his head.

'I need a gun and two boxes of army-issue morphine.'

Sellars was reaching for the whisky bottle, but he stopped, looked at him.

'What for?' he asked.

'I need a gun and two boxes of army-issue morphine,' Gunner said again.

Sellars sat back, looked like he was deciding.

'If I give you them, and it's an if, you owe me. Big time.'

Gunner nodded.

'I know,' he said. 'Believe me, I know.'

Sellars nodded to Tam and he lumbered off, came back a minute later with the two boxes in his hand and a gun wrapped in an oilcloth. Gunner looked at them, ran his tongue around his dry mouth. Sellars took them and handed them over. Leant into him so Tam couldn't hear.

'You be careful, Mr Gunner. My brother needs you. You know what you're doing?'

Gunner nodded and Sellars broke away.

'Get the cunt out of here, Tam. Think I'm ready for round two with her next door.'

Gunner was halfway out the door when Sellars shouted after him. 'You're racking up the debts, Gunner! Remember they'll get called in. They always do.'

48

Gunner hurried down the stairs, two boxes nestled in his pockets and the gun shoved into his waistband. Sellars was right. Gunner did owe now. Owed big time. But he had what he wanted, and hopefully in a couple of days he'd be on a train to somewhere and well away from Sellars. And who knew if he would still be there when he got back.

The weight of the morphine boxes in his hand was reassuring. All he wanted to do was duck into a close and stick one of the syrettes into his thigh, but he couldn't. Not yet.

The sun had come up, edges of the factories in the distance ringed in a yellowy pink. The barracks still looked quiet. There were a couple of soldiers sitting outside the wee guardhouse on the left as you went in. Could they be keeping him in there? It was well out of the way of the rest of the goings-on at the barracks, he supposed, and he'd never seen the two soldiers sitting there before.

He hobbled up to the car, pulled the door open and got in.

'Give me that thing,' he said.

Victor handed over the old pistol and Gunner unwrapped the other from the oilcloth. He realised he'd forgotten to make sure it was loaded. He cracked it, six bullets in the chamber. He snapped it shut again.

'Where did you get that?' Victor looked amazed.

'Doesn't matter,' said Gunner. 'You know how to use it?'

Victor nodded uncertainly.

Gunner swore under his breath. 'It's an Enfield. Piece of piss.' He gave him a quick lesson, Victor concentrating hard.

'OK, I've got it,' he said, and held his hand out for the gun.

Gunner hesitated. 'You sure about this, Victor?'

'Never been more sure of anything.'

Gunner handed over the gun, 'Come on. Let's go and see what's going on.'

They walked down Maryhill Road towards the barracks, settled in behind one of the baffles in front of the closes opposite. Gunner lit one of the Black Cats he'd found in the glove compartment.

'This might be a long bloody wait,' he said. 'We could be here for hours.'

Victor shrugged.

They stood there staring at the barracks gate opposite. Apart from the two soldiers in front of the guardhouse periodically moving back and forward and stamping their feet, nothing happened. The first few people were up and about in the street, trams had started for the morning. Gunner kept running his fingers over the box in his pocket, all he wanted to do was get one of the syrettes out and inject himself, let the pain flow away, but he knew he couldn't. Had to try and keep alert.

'What's that?' Victor asked.

There were two cars making their way across the parade ground heading towards the gate.

Victor grabbed at Gunner. 'Come on.'

The long black cars pulled up outside the gatehouse. Two goons in suits got out, started talking to the two soldiers, left the back doors open.

'I think he's coming out, Victor,' said Gunner. 'You ready?'

No response. Gunner turned. Victor was standing off to the side, hand shaking, gun held down at his side.

'Victor! What the fuck's going on?'

Victor stood there, shaking his head. 'I can't, Joe, I just can't do . . .'

Gunner ran over, shook him. Nothing. He just looked at him like a whipped dog. Gunner pushed him away.

'Go, Victor! Just get out of here.'

Gunner ran across the road, jumping across the tram tracks, and made for the barracks gate just as Moore stepped out the gatehouse. Moore stopped, looked around, took out his cigarette case, and lit up. Blew a stream of smoke into the bright morning sunshine. The parade ground was empty, looked like everyone had been kept inside. He stood by the car, was plainly waiting for something. Or someone.

Gunner kept his eye on him, crept along the wall outside, and flattened himself against the side of the big stone gatepost. He peered round, no one was looking over at him, all eyes were on the gatehouse. He pulled the gun up, stuck it through the gate, balanced his hand on one of the slats. If he was lucky, he'd get one clear shot, two would be a miracle.

Moore turned to the gatehouse door, smiled, and Hess emerged, limping slightly, now dressed in a grey suit. He looked up at the sky, breathed in, let the sun hit his face. Gunner pulled the hammer back, felt it click into position. He aimed for Hess's body, figured that way he had a better chance of hitting him, and started to squeeze the trigger. Suddenly there was a shout, Moore nudged Hess and they both turned towards the parade ground.

Fraser was running across the ground towards them with a big grin on his face. He was holding an envelope up, must have forgotten to give them something. He reached them, mimed exhaustion. Hess held out his hand for the envelope and Fraser pulled a revolver out from under his coat, pointed it at Hess and shot him twice in the body.

The two cracks electrified everything. Hess dropped and Moore tried to grab him. He caught him and managed to push the screaming Hess into the back of the car. He got in after him, shouted at the driver and it accelerated off, doors wide open. One of the soldiers only just managed to get the gate open before the car hit it. Gunner had the impression of a grey suit covered in blood as the car sped past him, a glimpse of Moore's face as he leant over to pull the door shut.

Fraser ran down the parade ground still firing shots, the last one reducing the back window of the car to a jigsaw of shattered glass. The two goons moved quickly, didn't even try to get Fraser to surrender. They emptied their revolvers into him, his body jerking, erupting blood into the harsh sunlight. Gunner turned his head away as one of the bullets took the top of his head off.

Before Gunner had a chance to move into the parade ground, the other car came barrelling towards the gate. It screeched to a halt by Fraser's body and one of the goons jumped out, dragged the lifeless form onto the back seat, and pulled the door shut behind him. The other one stopped for a minute, saw Gunner. He held his gun up, wasn't sure what to do. He gave Gunner one last look and got in. The car accelerated off in pursuit of the other one.

And then, as soon as it had started, it was over. Gunner stood there, gun at his side, still trying to take in what had happened. All that was left was some blood on the parade ground and rubber skid marks from the tyres of the cars.

Gunner put the gun in his pocket and sat on the wee wall by the gatehouse. Put his head in his hands. Why had Fraser shot Hess? Why would he do that? He took his cigarettes out with shaking hands and managed to light one. There was traffic on Maryhill Road now; a fat woman passed, pushing a pram full of washing, a fish van stopping across the street.

Was Hess dead? Fraser certainly was. He knew that. He could still see his head exploding as the bullet hit. Gunner's hands wrapped around the box in his pocket. He stood up. Dropped his cigarette on the ground and ground it out. None of it added up. There was a figure coming across the parade ground towards him. Yelled at him to wait. He stopped in front of Gunner, a grin on his face.

'That was a bit of a to-do,' Nickerson said. 'You OK?'

Gunner nodded. Couldn't believe it.

'What are you doing here? I thought—'

Nickerson held up his hands.

'I told you, Gunner. Things change in the Secret Service, things change all the time.' He looked round, breathed in the morning air. He turned to Gunner again. He held out a silver flask. Gunner took a deep gulp. Whisky. The good stuff.

'You weren't meant to see that, obviously. Nobody was.'

Nickerson took a hit himself, grimaced.

'Good stuff, that.'

He sat down on the wall and motioned Gunner to sit beside him.

'It was all supposed to happen in the guardhouse, but Danielson was late.' He looked down at the pool of blood on the ground and screwed up his nose. 'Still, needs must.'

'Danielson?' asked Gunner.

Nickerson smiled. 'Sorry, Fraser. His father was a German Jew, a schoolteacher here. He went back to Berlin in thirty-seven to try and get his sister out. Was killed on the direct orders of Hess. An undesirable, apparently. So Fraser bore a rather useful grudge. Very convincing he was too, quite the young Nazi. I told him there was a distinct chance he wasn't going to come out of this alive, but he was determined.'

'You told him?'

Nickerson nodded.

'Wasn't only Moore who was plotting away. Danielson was one of mine.'

He held the flask up.

'To Danielson. A good man gone.'

'Poor kid,' said Gunner. I didn't realise he was one of the good guys.'

'As with most wars' – Nickerson grimaced – 'the young are expendable so the old can stay in power, and ever it was so.'

He took another swig from the flask.

'Right. No point getting maudlin.'

'As soon as Hitler realises it's all gone very wrong, he'll deny any knowledge of what Hess was up to. Herr Hess's goose is cooked either way. As are the gooses – geese? – of Mr Moore and his mob. He'll be running for the hills.'

'What'll happen to Hess?' asked Gunner.

Nickerson shrugged, smiled. He wasn't going to tell him that.

He nodded towards their old quarters, the Major's house. He stood up, brushed the ash off his tweed suit. 'Shall we?'

They walked across the parade ground, a couple of soldiers with buckets and mops hurrying past them heading for the puddles of blood at the gate.

'Nothing you saw today happened. That clear?' said Nickerson. He stopped, looked at Gunner. 'You sure you can keep your mouth shut?'

Gunner nodded.

Nickerson clapped him on the back.

'Good man. I'm trusting you, Gunner. Don't let me down.'

'Rudolf Hess shot on the Maryhill Road in Glasgow,' said Gunner. 'Nobody's going to believe a fairy story like that, are they?'

Nickerson shook his head. 'Not by the time I'm finished. No.'

The barracks was coming to life again. The doors over by the mess opened and forty or so young recruits spilled out, a sergeant shouting the odds behind them.

'There's something else, Gunner,' said Nickerson. 'Something I need to talk to you about.'

'That doesn't sound good,' said Gunner.

Nickerson shook his head, 'On the contrary, I want to offer you a job.'

It was the last thing Gunner was expecting. 'What?'

'You're a good man, Gunner. You can handle yourself. We need people like that. This war is being fought in far more places than people know. It's important work, vital work. I wouldn't ask you if I didn't think you were up to it.'

Gunner shook his head.

'I'm a polis, it's what I've always been. Hopefully the eye'll get better and soon as the war's over I'll be back here doing my job. Thanks, but no thanks.'

Nickerson didn't look too bothered at Gunner's refusal.

'To be entirely honest, your eye might well get better but I doubt the leg will, not with the shitty treatment you'll get here. Seems to me you'll end up pushing paper about in an office, trying not to resent every other policeman that's out there doing the job you used to do. And I hate to bring it up, but you have a brother who is on the run.'

'I thought Victor was working for you?'

Nickerson shook his head.

'Don't know anything about that, I'm afraid. All I know is he's been charged with treason.'

'You'd really just leave him hanging out to dry?'

Nickerson nodded.

'I need to win this war whatever it takes.'

'Bastard,' said Gunner. 'You fucking bastard.'

'Your bastard, though. You come and work for me, I can make that go away. Your brother goes scot-free. If you don't, well . . . You've got about five minutes to think about it. I need to be back in London. Car's coming to take me to the airfield.'

Nickerson walked up to the Major's house, taking a swig from his flask as he walked. Gunner stood for a minute, lit a cigarette, watched the soldiers scrubbing the parade ground. A stream of reddish soapy water ran down the slope and into the gutter.

What would happen to Victor if he didn't say yes to Nickerson? Victor would be found and shot, that's what. And he was right, he couldn't face a life behind a desk.

A group of lads emerged from one of the barracks buildings,

looked like they had some leave, all pushing and shoving each other, laughter and insults. He watched them head for the gate, finished his cigarette, flicked the butt away, and walked into the house where Nickerson was waiting.

Epilogue

The sun was high in the sky, temperature up in the eighties already. The hospital grounds looked immaculate on this sunny day. Gunner had just set off on his daily circuit. 'Help build up the muscles,' the doctor had said. 'Walk a mile a day.' So he did. The first week or so he was in agony at the end of it, having to stop four or five times. Now, on a good day, he could make it round without stopping.

This hospital was nothing like the one he'd been in before. This was more like a country house. No enlisted men here. Here it was all senior officers being looked after by consultants, and more nurses than you could imagine. Nickerson wanted him better quickly and Gunner wasn't complaining. As far as he was concerned, all was well with the world. He'd be more than happy spending the rest of the war here pottering around, stealing the occasional morphine syrette from the drugs trolley.

His leg was playing up today. He stopped halfway round the ground and sat on a wall watching the river flow by, enamel cup of tea in his hand, first cigarette of the day in his mouth. He took a drag, then took the letters out his pocket. Two, picked up from Reception that morning. The first one was a telegram, he knew who that was from, that could wait. The second one was more of a mystery.

A letter with a Glasgow postmark, thought he recognised the writing. Addressed to him at his regiment: that had been scored out and the hospital's address scrawled in red pen. He slid his hand along the flap and opened out the sheet of blue onion-skin paper. There was a shout from the lawn behind him. Gunner looked up. A battered football was rolling down the hill towards him. He kicked it back up, acknowledging the cheers as it went wide and hit a nurse carrying a tray. He shouted sorry, sat back down, looked at the letter.

> *Dear Joe*
>
> *Just a note, thought you might be interested. Read in the paper that they picked a body out the canal last week, a tall middle-aged man, thin, receding hairline. No fingertips, two bullet wounds in his side, not fatal, and a bullet wound in the back of the head that definitely was.*
>
> *Must be another lookalike? Who else could it be? Eh?*
>
> *I'm in a conchie camp out by Ayr. This one's a lot better, no drunk farmers kicking fuck out you, for one thing. Not sure how you managed to wangle that, but thank you. Not sure where you are but hopefully this will get to you somehow.*
>
> *I'll never forget what you did when I couldn't.*
>
> *Victor*

Gunner folded the letter up and put it into the top pocket of his battle dress. Opened the telegram.

CAR WILL PICK YOU UP THIS AFTERNOON STOP HOLIDAY'S OVER STOP TIME TO START WORK STOP NICKERSON

Acknowledgements

Thanks to Isobel Dixon and all at Blake Friedmann. Thanks to Yassine Belkacemi and all at Baskerville, John Murray.

Thanks to Nick de Somogyi and the staff of The Glasgow Room at The Mitchell.